'... ...s and ultimately enriches'
Heather Morris, author of *The Tattooist of Auschwitz*

'A tear-jerker. Bookworms are calling it a cross between *The Diary of Anne Frank* and *The Boy in the Striped Pyjamas* and it's a reading list essential'

Maximum Pop

'The best YA novel about the Holocaust I have read. The story it threads together is gripping, moving and important ... deeply-researched, but wears its learning so lightly that the history is woven seamlessly into the fabric of the colourful story'
Robert Eaglestone, Professor of Contemporary Literature and Thought, Holocaust Research Institute, University of London

'In Auschwitz, teenagers Ella and Rose survive because they create clothes for the Commandant's wife. Despite the dark situation, the friends' compassion, friendship and humanity win out'

Candis magazine

'This powerful young-adult Holocaust novel is an incredibly moving and important read that resonates with its message of hope and compassion'

Culture Fly

'A sensitive and brilliantly-written look at the Holocaust'
Book Murmuration

'Compelling, illuminating . . . and female'
Notes on Paper

'A truly mesmerising tale of hope, sacrifice and friendship and I loved it!'
Pretty Little Memoirs

'An affecting and enlightening read'
Black Plume

'Adlington's writing is beautiful and often moving. Keep the handkerchief ready'
The Lady

'Fashion and Auschwitz may seem an unlikely pairing . . . but this story is tremendously thought-provoking about the horrors of the Holocaust and the deeper meaning of clothes and the way you present yourself to the world . . . *The Red Ribbon* is a moving story of friendship, kindness and heroism under impossible circumstances'
Booktrust

'Gritty historical fiction with a symbol of hope'
Times Educational Supplement

SUMMERLAND

ALSO BY LUCY ADLINGTON
FROM HOT KEY BOOKS

The Red Ribbon

SUMMERLAND

LUCY ADLINGTON

HOT
KEY
BOOKS

First published in Great Britain in 2019 by
HOT KEY BOOKS
80–81 Wimpole St, London W1G 9RE
www.hotkeybooks.com

This is a work of fiction. Names, places, events and incidents are either the
products of the author's imagination or used fictitiously. Any resemblance
to actual persons, living or dead, is purely coincidental.

A CIP catalogue record for this book is available from the British Library.

ISBN: 978-1-4714-0827-4
also available as an ebook

1

This book is typeset using Atomik ePublisher
Printed and bound in Great Britain by Clays Ltd, Elcograf S.p.A.

Hot Key Books is an imprint of Bonnier Books UK
www.bonnierbooks.co.uk

In memory of the real Hidden Children.
Persecuted and driven into fearful secrecy, they lost
their identities, their families, their youth.
And in tribute to those who kept love,
trust and joy alive.

Contents

Fish-Paste Sandwiches

There are lots of stories about war. Stories about glory. Suffering. Survival. But who talks about what happens afterwards, about life now, when we've scrambled out from under the rubble and stopped waving flags of victory or surrender? Who dares mention what we've become?

Not me. I don't talk. I watch, mostly, and wait.

That day – the day we blew across the sea to England – I was so excited it felt as if minnows were swimming around inside me. There was so much to see in the port . . . ropes, cranes, sailors, seagulls . . . rainbows in oil slicks and fish guts in buckets.

'Stick together!' cried our Red Cross escorts. There were nearly fifty of us in our group, aged five to sixteen. Forty-seven orphans of war, and me. Leftovers.

We lurched up a gangway onto the ship. Once that was pulled in, the only escape route was overboard.

'Keep away from the railings!' yelled a Red Cross woman. Then, in a quieter voice, 'Honestly, it's like herding cats.'

I hid in the middle of the group, holding tight to my case. The air was a fug of fuel and salt spray. The deck thrummed.

I'd never been to sea before. 'One day we'll go to England,' my mutti had said, a lifetime ago. 'When the sun shines, it's the most beautiful country in the world. A true land of summer.'

October clouds hid the sun now. Down we plunged into the murky green, then up to the white wave-tops. I wondered which bright spark had thought it was a good idea to give us fish-paste sandwiches for lunch. They looked and smelled horrible, but when you've sucked on pebbles out of hunger, you're not too fussy. I was saving mine for later, which was just as well, because the other children hung like limp monkeys over the railings, sicking theirs up.

I turned my face to the sky, amazed at how wide it was.

Behind us . . . Europe, its ghosts swaying on the dawn beaches, thick as dune grass. Ahead of us . . . England. A new life.

Had I been followed?

Landfall.

Crowds pulsing and pushing. Smells of sweat and wet clothes. Rain on the docks. I was hurried along with everyone else, off the ship, onto English ground, into a huge wooden hall that creaked as the wind gusted. *Customs*, said a sign. The crowd slowed. Men in uniforms ahead!

Keep calm. Act natural.

My fingers played a soundless piano tune against my thigh, a rhapsody by an Englishwoman my mutti had admired called Rebecca Clarke. The music was half ominous, half hopeful. I understood that feeling.

'Stay together! That means you too, Arek,' shouted one of the Red Cross women. Betty, her name was. *Poor Betty*, the kids called her behind her back. Always with a sniffle and no hanky. Arek was a Polish boy who'd survived a hell worse than hell by hiding in a toilet pit. Now he was free, it was as if his arms and legs had to be all places at once. I knew how it felt to be so trapped you wanted to run mad like a crazy spider. Instead I kept calm and ladylike, as I'd been taught.

While Betty checked names, another Red Cross lady – Margaret – tried to line us up in order. Margaret had been a hockey player before the war – what was *hockey*? – and said she loved children, though she probably meant normal kids who picked flowers, not fights. Ones who didn't lick the plate when the food was all gone. I'd been normal once, I think. It was hard to remember. I'd been happy before the war. There'd been a boat on a lake – a wooden toy with a cotton sail. A tall man with sun behind his shoulders.

'Brigitta Iggle?'

I blinked and the memory vanished. Someone had said a name I knew – the name I used, pronounced wrong. It was spelled *Igeul* in German, like *eagle* in English, and it meant hedgehog.

Betty tapped her fingers on a clipboard. Her woollen gloves had unravelled at the tips.

Margaret squinted at the list of names. 'Brigitta? Like Bridget . . . ?'

They both glanced round the group, eyes passing right over me.

Betty sneezed and called out again. 'Is there a Bridget Iggle?'

Much as I preferred being invisible, I didn't want to be left off the list. I absolutely had to be let into England.

'Here!' I called. When no one looked my way, I realised no sound had come out. Too many years of just whispering, or talking with fingertips only. I raised my hand.

'Oh, her,' said Betty. 'The dark one. *Now* I remember: she kicked up a stink at the clinic when she had to undress for the examination. In the end I told her to keep her underthings on. Hey, you, Arek, get *down* from that table! I swear that boy's got ants in his pants – he *never* sits still. Er, what was I saying?'

'About Brigitta,' Margaret prompted.

'Oh yes. Not a bad-looking kid. She'll be a heartbreaker before long. A couple of eggs short of dozen of course,' she added, tapping the side of her head.

'Hush,' said Margaret. 'She'll hear you.'

'Her? Doesn't speak a word of English, or any language, it seems. Doesn't speak at all.'

'Poor thing. Poor all of them. No homes, no parents . . .'

'Oh, children are like rubber, don't you worry. They soon bounce back. Even after . . .' Betty's voice trailed off. She sniffed and quickly looked back at her clipboard and stabbed the list of names. 'How on *earth* do I pronounce *this*? Why can't the Polish language have more vowels and fewer consonants? Arek Whateveryournameis, put whateverthatthingis *down* and line up with the rest of us . . .'

The crowd shuffled forward, closer to the men in uniforms with shining buttons. Uniforms meant trouble. Questions. My heart was racing so fast the beats blurred into one continuous throb. I looked down at my hands, now fingering a tricky bit of Beethoven on the wool of my skirt.

4

I can't do this.

I have to do this.

One by one the officials crooked a finger for someone to step up and show their papers. My turn.

Do what everyone else does.

A customs man behind a big wooden desk looked me up and down. What did he see? A dark-haired girl in a red check coat, brown cardigan, brown skirt, brown socks, brown shoes. It was a smart coat at least, though it had been through a lot. All my clothes were cast-offs. A bit like me.

'Name?'

I was paralysed, unable to speak.

'She's Bridget Iggle,' said Betty, looming over my shoulder.

The man scanned my creased identity papers. 'From Germany?'

I shook my head and mouthed, 'Austria. Vienna.'

'Says here you trained as a seamstress.'

What should I reply to that?

The customs man frowned at Betty. 'Here, you, miss, ask her if she's a seamstress.'

'Like I know!' Betty spluttered. 'My job's just to fetch them here. I barely learned how to say *parlez-vous* in school, let alone German.' She turned to me and did a pantomime of sewing.

I nodded.

'Coming to England to work?' continued the customs man. Another nod.

'Anything to declare?'

I handed over my brown cardboard case, given to me at the Red Cross refugee centre in Berlin. The customs man clicked

5

the lid and opened it. It didn't take long for him to search through all I owned in the world.

One nightshirt.

One spare set of underwear.

One small book with tiny, tiny writing.

And, most precious of all: one grey glove. Just the one.

'Anything else?'

I shrank away. They wouldn't do a body search, would they? That would be disastrous. Then I remembered my uneaten sandwich. Wordlessly I pulled it out of my pocket and handed it over. The customs man took one sniff at the fish paste and shoved the whole sandwich back at me. 'Move along now. Nothing to declare.'

I moved along, head down, eyes down. Eventually I allowed myself a quiet smile.

Nothing to declare, the man had said? Well, we all have our secrets. No one needed to know about the knife in my sock.

Bacon Butties

'Late through customs and only just made it to the train,' Betty fretted. ' Oi – Arek, get down from that rack – it's for luggage, not boys.'

We tumbled into the carriage, a mess of scabbed knees, sharp elbows and suitcase corners. The train seats were hairy. I got jammed between a soot-speckled window and a little Czech girl who had yet to take her thumb out of her mouth. She stroked her nose with a forefinger as she sucked.

An Englishman in a cheap coat and thin leather gloves pushed through to the seats opposite. 'Shift up,' he told the two Polish boys who were trying the seats out for bounce. The man's teeth were a spectrum of yellow, black and gold. He made a point of spreading his buttocks as wide as he could across the seat, then he opened his newspaper. The headlines were bold.

NAZI TRIALS IN NUREMBERG! WAR CRIMINALS TO BE HANGED!

JUSTICE MUST BE DONE!

NAZI SPIES FEARED HIDING IN ENGLAND!

So the few Nazi leaders who'd been captured alive at the end of the fighting were on trial for their crimes. Would the judges one day catch up with all the other little Hitlers who'd carried out the orders? I could think of a few. Before I could read more, the man folded the newspaper and took his lunch out of a bag. It was a floury bread roll cut in half, with two slices of warm fatty bacon dropping out of the side.

Arek and the other refugees were drawn to the smell like hungry dogs.

The man flapped his newspaper at them. 'Get away, greedy beggars! A fella ought to be able to eat a bacon butty in peace. Hey, you, nurse! Are you in charge of these brats? Keep them under control or I'll have them thrown off the train.'

Margaret went pink. 'Boys, *sit down*. You will get fed again, I promise.'

'Ruddy foreigners,' said the man, through a mouthful. 'No manners! I blame the parents. They ought –'

'They don't have any parents,' Margaret snapped. 'They're Jewish survivors of the Horror Camps, if you must know. I dare say you must've read about them in the papers – Auschwitz and Belsen and suchlike. We managed to get permission for one thousand orphaned survivors to come and find new homes in Britain. Unfortunately we couldn't actually find one thousand camp children left alive. Not even eight hundred. This is the last batch.'

The man looked down at his bacon butty – what was a *butty?* – then he looked at the boys clustered round him. 'Oh. Well. They can have some if they like . . .'

'They're *Jewish*. They don't eat pork.'

I flinched. What was Margaret thinking, saying the J-word out loud? Anyone could be listening!

The man wiped greasy fingers on his trousers. 'Shocking what 'Itler did to them Jews,' he said, picking at a piece of rind stuck in his teeth. Then he smiled at the little Czech girl sitting next to me. 'Don't cry, sweetie. You're safe now. It couldn't happen here. This is England.'

I hadn't noticed the girl crying. What was I supposed to do? I remembered my mama's warm, firm voice: *Here, hold my hand. Don't let go.* I felt for the Czech girl's hand and gave it a squeeze. With a quiet sob, she turned and burrowed into me.

There was a crackle from my coat lining. Had anyone else heard it?

The Englishman nodded at me. 'You're a good girl, you are.'

I held myself still. *That's what you think.*

Whistles, pistons, smoke and steam. On we rushed, to our future. Who'd welcome us? Who'd want us? Who'd want me?

A faint sun shone on hedges, fields and villages. Kids pressed flat against the train windows, pointing things out and chattering away in half a dozen languages. Arek got locked in the lavatory and Margaret nearly blew a gasket trying to get him out again. Farms and countryside gave way to factories and wasteland, and rows of red-brick houses with pigeons on the roof tiles and washing strung in the yards.

'This is it, this is London!' cried Betty. 'Make sure you've got everything. Whatever you do, stay together and don't –' The rest of her words were lost in a very wet sneeze.

More clambering, shoving, lugging and bickering. I had my

suitcase tight in one hand and the Czech girl limpeted to the other.

Just as Arek tripped off the train and onto the platform there was a shout. 'There they are!' A cluster of men in hats jogged towards our carriage. Questions shot out like bullets. 'How do you like England? Are you happy to be here? What was it like in the Nazi camps?'

Then they hoisted up cameras with bulbs that flashed and shattered, crunching underfoot. 'You there, the pretty dark girl, smile for us!'

Too late I turned my head away. Too late I yanked my hand from the little Czech girl's and raised it to my face. I was stabbed by the lights and caught on film.

So I did what any self-respecting, honest citizen wouldn't do. I ran.

I burst out of the station, heart pounding, almost straight into a jam of traffic. Horns blared. 'Watch where you're going, darlin'!'

I dodged cars, jumped puddles and slid between strangers on the far pavement. Then I slowed. You might look normal running *towards* a station, maybe late for a train, but you stand out running away. It's best to blend in and be what everyone expects. Hide in plain sight.

London looked endless and I was lost, of course. Still, if I didn't know where I was, no one could track me down. But what if I ever wanted to be found? To answer that question I had to get to Summerland, which meant un-losing myself.

Where are we, Mutti? I used to ask my mama.

She'd peer through keyholes, or out from under beds, or along the moon-silver stones of a secret pathway, wherever we'd been hiding at the time. You could criss-cross an atlas with all the places in Europe we went, looking for refuge.

Where are we? I'd ask, wondering if it was Romania, Moravia or Bavaria, and she'd say, 'We're exactly where we are on the surface of the planet, and we're together. That's all you need to know right now.'

Before the war I'd known exactly where I was. I'd be swinging my legs at the dinner table as grown-ups talked and joked. Making dens among the fallen leaves in the park. Running to school with a bouncing satchel. Were these memories or did I make them up to pass the years of hiding, when we were everywhere and nowhere at once?

Now I'd made it to the speck of the planet called London. I wished I could swing around lamp posts in celebration. I didn't of course. A nice girl wouldn't do such a thing, so neither did I.

London is a place of magic and marvels, my mama once told me, all in whispers. *Close your eyes, Liebling, and picture the city – a skyline of towers and spires. A river with ships that sail across every ocean on the planet, carrying sheep wool and spices, tree logs and diamonds . . . people and pineapples, cottons and queens. London is the heart of an empire. Unconquered. Defiant!*

Did I feel defiant? Definitely. Cold and overwhelmed too.

I crossed the river. *The Thames*, they called it, pronounced *tems*. It was brown and clogged with boats. I wished I could stop and gaze out over the sliding, slapping water. You could watch boats for hours, I reckoned, and never get tired of wondering where they'd been and where they were going. Instead I had my own journey to make. To the one place on the planet where I might find what I was looking for.

11

Which way was Summerland?

Everything everywhere, all mine for the seeing, as long as I kept moving. Stone lions crowned with pigeons . . . a red bus splattered with an ad for toothpaste . . . men in turbans talking with such animation their beards bounced . . . a blind accordion player at the underground railway steps, my heart squeezing with every wheezy note she played.

Mizzle turned to drizzle turned to rain. London people pulled down their hats and crouched under sudden umbrella sproutings. I thought they'd look happier that they'd won the war, not so pinched and tired. Didn't they realise they had it better than Berlin? Yes, they'd been bombed, and there were rubble hills between the buildings, but no one was fighting to eat clumps of stringy nettles growing in the debris, or chasing rats along buckled train lines. I shivered at the memory.

In Berlin it was women who cleared the bomb ruins at the end of the war, one brick at a time, one barrow after another. I'd done my fair share of chipping mortar from old bricks so they could be used again. Here in London, it was men with cranes who worked rebuilding. White, brown, black faces – the builders all wore wool caps but their hands were bare and their skin, whatever the colour, looked tough like gloves. Were they glad the bombs had fallen because now they had work and a pay packet every week?

'We'll bomb the Brits and all their filthy Jews into oblivion!' Herr Trautwein used to boast when he came home from work. Herr Trout-face, with a shiny swastika on his lapel and a voice that carried through the apartment to where I was hiding.

Herr Trout-face, manager in a factory near Berlin, building aeroplanes for the Luftwaffe so they could blow up the world. Frau Trout-face clucked and agreed with her husband, as all good Nazi wives should. My mama said nothing as she served them their dinner. The Trautweins didn't know she was a Jew. Had no idea I was crouched in their spare-room wardrobe.

Oh God – I couldn't go back there. Not to that cramped darkness with Frau Trautwein's fur coat tickling my nose and the fear that one sneeze would have me dragged into daylight to be shot.

This world I now had to roam in, it was all suddenly too much. I ducked into a doorway and held my suitcase close. I clicked the clasps open and checked that my one grey glove was dry. Such a small thing, and so seemingly insignificant, yet that glove was the real reason I'd come to England: I had to find the other glove to make a matching pair.

One by one the street lamps came on, making the rain shine silver. People poured out of the buildings, leaving the windows dark behind them. They all had somewhere to go. I did too, only the old fear gripped me: if I moved I'd be caught.

Across the street a boy on a bike skidded to a stop outside a grand building of golden stone, with carved lions guarding the entrance. One window in this building was still bright. I saw the silhouette of a man standing there, looking out, as if searching for someone. I wondered if he'd find whoever he was looking for. If I would. Then the blind was drawn and the man moved away.

The boy on the bike slapped a bundle of evening-edition papers on the pavement by a news kiosk. I thought of the reporters and photographers back at the station. It was the worst luck I'd been caught on camera. Someone might see me. Accuse me. Arrest me. Better to be invisible. So here I was. Unseen. Unknown. One small soul, lost among the ghosts.

Hot Buttered Toast

I'm not afraid of ghosts. Some people are, but I don't know why. The dead don't harm us – they leave that task to the living. I'd been seeing ghosts ever since I climbed out of the rubble after the bomb blast in Berlin, powdered with brick dust that stuck to the blood.

Herr Trautwein once bragged, 'The RAF will never drop a single bomb on German soil!' That was shortly after Mama got the job as their housekeeper – on false papers of course. She'd long since destroyed her proper passport, stamped with a *J* for *Jude* – Jew. She used the last of our precious money to pay for a false identity. I had to memorise her fake name. I was used to that – forgetting who we really were, to remember who we had to be.

This was after the other hiding places had failed, maybe two or three years into the war. I forget dates as well as places. I carry tunes in my head instead. Mama smuggled me into the apartment while both Trauts were out. Frau Trautwein went to the Nazi Women's League meetings, where they boasted about their offspring and knitted children's clothes for charity. The Trauts had specified *no dependents* on the job description, but Mama was desperate for work, and the job came with food and shelter. It was cold living rough. We hadn't eaten much for days, just raw potatoes we dug straight from the ground in someone's allotment.

How ironic, that after everywhere in Europe we'd searched for safety, we ended up in Berlin, the heart of the regime working to stamp Jews out. The only thing more outrageous would be turning up at Hitler's bunker looking for a bed and a bite to eat.

'They won't expect us here,' Mutti explained. 'They think Berlin is Jew-free.'

They were wrong. We saw others like us, scuttling about after curfew, or curled up in the sewers. Jews in hiding were called *submarines*, because they were under the surface. Jews not hiding were called dead.

So Herr Trautwein helped build aeroplanes to bomb Britain, and Britain retaliated with bombs on Germany. By the time all the bombs had fallen it was hard to tell ghosts from flesh-and-blood people, we were all so faint and grey.

Here in London ghosts were everywhere, dressed in all kinds of clothes – uniforms, evening gowns, shawls, short skirts, whatever they'd been wearing when they died. Some of them noticed me as I pushed between warm living bodies in an underground station to find a map of the rail network. Mostly the dead minded their own business, travelling in the groove of their last living moment.

Long ago one magic summer Mama had travelled across London by car. A *Silver Ghost*, she'd called it. 'But you'll need to get the train,' she told me. 'Look for King's Cross station.'

From the name I expected a king and a cross, or at least a crown. Instead I found arched girders thick with pigeon droppings.

'All fares!'

The ticket inspector was moving along the train carriage. I knew this game. I'd played it before, in Berlin, keeping ahead of the uniform then jumping out at a station, sprinting along the platform and dodging into one of the compartments that had already been checked, just as the train moved off again. It was a trick I'd learned from other feral children after the war was over. We were like packs of rats, scavenging all over the skeleton of the city. If I hadn't heard that the Red Cross were helping Jewish refugees get to England, I might have been stuck there still.

I squished into a compartment and sat down, suitcase tucked between my legs. Other passengers wrinkled their noses. Was it me that smelled bad or my sandwich? Hard to tell. Ignoring the disapproval, I fed the fish paste to the wolf in my stomach.

A young soldier opposite was reading the evening newspaper. My heart jolted at the headline.

NEW HOMES IN ENGLAND FOR NAZI VICTIMS

There was a photograph of a flash-bright face and a check coat. A picture of *me*, being ambushed by those idiot reporters. This was a disaster! What if I was recognised and caught before I got to Summerland? The soldier caught me staring. He folded the newspaper – thank God – and leaned forward with a stained-tooth smile.

'Going far, darlin'?'

I pretended not to hear.

A hefty woman next to him nodded at the newspaper headline. 'Look at this: more foreigners flooding the country, coming here to sponge off us hardworking English. A disgrace, I call it.'

Please don't look at the picture.

The soldier ignored her and spoke to me. 'Come on, darlin', smile – it might never happen.'

'Aw, leave her alone,' said his mate, a sailor.

The soldier casually put his hand on my knee. 'Just being friendly, aren't I? A pretty girl out on her own likes a bit of company.'

'You wouldn't think that if it was your sister,' said the sailor.

The soldier pulled his hand back quickly, saving me from having to break his wrist or stab him through the palm with my knife.

'Less of that hanky-panky if you please,' huffed the hefty woman. 'Honestly, girls today don't know how to behave! I blame the war – giving young people too much freedom. Girls going away from home and wearing trousers and who knows what. No wonder the world's in such a mess.'

'Mind your own business!' scowled the soldier. 'And the world'd be even more of a mess if we hadn't gone over there to sort old Hitler out. Why shouldn't we have a bit of fun, now we're back?' He eyed me in a way that made me wish I had the protection of trousers, not a flimsy skirt over bare legs. At least he'd forgotten about the newspaper.

He went to light a cigarette in the train corridor. The sailor got up to follow him.

'Look after yourself,' he mumbled as he brushed past.

I watched them slouch and smoke and joke, feeling jealous. It was easy for men to do things. Girls were always getting warned about what might be done to them. Mama said it was safer to be a girl in wartime. In the early months they'd only been rounding up men and boys. Arresting anyone who might be a threat. There'd been three of us back then – me, Mama and Papa. We were waiting to hear from England, about a safe place to live. Then all the Jewish men in town got taken. 'I'll find you!' Papa said, as they dragged him along the street, away from me and Mama.

He never did.

It was so long ago I couldn't remember his face or his voice. I stared into the glass of the train window, thinking how things could have been different.

The hefty woman who didn't like foreigners fell asleep. She snored. When the train reached the station she was supposed to get off at, I didn't bother to shake her awake. My own eyes were so heavy. but I had to keep alert to check every single station name. It was only safe to sleep when you were properly hidden, or if Mama was on guard. Not safe now. Definitely mustn't, wouldn't . . .

'All fares!'

I must've nodded off, propped up against the window. We

19

came to a halt. The carriage was empty. Just me and . . . the ticket inspector!

Instinct kicked in: hide or get away. Nowhere to hide. I fumbled for the door handle and tumbled out onto the platform with my case. A whistle blew. Doors slammed shut. The train pulled off and I was alone in a circle of lamplight, rain spattering down.

The station name sign was underneath a basket of drowned flowers: *East Summer*. Mama must have been watching out for me, because it was the very place on the planet I needed to be.

Beyond the lamps of the station all was dark. Wet hedges edged a lane, making a black border to wide miles of windswept unknown. I felt a sense of emptiness – a space left behind in time.

Head down I trudged along the lane . . . and walked straight into a policeman. Without hesitation, I turned and ran – straight into the hedge. A beast loomed up, all white eyes and steaming breath. It bellowed. I yelped and fell. The policeman hoisted me to my feet.

'All right, all right, it's only one of Old Rory's cows having a moo at you.'

A *cow*? Of course it was a cow. How stupid to panic. I had to think clearly. Behave normally. Mama had taught me how to produce real-seeming tears if necessary. She said to use this technique only as a last resort, because sometimes looking weak was the last thing you wanted.

The policeman planted his feet wide.

'To be fair, it's more likely to be a bull – not nearly so stroppy as the cows. Old Rory's got them to pasture on the old East Summer airfield now it's closed. New here, aren't you? A bit lost and wet by the look of it. Hang on, let me get me bike light and we'll see what's what.'

I knew all about policemen. They sometimes started with a pretence of friendliness. Next thing you knew, there'd be a concrete prison cell, questions, beatings . . . unbearable things. Once in Berlin my mother had been missing for three days. They'd picked her off the street and interrogated her – *What's your name? Where do you live? Are you hiding something?* By the time she came back, Frau Trautwein was furious. Without her trusty housekeeper she'd had to do her own cooking and cleaning and shopping. Mama apologised and said it had all been a misunderstanding, she'd get right back to work as soon as she'd changed out of her bloodied clothes.

It had been one of the worst times of my life, those three days of not knowing. Of not daring to leave my hiding place to go look for her. Of being twisted with hunger because the potato peelings Mama had left me were soon gone. Of being parched with thirst because I couldn't turn on the taps without the Trauts hearing, yet sick from the stench of the jar I had to pee in.

Mama came to me as soon as it was safe. *My darling, I'm sorry, so sorry, you poor dear* . . . That night, when the Trauts had scuttled down to the bomb shelter and searchlights criss-crossed the sky, Mama walked me around the apartment until my legs worked again. Usually we'd play silent piano duets when we were alone together. After her time with the police Mama couldn't play anything until her broken fingers had mended.

Never trust a policeman, she said.

This English policeman was wide and tall, made taller by a strange helmet with a silver badge. He had gingery whiskers on his chin, and hairs coming out of his nose too.

He seemed surprised when I handed him my papers. He took them anyway and read them through.

'Brigitta . . . *Iggle? Eegoyle?* Austrian, are you? Hitler's homeland, eh? He should've stayed there, painting houses or whatever he did before trying to rule the world. Hmm, you don't look much like a Nazi to me. Says here you're with the Red Cross – a refugee.'

I nodded.

'From . . . how d'you say this . . . ? *Auswitsh?* Blimey – heard about that on the wireless. Bloody awful it sounds, killing babies and everything. Like that Belsen place. Mr Oakley in the village, he can tell you about Belsen, except he won't, it was so nasty. Don't worry, you won't find folks so badly behaved here in England, at least not in the village. Out towards town there's the glove factory, Gant's, and they do employ a lot of *foreigners*. No offence.'

And then, instead of locking me up, or kicking me into the gutter, or shooting me on the spot, the policeman gave me back my papers and he smiled.

He smiled.

'I'm Constable Ribble. Where d'you need to get to, petal? I'll give you a croggie on me bike.'

In my suitcase I had a dictionary. It was a tiny thing, with pages too small to be any use as toilet paper, which is probably why it hadn't been ripped up like other books. It was one of the few things I'd salvaged from the wreckage of the Trautwein building after the bombs. *Midget Dictionary German–English English–German* it said on the cover. I desperately wanted to check it now to see what on earth *croggie* meant, and why this Ribble had called me a *petal*. Wasn't that something to do with a flower? Did I look floral? The constable's dialect was nothing like the elegant English my mother had forced me to learn. I was in a place called Yorkshire now.

You must speak like a local to avoid suspicion, Mama said, when we were looking for safe places to stay. *If in doubt, say nothing.*

Constable Ribble pointed to the seat of his bicycle and mimed him pedalling with me balancing.

'A CROG-GIE!' he repeated, loudly and slowly. 'No? Suit yourself. I'll walk you back to the village anyhoo. I usually come to the station to pick up the evening papers that folk leave on the train – something to read while I'm dunking me biscuits on the evening shift. Nice time of evening this, 'cept for the rain. Most folk are snug and dry indoors, minding their own business, just a few rascals creeping round where they oughtn't to be. Don't suppose that's you, is it? Up to no good?'

Although he acted bluff, his eyes were sharp.

I produced a smile.

* * *

The lane led downhill until the hedges gave way to houses with warm chinks of light showing at curtained windows. Soon we were on a street with pavements, a pub – open, a shop – shut, and one solitary lamp post shining by a telephone box. A wide stream ran through the village and there was a pond.

Ribble stopped by a small stone building with a blue lamp that said *POLICE*.

'Why don't you and I get out of this rain for a bit . . . ? I'll fix us a brew and rustle up biccies. No?'

Very no. *Brew* and *biccies* could mean any kind of torture device.

'In that case,' he said, 'you'd better tell me where you're heading. Can't have you wandering around the village, scaring the cows and whatnot.'

After so many months and so many miles it was time to commit. I lifted my chin and took a deep breath. I said it out loud. 'Summerland.'

'Summerland? You mean the big 'ouse? That's easy. Cross that there bridge, follow the avenue and you can't miss it. Say 'ow-do to the missus for me. You sure you're all right? Fair enough. Goodnight for now then, Miss Eegoil . . .'

I went over the arch of a bridge, with invisible water rushing beneath, and came to the start of a long avenue. Ranks of tall tree sentinels marched along either side. Beyond the trees were shadowed lawns, lumped with grey-grassy humps like the burial mounds of giant ancestors.

I breathed in big gulps of the freshest air ever tasted. The last time I was in the country it had been somewhere in Poland, scorching hot and so dry we drank out of puddles until these dried up. We'd been hidden in a sty, fighting bad-tempered pigs for a share of the slops. They were bacon by Christmas; we somehow stayed alive.

Now I walked alone in the English countryside, holding my case, humming a few bars of music over and over to calm my mind. My hands, gloveless, were so cold I could barely feel the suitcase handle in one hand or my knife in the other. Would I need it? I'd soon find out.

Ahead, in a dip among wet fields and beyond gates of black curling metal, was Summerland Hall – a place of fairy tales told in dawn light, in the last moments before doors were locked on me and I was left to sleep, while humans outside began their day. A house of wonders. A refuge.

I'd expected lights, warmth, glitter, not this picture of abandonment. Row upon row of blank windows, with ivy growing from ground to chimney-pots, as if trying to pull the house apart, brick by brick. In the middle of the roof was a clock tower. The hands on the clock were stuck on twelve.

To the left of the house a cold black lake spread towards bristling trees. There was a terrace with an ornamental pond. It was studded with a silent fountain and the cracked glass of a conservatory. To the right, a high brick arch and more brick buildings, all matted with dark leaves.

The gates were half open. An invitation or a trap? I crossed the gravelled forecourt to the house. Every step I took sounded as loud as an orchestra playing chords out of tune.

Stone stairs, mottled with moss, lured me to a huge front

door. I reached for the lion's head knocker. It was heavier than expected . . .

Bang! Bang! Bang!

That surely woke the ghosts . . . Yes, here they came, the Summerland spectres, drifting to the downstairs windows. Young men mostly. I saw the fluff of hopeful moustaches and cropped, combed hair. A hint of uniforms. War-dead.

Bang! Bang! Bang!

Would no one living answer?

The sound echoed and the ghosts rippled. Silence. Then I nearly leaped out of my skin when a very unghostly set of knuckles rapped on glass. A white face with red cheeks was at the window by the door.

'There's nobody home!' came a muffled voice. 'Who are you anyway? Well? Cat got your tongue?'

Why would a cat have my tongue? I stuck it out to show that no such mutilation had occurred.

The woman stared.

'Just my luck, an escaped lunatic. You'd better come in. I don't want to be cleaning your drowned corpse off the steps in the morning. No, not this door. It doesn't open. Go round.' She pointed to the right side of the house and mouthed the words again: 'Go. Round.'

Through the arch was a garage, protected by a big rusty padlock. There were collapsing sheds and shadows. Wet cobbles made me slip, brambles tore at my bare legs. A light shone out.

'This way, hurry up . . .'

I fell up a doorstep. My suitcase handle snapped and the case dropped to the floor.

'That's one way to make an entrance!'

Strong hands had me upright and propelled me across stone flagstones to a chair. I found myself sitting at a wooden table, scrubbed bone-white clean. The table was by a great black oven range, blissfully warm. All around were high shelves stacked with pans and kitchen bits. Up above, snow-white laundry hung from a wooden winter-hedge. In the middle of it all, the woman. She had brown hair skewered into a knot at the nape of her neck, a cardigan with sleeves pushed up to show powerful arms and a starch-stiff apron almost down to her slippers.

'Dripping all over my floor,' she muttered as she threw me a towel. 'Give me your coat and we'll set it to dry. Fine. Keep it on and catch a fever, no skin off my nose. You will take your shoes off, mind. My kitchen, my rules.'

I bent and tugged at the laces, transferring the knife into my sock. As soon as my shoes were off, the woman grabbed them. She stuffed each shoe with newspaper and put them in front of the range. If I had to run, I'd need to lunge for my shoes before I made it to the door. So I might as well dry my coat as well. It had precious things hidden inside the lining. I handed it over to the woman.

She watched me squeeze rain from my braids.

'I saw you had a tongue. Can you use it? Can you talk?'

Speak to no one. Tell them nothing. These were my instructions, drummed in week after week, year after year. Talking didn't come easily. Carefully I sounded out some English words.

The woman frowned. 'Speak up! I've heard gnats shout louder.'

27

Slowly my hand inched down one leg to the knife again. 'You are . . . Barbara Summer?'

There. I'd said it. I'd named her, the woman I'd come all this way to find. The one who maybe needed a knife in her heart. It was her fault there was only one grey glove.

To be fair, this woman didn't look like a wicked witch. In fact, she laughed.

'Lady Summer? Get away! I'm Sophie Rover – Summerland's housekeeper, cook and general dogsbody. No more, no less. Lady Summer indeed! Her Ladyship and maid are away till tomorrow, and just as well. Neither of them would take kindly to beggars knocking on the front door. Me, I've been in the army. I've seen a bit more of life, so I know when someone needs a good cup of tea and a sit-down.'

As she talked she put the kettle on to boil, set a chopping board on the table, took a loaf of bread from a white enamel tin and fetched a knife from a drawer. I left my knife where it was. Sophie Rover's was much bigger.

She cut two thick slices of bread and set it to toast on the range. Next she lifted the lid on a glistening golden-yellow block. Real butter. Not pale margarine, not white lard, not dark oil. Real butter on white bread.

'Hot buttered toast and a brew!' said Mrs Rover. 'Nothing quite like it for setting you right. And you look proper famished. I'm used to feeding a hundred fellas at a time, back in my army days. Getting some colour in *your* cheeks will be a doddle. Now, here's your tea – extra sugar – and here's your toast. Ask no questions how come we've got more

28

butter than the piddly ration amount. You make short work of that, then we'll get down to brass tacks: what's your name, where are you from, and what bad luck brings you here to Summerland?'

Porridge with Jam

I told her nothing but my name. My business was with Barbara Summer.

Mrs Rover didn't push for more. She bustled about tidying up in the kitchen while I wolfed down the toast and gulped my mug of tea. Mama had warned me that English people liked brown water with milk in. It was strange but warming and sweet. I liked it.

What now? Spend the night in one of those outbuildings and wait for Lady Summer to return? I reached for my coat.

'Leave that. I'd not put a cat out on a night as wet as this, not even a silent cat like you. Vera Baggs – that's my lady's maid – she won't approve of me letting you stay, and that's reason enough for me, unless you've got anywhere else to go?'

I shook my head.

'Thought not. Bring your case and follow me.'

She led the way through a series of workrooms, up two twisting flights of bare stone steps and along a narrow corridor lined with closed doors and shuttered windows. There was one bare bulb hanging from a cracked ceiling. We were in the attic.

'The lavvy's down that end. You know – *toilet?*'

30

I blushed and nodded that I understood.

'The flush is a bit temperamental. Give it a good yank.'

Yank? 'An American?'

'No! A *pull*.' She mimed jerking a rope. 'Here's your room. Old servants' quarters. As you've probably noticed, much of the house is under dust covers – not in use. We had bomber crews stationed here during the war. Nice lads, most of them. A bit wild at times, from what I've heard, and didn't leave the place fit for habitation, that's for sure. We've only just started opening up rooms again and getting stuff out of storage. Honestly, there's enough posh crockery and knick-knacks and sticks of furniture crammed in the attic to fill a jumble sale. All of it to be dusted off and put out on display again. Now Lady Summer has finally come back to live here, things are getting back to normal, even if His Lordship isn't . . . Well. Never mind about him.'

I looked at her. What was *normal?* I did have some memories – or were they dreams? – of being somewhere called home. We didn't have to hide. We lit candles on the Sabbath and only put clothes in wardrobes, and sang really loudly whenever we felt like it. Mama always said I learned music before words and walking.

'Here, give me a hand with the sheets . . .'

At the Berlin Red Cross centre we'd been trained in housework basics, so I knew how to make a beds even if I hadn't slept in one half my life. Girls coming to England as refugees were supposed to find a job as a domestic help, a factory worker or a field labourer. There was a factory near Summerland. The policeman Ribble had mentioned it. It

31

was called Gant's and it made gloves. The gloves they made had labels inside with the name spelled out in beautiful blue scrolling letters.

Gant's Gloves, England.

My glove was a Gant's glove, in soft dove grey.

'Back in a jiffy . . .' said Mrs Rover.

When she was gone, I sat on the bed for a moment and closed my eyes. A whole room all to myself!. It was very plain, with a narrow bed, a chest of drawers and . . .

Mrs Rover came back just as I was shoving the wardrobe out the bedroom door.

'What on earth are you doing?' she shouted.

'*Keine Garderobe!*' I said through clenched teeth. The damn thing was too heavy to shift quickly. The door kept swinging open.

'You can't just go moving furniture about! Stop that right now!'

'No wardrobe!' I repeated, in English this time.

'Fine. No ruddy wardrobe. Here . . .' Her beefy arms practically lifted the wardrobe off the ground. Together we got it out of the bedroom, into the corridor. I shut and latched the wardrobe door but did not lock it. If Mrs Rover hadn't been watching I would've taken the key and thrown it into the lake. I didn't need a reminder that I'd spent years of my life living in a box where I couldn't stretch taller than the coat hangers or wider than the span of the wood. Even now, out in the wide world, my body remembered how cramped and crazy it had been, how I'd felt I'd burst out of my skin and out of my mind if I had to keep still in there one minute longer.

Only at night could I creep out. Mama had taught me squats and press-ups and bicep curls – she'd learned gymnastics at her posh school – so I'd have some muscles at least, when I next needed them.

'You're stronger than you look,' said Mrs Rover thoughtfully. 'An oddball too, no mistake, but I'll say no more about furniture removals. Here – a fresh towel. If you need anything, my rooms are just off the kitchen, though I warn you, I can sleep through a bomb raid, sirens and all, so knock hard at the door.' She paused. 'You're not fanciful, are you? Some sensitive souls – not me – *some* fusspots, namely Vera Baggs – they reckon old Ursula the chambermaid haunts the top floor. Drowned herself in the lake, they say, after the Great War, in 1918. Unrequited passion or some such nonsense. No man's worth it. I'm married – I should know.'

I took the towel. 'Goodnight, Mrs Rover.'

'Goodnight, Brigitta.'

'Mrs Rover . . .'

'Yes?'

'Thank you.'

She gave me a long, long look, then nodded. 'You're welcome.'

Mrs Rover was right about the *lavvy*. After paying a call I found the lavatory pull was at the end of a long chain that set off a great thundering orchestra of clanking pipes. In the Trautwein apartment I hadn't been able use the toilet during the day, even if the Trauts were out, in case they came back early, or a neighbour called. I held it in as best I could until they were asleep. The evening they got the news their son was

33

dead, they didn't go to sleep, and it was beyond horrible to have to go in a tin in the wardrobe and hope they wouldn't smell it. I hated them more than ever that night, as they sobbed and said their son had died a hero's death for Hitler. *What about me?* Their son at least had had a chance at life. He'd been a pilot. Probably crashed in one of the planes made at his papa's factory.

How I'd wanted to burst out of the wardrobe that night to surprise the Trauts – to see their faces when they realised they'd been eating, breathing and snoring with a *Jew* child hidden among their save-for-Sunday clothes. Better still, I would have marched over to their piano and damn well played something LOUD to let music drown out their blubbering grief. I didn't of course. Even living in a wardrobe is better than being dead.

It took me a moment to realise I had an audience while in the Summerland toilet. A girl had wafted through the door and was sitting on an upturned bucket, a mop in her hand. She was a faint ghost, barely visible. As time passes, ghosts lose whatever tethers they have to life. Only recent ghosts look close to solid.

'Are you Ursula who drowned in the lake? Were you watching me pee?'

Ursula picked up her mop and went through the motions of wiping the floor.

I stepped round her. Walking through a ghost's nothingness is very unpleasant.

The plumbing noise had brought a whole cloud of spectres up to the attic floor. They were mostly pale young men in faded uniforms. More war-dead. Probably the airmen Sophie

Rover had talked about. These were more like boys than men. British and Polish, I thought, from the uniforms. Lots of Poles escaped to England so they could join the Allies against Hitler. England had been their refuge. These had obviously died a long way from home. They jostled for a view of me. One guy with a football under his arm jerked his head to me, as if inviting me for a kickaround.

'Maybe tomorrow night,' I whispered with a yawn. The strangeness of the day was catching up with me. I'd crossed a sea since breakfast and travelled miles in an unknown land to get to this house of shadows and secrets.

I trailed my fingertips along the wall back to my room. Summerland was real, not just the stuff of stories and promises. *A safe place*, my mama had said. *I'll find you*, my papa had called out.

Using my coat as a pillow, I curled up under the bed, not on top of it. I slept with my one grey glove curled in the palm of my hand.

Waking. Complete confusion. Where was I? Who was I? Was it day? I had no idea of time. The wristwatch I'd stolen from a dead man in Berlin had, in turn, been taken from me by a Russian soldier who already boasted five watches going up his arm. When I crawled out from under the bed I saw the sun was shining. For years daylight had been the danger time when I had to stay out of sight. It was still a novelty to open curtains and see blue sky.

The bedroom window looked down on a jumble of slate roofs, an overgrown vegetable garden, a chicken hut and a row of washing. The red-check tablecloth pegged on the line was a bit of everyday magic – a sign that things were normal. No war here. I'd been right to come. There was a song Mama used to sing: 'It's a Lovely Day Tomorrow'.

I dusted myself off a bit and headed for the kitchen, suitcase packed and tucked under one arm. I paused on the landing. There was an archway onto another corridor, this one grander than the attic hallway. All the doors were closed. Along the walls were framed paintings, some draped in white sheets. There was a small table set with a bowl of bright fruit – oranges. I walked softly towards them. Slowly a sheet slipped from the nearest picture. A murky portrait: grim man, grimmer woman and good-looking boy. Judging by their modern clothes, I guessed that had to be the recent Summer family. I studied their faces. Father, mother, son, all together. A bit like my family before the war, except we lived in cramped lodgings and knew how to smile.

If things had been different . . .

Things were what they were. I reached out for the oranges instead, remembering a long-ago smell of dimpled peel. These oranges were fake. Cold, hard glass.

If I'd known what was waiting in the kitchen I'd've been out of the house like a shot.

'Ah,' said the policeman.

This wasn't fair! Police generally came at night. At 3 a.m. or just before dawn. Heavy boots on the stairs. A pounding at the door. Shouting, punching, handcuffs. Gunshots. Here was one in daylight.

36

'Morning!' said Mrs Rover. 'I've kept some porridge hot. You've already met Constable Ribble, haven't you?'

I calculated the odds of getting past him to the back door then into the woods beyond the lake, where he couldn't follow by bicycle.

Mrs Rover pressed me into a chair and held me there. 'Here you go – proper Scottish oats soaked in lovely creamy milk.'

The policeman was opposite me. He leaned forward with a frown so severe it made my heart race. 'Downright criminal, I call it. I won't let you get away with it!'

I waited for the truncheon blows and the handcuffs.

'Get away with what?' asked Mrs Rover.

He nodded at my bowl. 'Eating porridge without a swirl of jam in the middle. Haven't you any jam?'

'You know better than to ask a question like that, cheeky blighter.' Off she went to a larder, still talking. 'When I was in the army I'd be boiling up jam by the barrowful. So much jam, it used to explode all over the ceiling at times. Raspberry, plum, damson, I've jammed them all. Try this, Brigitta. Strawberry. The last batch made before they dug up the fruit patch for an air-raid shelter. Master Joseph used to love it . . .' Her face darkened. 'Poor lad.'

'Poor fellow,' echoed the constable.

Master Joseph . . . would that be Lady Summer's son? The one from the portrait?

Keeping a close eye on the policeman, I dipped my spoon in the jam jar and drew out a blob of lovely, rich red stickiness.

'Go on. Drop it in the middle and make a spiral. It'll go pink.'

Under orders, I did just that. I took a mouthful. *Jam!* An explosion of sweetness! I'd forgotten there could be such treats.

'Good, isn't it?' Mrs Rover passed a teaspoon to Ribble so he could dip into the jar. 'Can't imagine there's a lot of jam in that *Auswitsh* place, or wherever you've been, Brigitta. Stick around and I'll make my famous jam roly-poly. I served that to the chaps evacuated from Dunkirk. On their last legs, they were. My puddings didn't half make them up and ready to fight the Jerries again. No offence,' she added quickly.

'I'm Austrian,' I said between mouthfuls.

Later I'd have to get my dictionary out and check all the new words – *porridge* . . . *spiral* . . . *roly-poly* . . . I'd heard of *Dunkirk* via clandestine radio. It was when the Germans kicked the Brits out of France in 1940. During Dunkirk I'd been under the floorboards of a warehouse – in Poland, I think – trying not to sneeze from the dust. Above me were plundered Jewish Kiddush cups and Hanukkah candelabra. I supposed they were to be melted down. Me too, if I'd been found.

Constable Ribble puffed out his chest and fixed his eyes on me. 'And now . . . we'd best get down to business, young miss.'

I froze, spoon halfway to my mouth.

'Yes, after our meeting on the lane last night, well, I just thought I'd drop in and see how you were getting on here at Summerland.'

There was a long pause. I stared at my pink porridge.

Mrs Rover saved me by giving Ribble a friendly flick with her tea towel. 'Leave the girl alone. Go catch some burglars, or poachers, or black marketeers, or whatever it is you do to justify your wages.'

He picked his helmet up and set his mug by the sink. 'I may look slow, but there's not a lot that I miss, Mrs Rover. I've been reading in the papers about Nazi spies hiding in the hedges and Hitler's henchmen escaping dressed as nuns and suchlike. Wouldn't want to find one of those in the shrubbery, now would you?'

He winked at me as he left. What sort of country was this, where the police *winked* and let you put jam in your porridge?

A bell rang – one of several on a long board in the kitchen, each labelled. The jangling one was for the drawing room.

'Drat and botherations!' cried Mrs Rover. 'Quick, Brigitta, wash your hands and run a comb through your hair, and I'll plait it up again. That'll be Lady Summer. She got back before you were up, you lazybones, with Miss Bossy Baggs the maid – that's Miss Vera Baggs to you – and she's wanting to see you, sharpish.'

I suddenly lost my appetite.

Mrs Rover bustled me out of the kitchen and along a stone passageway. It was lined with toilet cubicles. Fifteen of them, painted air force blue.

'Don't ask,' she said grimly.

We pushed through a door padded with thick green felt and into the main part of the house. It was vast, quiet and dim. On the walls more giant portraits and speckled mirrors. Through open doors glimpses of shuttered rooms. Furniture was draped in sheets, like ghosts you could sit on. Then, an archway, a ballroom and, *good God* . . . a piano! A proper concert grand. I stopped short. My fingers fluttered. This house was too quiet. It needed music. *I* needed music. Music, laughter, fun, freedom . . .

Not since before the war had I played a real note on a real piano, not once. My fingers had mapped out whole concertos on Fish-face Traut's piano without ever pressing a key down to hear unseen hammers vibrate invisible wires for sound. I stayed with that imagined sensation for a moment. What would it be like to make music again . . . ?

'Quick march!' ordered Mrs Rover. 'Come on – left right, left right. Here . . . halt!' We stopped outside a white door. She tapped politely. The door opened. A bony finger beckoned – *come in* – then a palm splayed – *wait there* – and the finger gestured *shh*, before flicking a dismissal at Mrs Rover.

Lady Summer was on the telephone.

Her voice was not how I'd imagined. She was not the gracious, welcoming queen of a fairy-tale house at all. She didn't sound like summer roses or fresh strawberries on the lawn; more like the glass oranges upstairs – cold and repelling. She held the black phone receiver away from her mouth as if it might somehow contaminate her.

'Let me remind you, you upstart ministry *mouse*, when I very generously allowed the air force to use Summerland for the duration of the war, it was on the understanding that the men billeted here would respect its age and heritage, and yet I return to find everything in a *deplorable* condition.'

I didn't need a dictionary to tell me what *deplorable* meant – her tone was enough.

'You have already had my report about the Nissen huts on the lawn, the golf balls clogging the fountain and the *fifteen* military conveniences lining my back passage . . . Excuse me! Do you find this *amusing*? I can assure you I do *not*. Nor did I smile to find beer bottles inside the piano and male underpants over the hall chandelier. Yes, I said *underpants*. I sacrificed my husband to this war . . . yes . . . I should think you *are* sorry to hear that . . . If you must know, he was run over in the blackout, but my son, my only son, was shot down during a bombing raid over Germany, so you see I have paid my dues! It's time *you* paid for the damage done to the ancestral home, and *that* is my final word!'

She smashed the receiver onto the phone cradle and stood for a moment, containing her anger. Like the table and chairs, Lady Barbara Summer was all angles and spindly with it. Her dress, hanging from skeletal shoulders, blended with the lemon pastels of the cushions and curtains. Like the cushions, her figure was flat. Her cheeks were chalk white, with two spots of red rouge to match the dab of red on her lips. Her hair was set in perfectly parallel waves.

As she turned towards me her dress wafted at the hem like a cobweb and a hint of perfume sent me tumbling back in time to a memory I never knew I had – a bottle with a ribbon – a spray of scent – my papa kissing my mother . . .

Pay attention.

'So – you are the uninvited guest? My housekeeper does have an unnatural weakness for waifs and strays. What is your name?'

'Brigitta Igeul.'

'German, I suppose.'

'Austrian.'

'Hardly, with *that* accent. I was a pupil at a very exclusive finishing school in Switzerland, you know. One of my dearest friends at that time was German. I know the accent when I hear it.'

'I have been in Berlin, at the end of the war.'

'Poor you,' she said, without emotion. 'Mrs Rover tells me you are a Jew. That you were in one of the Nazi camps during the war. Auschwitz, in Poland.'

I nodded.

'She should not have let you stay here without my permission. What dark hair you have – is it verminous?'

'No.'

'Your identity papers state you are fifteen years of age?'

'Yes.' To be honest, I no longer remembered birthdays. I knew my supposed age because it was written on all the documents.

Lady Summer began to circle me. I felt naked under her gaze and dizzy from her perfume. Mama used the same scent, before the war; I was sure of it now.

'You have good posture, I'll concede that. Clean nails. Shabby clothes – par for the course these days. People have let standards slip. When I was a girl . . .'

Her voice drifted. Her fingers brushed the frame of a photo on the desk. It showed a boy in white sports gear, holding a flat wooden bat. Her son, I supposed, shot down over Germany. I envied him his grin, his short floppy hair and easy pose.

Now. Now was my chance. To show her the glove. To ask her, tell her, stab her – I wasn't sure yet. All this time I'd thought of Summerland as a refuge, or a meeting place. Was it just a might-have-been? A cruel, unwelcoming joke? Mama had said it would be safe here. Had she lied?

I drew myself tall. 'Lady Summer . . .'

There was a scratchy sort of knock at the door. She turned and the moment was gone.

'Only me,' said the creature who slid through the narrow gap. She was all soft and formless, from the droop of her cheeks to her sloping shoulders and puffy fingers. 'I heard voices and wondered if you needed anything, my lady. No trouble at all if you do. I'm here to help . . . Oh. This must be the *refugee*. As if our rations weren't stretched quite far enough already.'

'Thank you, Miss Baggs. As I am sure you are aware, our sturdy Mrs Rover is capable of feeding an army so we need not worry on that score.'

Miss Baggs rippled. 'Perhaps you are not aware that Mrs Rover has been giving this refugee *jam* with her porridge, my lady. *I* never have such a luxury.'

'No, I don't imagine you do.'

I tried again. 'Lady Summer –'

She interrupted me. 'I understand that the Red Cross arranged your visa and passage to England?'

'Yes.'

'You should say, *Yes, ma'am*,' corrected Miss Baggs.

'Curious,' said Lady Summer. 'You were sent here even though I offered no such hospitality. Do I know you?'

Not yet.

She smoothed the fine wool of her dress. 'Your documents state you are a seamstress. Do you sew well?'

That question made Miss Baggs wobble with indignation. 'I do *not* need any help managing your wardrobe, my lady,

43

unless you think my standards have somehow slipped and you no longer wish to honour me with the position of maid and companion, in which case please accept my resignation right now at this very exact moment, offered freely, despite my many years of faultless service –'

'That will do, Vera. Can you sew, Brigitta?'

'N-no.'

'There!' exclaimed Miss Baggs. 'She can't sew, so she needn't be here.'

Stop stammering like a frightened child, I told myself. *You're trained to handle interrogation*. Despite months spent planning this moment, every speech I'd ever prepared flew out of my head. What was I supposed to tell her? The truth? Could I just blurt out what I wanted . . . what I hoped for . . . what I was?

Hardly.

I'd wait until the nasty Baggs woman was out of the way, until I could be certain who to trust. There were things I could find out on my own first, I was sure of it. Besides, if I stayed at Summerland there could be more of that hot, sweet porridge. There might even be music.

I found my voice and spoke quickly. 'I can work, my lady. I can clean your house. Take beer bottles out of the piano. Take underpants off the . . .' I waved my hand towards the light fitting, since I couldn't remember the English word she'd used.

Lady Summer folded her arms. Her elbows stuck out like knife points. 'Thank you, that will do. And yet . . . there's something about you, Brigitta Igeul.' She pronounced my name perfectly.

The telephone bell jangled, making us all jump. Lady Summer

snatched up the receiver. 'I *said* that was my last word, you incompetent little desk-weasel! I beg your pardon? . . . Oh, *Matron*. My apologies. I was not expecting your call.'

As she listened her body sagged like a piece of perished elastic. 'Being discharged? When? For certain?'

Miss Baggs sidled closer to me and muttered, 'There *is* something about you, missy. My lady may be gullible, but I'm no fool. I'll be watching you . . .'

She couldn't say anything more because she wanted to listen in to the telephone conversation, and Lady Summer's voice had dwindled almost to a whisper.

'No, no problem at all. I understand it has been a long convalescence and his spirits aren't . . . what they ought to be. He is coming home, that is the important thing. Where he belongs. We'll be ready.'

Slowly she put the receiver down. I couldn't tell if she was happy or nervous or both. Once she was facing us again her face was composed under its mask of powder and rouge.

'Well, it seems your arrival is timely after all, Brigitta. That was the hospital. There is a patient arriving a week on Saturday. My son. We will need to prepare his rooms. You say you can work? There is no shortage of that required in Summerland. I intend to have this house restored to its former glory, in honour of my boy, and the long, illustrious line of Summer men. In the meanwhile, Mrs Rover will give all instructions.'

She glided to a strip of embroidered cloth near the door and gave it a pull. In the depths of the house, a bell rang. Before I could leave, her voice jerked me to a stop as sharply as if one of my plaits had been pulled.

45

'Oh, and Brigitta – regarding your time in that Nazi camp, you will say nothing of it, do you understand? You will not speak of Germany or about anything connected with the war. All that is past. We have to look forward now . . .'

Apple-and-Blackberry Crumble

In the days that followed, Summerland was no longer still or quiet. Together Sophie Rover and I threw open shutters, whipped off dust-sheets and lugged buckets of hot water made pink with stinging soap. I pretended I was Ursula, the ghost with a mop. It was important to be what people expected to see. An innocent refugee. A skivvy.

Holding a duster gave me a pretext to sidle into the many rooms at Summerland, looking for evidence of life here before the war. Mostly I found mouse droppings and empty spaces. The rooms I really wanted to search – Lady Summer's bedroom and study – were kept locked. She didn't trust me. Very wise.

'It once took an army to keep this place running,' Mrs Rover said. 'Not a speck of dust, not a moth or fly left alive. I came here as a girl once, for the Bonfire Night party. That's a big Summerland tradition for all the village. There were maids bobbing and menservants bowing and all sorts of pomp. Now it's just the two of us and useless Baggsy – who'd've thought?'

We were preparing a bedroom and sitting room for the

patient. I was glad of the work. It gave me something to do with my body, which was aching to run wild. I sloshed suds across floorboards and thought, This could have been my home, *should* have been my home. Mama had written to Barbara Summer before the war, begging her for refuge. Waiting for a reply, Mama told me about cricket and croquet and English roast beef. Lady Summer never answered. If she had, there would have been sponsorship and visas. We could have taken the ship across the Channel together. None of the horrors would have happened. No running, no hiding, no wood of the wardrobe pressing in on me day after day after day after day, night after night, year after year . . .

I took my fury out on the floor mopping, since I couldn't legally kill those I held responsible for my war.

'Steady on,' said Mrs Rover. 'We're trying to clean the place, not drown it.' She was scraping at a window which still had gummy strips of tapes criss-crossing each pane, to stop the glass shattering if a bomb fell. Just like the windows in the Trautwein apartment.

'No bombs now at least. A couple of strays fell in the woods back in '42 and hit the gamekeeper's cottage, killing poor Roman Varley's wife. I was at school with her. The village kids call the ruin the Bomb House and say it's haunted. I told them – no such thing as ghosts.'

A shadow moved past the bedroom door just as she said that. Who was it? Ursula? Too tall. An airman? Too . . . delicate. Sunshine ghosts are rare and almost impossible to see.

Mrs Rover's voice made the shadow vanish. 'Oi, Brigitta! Since your head is so full of cobwebs, you might as well run up the ladder and clear those dusty ones around the light fitting. Don't worry, I'm not going to look up your skirt!'

I was pulling it as far over my knees as I could.

'As if I'm bothered about seeing your knickers after three years in the army. My godfathers – there were some horrors! Big grey pants like barrage balloons, fastened with elastic above the knee . . . proper passion killers. Talking of passion . . .' Her voice dropped. '*You're* not, are you?'

'Not what?'

'Pregnant?'

'No! Impossible!' I nearly fell off the ladder at the very thought.

'That's what me and my Tim thought, when we were courting. We only ever did it standing up so I thought we'd be all right, but *no*. Had to get married, him in khaki, me in a borrowed frock. Turned out it was a false alarm, but I'm stuck with a husband now, off and on. My advice is, keep away from boys, Brigitta, especially when they get *that look*.'

Face flushed red, I twirled the feather duster. Most of the cobwebs seemed to get stuck to my arms. A dry, curled-up spider dropped on a strand in front of my face, very dead. It reminded me of a time when I'd been curled up in the dark myself, very alive, very aching to move. A thousand ghost spiders had run across my bare face and arms before skittering away. I'd tried playing music in my head, but that only made my skin tingle more. Suddenly I was right back in that wardrobe again and it seemed to be closing in around me, and it had been *ages* since Mama brought me anything to drink, and I heard footsteps across the rug, the key turning in the lock of the wardrobe, but it wasn't Mama, it had to be Frau Trautwein opening the door . . . I'd be seen, discovered, dragged away, killed, and the door was stuck so she jerked at it more and I tried to shrink small enough to run away like a spider only I felt as big as an elephant but then Herr Trautwein called to say he was home, so she left and I didn't die but I wanted to.

The memory was so fresh, so *real* my skin came up in bumps. I dropped the duster stick and opened my eyes to Summerland.

'Butterfingers!' came a sneer from the doorway. Not a ghost. This was the lumpy Vera Baggs. 'Lady Summer needs a few items from Oakleys'. I would go myself, if I wasn't so busy supervising preparations for the patient.'

'I'd go myself if I wasn't so busy actually *doing* the preparations,' huffed Mrs Rover. 'Here, Brigitta, could you pop down to Oakleys' – the village shop? It'll be good for you to get some fresh air and a bit of sunlight.'

'We can't trust *her*!' snapped Miss Baggs.

'What's she going to do? Single-handedly invade England and set up the next Third Reich?'

'I will go,' I said.

I'd never bought anything in a shop before. It would be an adventure.

Daylight was dazzling. A breeze wafted through the back door, bringing the promise of trees, fields, freedom. A yellow-white autumn sun shone over ivy leaves and red brick walls. I walked out by the terrace. The grass was dewy, the moss was green. White clouds floated in the fountain water, reflections from a blue, blue

50

sky. From the woods I heard the crack of timber being chopped. A spiral of smoke rose up through the branches. Woodcutters. There'd been a time in the war when we hid in a forest. We'd no matches for a fire and everything was wet. Mama wrapped me in her arms and hummed tunes from the *Peter and the Wolf* symphony, where the music brings all the characters to life.

I'm here, I told the breeze. Let blackbirds take my words to her, wherever her ghost was now.

A flash of movement behind me. A face at a window? Gone.

As soon as I was out of sight of the house, I ran; I couldn't help it. My shoes scuffed up grit, my braids flew out behind me. Not from danger or towards safety, just running for the sheer fun of it – amazing! I only slowed down when I reached the humpback bridge over the river. Water flowed silver. Some pooled in a pond edged with emerald grass.

Years ago there'd been a boy who fed the ducks. I remembered him. Except that couldn't be true, because who'd give their bread to *birds* when they could eat it themselves? Thanks to Sophie Rover I was now fuelled by big slabs of bread and butter, and a daily lunch of something called *meatuntooveg*, which was slices of meat with a mound of mashed potatoes, floods of thick gravy and a mush of greens. All that, followed by pudding. I could almost feel my body growing every night. I got too cramped under the bed and decided to sleep on the mattress. Being comfortable was nice, in a strange way.

In the village I got my bearings quickly enough. Left past the bridge was a clump of yew trees and a church spire. Ahead of me, next to the pond, was a triangle of grass, the police station, a pub – called the Clock Tower – and the village shop.

51

The sign above the shop window read: *A&E Oakley. Grocer's – Post Office.*

I was glad I'd spent time with the British Red Cross nurses in Berlin, getting used to the language. German I'd learned at school before the war; Czech and Polish at home from birth. Then, in hiding, my mother had taught me French and English. I could still feel the faint tickle of her fingertip, tracing letters in my palm. *A is for Apple, B is for Blackberry . . .*

In front of Oakleys' shop were rows of wooden crates, each full of a different type of vegetable. There was also a red post box. It matched the red telephone box on the triangle of grass. My heart quickened. I'd come to Summerland for . . . I wasn't quite sure what for now. Justice? Safety? A reunion? What if I did some hunting instead of just waiting for something to happen? There was a telephone book in the phone box. When things had got bad in Berlin, people ripped directories into squares for toilet paper. Then we had to use pages from the few books that hadn't already been burned for fuel. Frau Trautwein suggested sheet-music squares in the toilet, but my mother had objected. I couldn't say anything. I didn't exist.

I nipped into the box and flipped the flimsy pages, looking for a name I'd buried for years. It began with *g*, like *g* for glove and G for Gant's. I ran my finger down a page of surnames. G . . . G . . . G . . .

No Golanski.

He was dead. I knew it.

He couldn't be dead! He was my *papa* – large and warm and full of life. He'd taught me to whistle on grass stalks and had folded paper boats for my bathtub. Except it had been so long since I saw his face I had probably just invented memories of a papa while alone in the dark of the wardrobe, where there was no grass and no baths. Lots of fathers died in the war – why should mine be any different? Just because I desperately wanted him to be alive, that didn't mean it would happen. Why was I even holding out hope? Was he worth it? Hadn't he abandoned us anyway? Left us to suffer alone? Left me in this mess? The pig! He was alive and he didn't care about me. *I'll find you*, he said. What a lie. He wasn't even looking for me. Fine. I'd get addresses. Write letters. Find him first. And then . . . ?

The knife was still in my sock.

I fingered a few bars of music against my leg to collect myself before crossing the green to the shop. A bell tinkled as I opened the door. A group of people turned to say hello, then fell silent. A gigantic woman behind the counter – Mrs Oakley? – beckoned me forward. She had a flour-white face and a pinned-up lump of hair like a loaf of bread.

'Our Ribble said there was a foreigner at the big house. Looks like he was right. German, are you? I'd spit if wasn't unhygienic. Germans everywhere these days, like a ruddy invasion! There's half a dozen prisoners working at Home Farm and I don't know how many else up Old Rory's place. Get out of here. I won't serve you.'

The other customers nodded or tutted or just stared.

A man in a brown apron – Mr Oakley? – smiled, but warily,

because his wife was big and cross. 'Now then, Enid, it's not likely this pretty lass is out to start World War Three, are you, pet?'

Mrs Oakley sniffed. 'You know what happened to my dad – gassed by the Germans in the first war. Never been right in the head since.'

I thought I heard Mr Oakley mutter, 'Runs in the family.'

'And I always said Joseph Summer would come to grief if he joined the RAF, even if he did look proper smart in his uniform, bless him. Ruddy Huns – using his plane for target practice.'

'Poor lad,' said Mr Oakley. 'I remember him winning the last cricket tournament before the war, with that shot he put through the village-hall window. What a belter.'

'I have a list, from Lady Summer.' My accent sounded painfully un-English.

Mrs Oakley sniffed. 'If you *haf* a *leest* from Lady Summer, then I suppose I'll have to oblige. Put it on the counter.'

While her husband collected items from the shelves and tore strips of stamps from a big book, Mrs Oakley totted up numbers and wrote a tally in a ledger. She wasn't done with her spite though.

'You should be glad you Jews aren't all in concentration camps still, and I don't see why you'd be sent there if you hadn't done *something* wrong. No smoke without fire, I say.'

I smiled at Mrs Oakley, wishing I could gut her like a fish for tossing out such horrible opinions. Smiling while feeling homicidal was one of my mama's tips: *Never draw attention to yourself. Never argue. Smile if it helps.* Mutti did a lot of smiling in the Trautwein house so that we could both stay safe.

54

Mr Oakley handed me a parcel tied with string. He showed me to the door.

'Don't you mind my missus,' he said quietly. 'She has to put up with me and my nightmares. I've had a touch of bother since I got demobbed from the army earlier this year. I was one of the first lot of Brits into Belsen, one of them Horror Camps. The things I saw . . .' His hand clutched my shoulder. His eyes were looking past me and into a memory. 'We thought they were dead,' he murmured. 'We thought they were all dead. Then some of them moved . . .'

He pressed something into my hand. It was a twist of golden barley sugar.

You couldn't tell what people were like. You never knew who'd help you, who'd betray you. Who'd understand; who'd condemn. I looked at the barley sugar. I suddenly felt guilty about all the secrets and lies I carried.

I still ate the sweet.

Two men stood smoking outside the Clock Tower pub. One nodded to his mate as if to say, *That's her*. The other threw his cigarette end down and went inside to refill his pint glass. Were they local? Could they be spying on me? I hurried on, then . . . *blackberries!* A brambly hedge full of lovely fat fruit! I began to pick them, cramming them in my mouth. The only way to survive in bombed-out Berlin had been to eat the green shoots of weeds and glean whatever berries weren't poisonous. When I'd eaten so many blackberries I felt sick, I filled my coat pockets with more and set off back to Summerland.

My way was blocked.

A gang of village children had gathered on the arch of the bridge and they were armed. A tall boy with hair slicker than duck feathers threw the first stone.

'Varmint!' he shouted.

There was a yelp. Their target was a scrap of a child cowering on the far side of the bridge, next to a rusty bicycle.

'Varmint!' echoed one of the girls, maybe the tall boy's kid sister. Her stone missed the target.

A bigger, solid girl with a bob of yellow hair had a baby on her hip and a stone in her hand. Tugging at her skirt was a pudgy boy.

This big girl threw her stone, yelling, 'Thief!' She was a good shot. The target yelped again. Shifting the baby's weight, the big girl reached down to find another missile.

'*Thief thief thief!*' the whole gang chanted.

The pudgy little boy now had a stone in his hand too. '*Feef! Feef!*' he sang.

I shoved my way among the kids until I was between them and their victim, too mad to speak English, yelling in German instead. 'Stop right now or I'll rip your scrawny little heads off with my bare hands and throw them in the river for the ducks!'

The tall boy laughed. 'What's this? Some Nazi dropped in by parachute? What do *you* care if some dirty flea-ridden gypsy gets what's coming to her? Move!'

I faced him without fear. Take out the leader, win the pack.

The big girl suddenly flushed. 'Come on, Colin, it's not worth it. Andrew, put that stone down!'

'I want to frow it!' said the podgy boy.

'I said drop it!'

56

The tall boy – Colin – stepped towards me. 'If you weren't a girl, and quite a dishy one too, I'd sock you in the face.'

Bam! My fist flew out. Colin reeled back.

'My nose, my nose, she's broken my ruddy nose, I'm bleeding! Ow!'

For a moment the gang were just stunned, then Andrew – the podgy boy – pointed to the gore dripping from Colin's face. 'Blackberries!' he sang. 'Juicy ones!' That made the others laugh.

The kid on the ground didn't stick around to thank me for barging in. She scrambled to her feet, set her boots to the bicycle pedals and she was off – a blur of scabby knees and snot. Too small to sit on the saddle, her skinny arms tried to keep the handlebars straight. It can't have helped that both tyres were flat, and some of the wheel spokes were bent.

One of the other kids made as if to chase her.

'Don't bother,' said the big girl with the baby. 'Nellie Varley's got nits, and it's not as if Joseph Summer is ever going to need his bike again, is it?'

That shut everyone up.

The girl hoisted the baby higher on her hip and looked me over.

'Who are you?'

'Brigitta Igeul.'

'Brigitta *Eagle*? Ha, that's funny! I'm Angela Goose. From the vicarage.' Her pale hair swayed. She tucked it behind her ear. 'This is Daisy . . .' The baby blew bubbles. 'And this is Andrew, my little brother.'

'Not little!' protested Andrew. 'Is she a Nazi?'

'She's a *maniac*!' said Colin, wiping blackberries and blood off his face. 'Mind you, not a bad punch, for a girl.'

'It floored you,' said Angela airily.

'I wasn't expecting it. At any rate, it's not how we do things here in England. We're *civilised*.' I stared at the stone still in his hand. He tossed it away and marched off, muttering, 'Stupid foreigners. You wait – you'll be sorry you threw that stone, German girl.'

'*That* was Colin Oakley. He's nice really,' said Angela with a funny sort of sigh 'And that's his sister Poppy running after him. I suppose throwing stones isn't *exactly* civilised. It just sort of . . . happened.'

I looked at the tracks of the bicycle. 'The girl – Nellie?'

'Her? Just one of the Varley rats. They're thieves and poachers. Their dad, Roman Varley, practically lives at the pub, him and Uncle Tim. Hey, *are* you a Nazi? Silly question – you wouldn't say *yes* even if you were. Where are you going? . . . To Summerland? Us too! Tea with Auntie Sophie. You've got blackberries, we've got apples . . . that means one of Sophie's famous, unbeatable apple-and-blackberry crumbles! Andrew, get the fruit basket. Andrew, I said put that stone *down*.'

'Plop!' said Andrew happily as he dropped it in the river.

'Now bring the basket. Honestly, boys, they're *impossible*. At least baby Daisy is a girl. Why are you looking at me like that? She's not *my* baby, you idiot. She's my sister – aren't you, you big fat dumpling? Weighs a ton. Why don't you carry her for a bit?'

Without waiting for a reply Angela dumped the bundle

of baby in my arms. Daisy smelled of soap and sour milk and warmth and love.

'Look at your face! Like I've given you a live bomb! Mum always says girls are good with dolls and babies.'

'I like babies,' said Andrew, trying to hold my hand, even though I had a fistful of fruit.

Angela laughed suddenly. 'I say, Brigitta, you didn't half belt Colin! What a corker! That'll bring him down a peg or two. Hope you haven't really broken his nose – he's kind of dreamy. I rate him a solid seven out of ten, even though his parents just run the shop. He called you dishy too!' She glanced over at me. 'I suppose you are – all dark and mysterious. I'm not jealous.'

'You *love* Colin,' piped up Andrew.

Angela rounded on him. 'I do *not*. Don't listen to him, Brigitta. He's just a stupid kid.'

Listen? How could I help hearing? His voice was loud, but Angela's was even louder – so piercing it echoed down the avenue to Summerland. People in London had probably stopped in their tracks to listen in too. Much of her English was lost on me, but from the way this Angela Goose had trusted me to hold her baby sister, I did work out I had somehow acquired a friend . . . and a friend who made sure I was sitting at the table with them when the apple-and-blackberry crumble came hot from the oven – all golden sugar and crumbs on top, syrupy fruit beneath.

A friend who laughed when I tried thick yellow custard for the first time.

A friend? Not what I'd expected at all.

Trust no one.

59

Later that day I heard Vera Baggs complaining that I hadn't bought enough stamps at the shop. She wasn't to know I'd hidden a few inside my one grey glove from Gant's.

I'll find you.

Victoria Sponge Cake

After a week of cleaning from attics to cellars, I knew most of the corners and corridors of Summerland house. By day I worked hard, fuelled by big plates of food. Sophie Rover made me so many cups of tea I peed rivers. Luckily there were fifteen military toilets in the kitchen corridor, so I could take my pick. After dark, while the living people slept, I crept through silent swirls of ghosts.

Airmen were everywhere. Some sprawled on ratty armchairs smoking, joking, playing cards. Some clustered round a dartboard set at the end of the ballroom, hung in front of an especially pompous portrait. The board had warped wires so the darts were firing off all over the place. Beer bottles chinked. Backs were slapped. It looked so much fun.

A young guy, jacket undone and shoeless, winked at me. *Want to play?* An open panelled door showed shelves crammed with board games and sports gear. He took out a cricket bat and tossed a red-grey ball in the air.

I smiled, but said no. I couldn't bat a ghost ball anyway, even if I'd ever learned cricket. The thing I really wanted to play was the gorgeous grand piano. I dug my nails into my palms to persuade myself I couldn't risk it. Not the noise, not the memories.

Each time I crept to Lady Summer's study, the door was locked. I desperately wanted a look through her things. Maybe I'd find a photograph album from before the war – a clue for where to search, for the missing glove, for answers. One night the ghost with the cricket bat sauntered up, disappeared through the door and came out again, grinning. Breaking and entering was easy for the dead.

Saturday came around – the day the patient was to be delivered. Lady Summer came to check his rooms were ready. She was shaking with nervous energy.

I was cleaning a silver dressing-table set – a comb, shaving soap and cut-throat razor.

'Careful with those. They belonged to my late husband.'

'Yes, ma'am.'

'I had a friend once. A German girl. She always brushed her hair with a silver-backed brush, one hundred strokes a night. I never thought –'

I wasn't to find out what Lady Summer hadn't thought. Vera Baggs arrived with her usual *Oh, am I interrupting?* entrance.

'Angela Goose from the vicarage is here, my lady. She'd like to know, did you want anything from town today? Mrs Goose is going in on the bus, but I can run any errands you'd like, no trouble at all. My rheumatism isn't *so* bad today and the rain *may* hold off.'

Lady Summer blinked. 'No. Brigitta can do the errands.

My son will need new nightclothes, and I don't want her here when the ambulance arrives.'

'I don't want her here full stop,' muttered Miss Baggs.

Like jam between sponge, I got sandwiched between Angela Goose and her mother on the bus into town. Mrs Goose obviously aspired to be elegant, but couldn't help being homey instead, like a woman who sat through opera but who'd rather bob up and down to a brass band.

She caught me staring at the knobbly handbag hooked over her arm and patted it proudly. 'Crocodile skin.'

I was thinking of a bus ride I'd had with Mama, when we still had money to pay for tickets and we were still allowed on public transport. It was in Warsaw, in Poland. We weren't wearing yellow stars, as all Jews had to do by then. We were pretending to be normal human beings. I was in a dress. My hair was shorter, with a stupid ribbon bow at the front. A woman across from us kept staring and staring. She'd had a crocodile leather bag too. Mama decided we'd better get off the bus early. *Filthy Jews*, the woman hissed as we left.

We hadn't been filthy. I'd washed behind my ears and under my fingernails and my shoes were polished. I asked Mama, *What did she mean?* That was when Mama decided we had to hide for real. She told me we were going to be smuggled into a Christian convent, where the nuns would look after us. I'd have to be a good girl – could I do that? *Yes, Mama. Of course, Mama.* I didn't want to be dragged away to prison.

Angela prodded me in the side. 'Hey, Dolly Daydream – you were miles away.'

Miles away and years ago. Would I pass for normal now?

Leaving the house that morning, I'd gone through the kitchen to the back door. There was another door apart from the big front portal which was always jammed shut, but only 'proper people' were to use that, not servants. Angela Goose had been waiting in the kitchen, cooing at baby Daisy in a basket near the range. 'You're so yummy I could eat you all up!'

Yummy. That seemed a nice word.

Sophie Rover had been rolling pastry and listening to the wireless. It was news from the Nuremberg trials. Witness reports about horrors at Auschwitz. She saw me and twiddled the dial with floury fingers until music came on.

'Beethoven,' I said, without thinking. 'Fifth Symphony.'

Mrs Rover stared. 'By 'eck, you know the classy stuff.'

I looked at my feet. The first booming notes of Beethoven's Fifth had been played on the BBC's radio broadcasts to Europe. We thought of it as victory music. We secretly tuned in as often as we could. That was only when the Trautweins were out, of course, and Mama was always careful to have the volume so low the neighbours wouldn't hear . . . and to reset the dial to Hitler's usual bombastic lies as soon as we were done.

'Classical music's *boring*,' cried Angela. 'Come on, B, or we'll miss the bus. Ta ta for now, Auntie Sophie, and thanks for minding baby Daisy!'

'Wait up, Brigitta,' said Mrs Rover suddenly. 'Have a spot of pocket money. You've worked hard all week. You might see something you like. Off you go – enjoy yourselves!'

Vera Baggs oozed in from the main house. 'Watch yourselves,

more like. Behave properly, Brigitta, and don't talk to strange men.'

Why did I need to watch myself when it seemed as if everyone else was watching me already?

On the bus, Mrs Goose rummaged in a string bag and pulled out a rainbow jumble of needles and wool.

Angela groaned. 'Mum's trying to teach me how to knit jumpers for the local W.I., which stands for Wibbling Idiots –'

'Don't listen to her nonsense,' said Mrs Goose. 'The *Women's Institutes* are making jumpers for orphans in Europe. We do them in stripes to use up odd bits of wool.'

I stared out of the bus as we came to a junction and there was a massive brick building like a ship. I twisted in my seat to read the sign over the entrance way. *Gant's*.

'That's Gant's, that,' said Mrs Goose. 'Belongs to the Summer family. It's back to making gloves now, but it was all bombs and bullets during the war – munitions, you know.'

So that was how it was. Lady Summer owned the factory that made the bombs that blew people up.

After a bad-tempered attempt to loop wool and poke needles, Angela flung the knitting down.

'Mum, I don't see why we should send jumpers to Germany – no offence – when we're short of everything here. Charity begins at home, after all. I'm sick of shortages and hand-me-downs, and even *bread* on ration. Next thing, we'll be needing coupons for air. I wish they'd ration homework – I've got tons, and I don't see why I have to do it. It's not like I'll *need* any of that stuff once I get a job. Brigitta, what do you want to be when you grow up?'

Before I could answer, she told me a long list of spectacular careers she'd be perfectly brilliant at.

I tuned her out and played a little music in my head. Debussy, not gloomy Beethoven. *Reflections in the Water* made me think of a lake sparkling with summer sunshine, not puddles and clouds. When I was very, very small Mama once had played *Reflections* in a concert hall, but I couldn't remember anything except that the seats were hard and people clapped a lot.

To give my fingers something to do since I didn't have a piano, I took up Angela's knitting. It was second nature to me, to read a pattern and work the stitches. What else could I do in hiding, when it was too dark for books and I'd run through my musical repertoire? Before the wardrobe, Mama and I knitted our way across Europe as we tried to find a country safe for Jews. We unravelled old knitwear, washed and wound the wool, then made it up into new garments to sell. Baby clothes bought train tickets. Sturdy socks paid for potatoes.

'Ooh, look . . .' Angela jabbed me in the ribs and pointed to a boy about my age on the street outside. 'He's eight out of ten all right.'

I looked. He was OK.

'Don't you like boys?'

I blinked. What was the right answer?

'I'd smooch him, wouldn't you?' she said. 'Quick, Mum, this is our stop!'

'Brollies up!' said Mrs Goose cheerfully. Her umbrella had a duck's head for a handle.

Angela dawdled, waiting for the eight-out-of-ten boy to pass. When he did, she winked. He winked back. Mrs Goose twirled her umbrella to shield her daughter before she shooed us both through the rain.

'Here we are. Victoria Department Store.' Mrs Goose announced. 'Bombed in the Blitz and all rebuilt now. Have you ever seen anything like it?'

I had, once, running down a street lit with flames. *Hold my hand*, Mama ordered, as if I could have slipped free, her grasp was so tight. Shop windows were smeared with hate, or cracked, or shattered completely. *Don't buy from Jews! Jews OUT!!* Our shoes crunched on broken glass. Shop dummies were tumbled about, missing clothes and arms and heads. I thought we'd run forever, but Mama stopped suddenly. She pulled me into one of the shops and began grabbing things from a pile on the floor.

'We'll have these, these and . . . this. Quick, come on.'

'That's stealing.'

She gave a harsh laugh. 'These Jews don't need it as much as we do.'

I remember the dress she gave me to wear. It was blue with a white collar. I hated it. I tried my hardest to grow out of it. When it was finally splitting at the seams Mama somehow found me another one. Red with acorn buttons down the front. I hated that one too. By then my hair was down to my shoulders. Long enough for braids, which I also hated.

'Very pretty,' Mama said.

* * *

'This shop is *amazing*,' Angela gushed. 'It's called Victoria after the old queen. There are four floors and a lift, and a cafe. Mumsie, you did say we could have cake . . .'

'We'll see. Come along, Brigitta. I'll give a list of Lady Summer's requirements to an assistant and they'll put it on the Summerland account. Brigitta? Are you listening?'

I was staring at the gloves. There were hundreds and hundreds of them in trays, in boxes, on wooden display forms, all waiting for hands. Dark, coloured, pure white . . . plain, pearled, embroidered, leather, woollen, lace . . .

Gants for Gloves! cheered a happy sign.

I looked for grey gloves, wrist length, with tiny button fastenings, like the one tucked safely in my skirt waistband. I'd had to leave my suitcase unattended in Summerland, but I'd brought my secrets with me. I knew I wouldn't find the glove to match mine here though. My papa had it. Or he'd lost it, thrown it away, forgotten it. Forgotten me.

'Brigitta!' Mrs Goose parped like a horn and directed me towards a lift. It took all my courage to step inside the metal box and let the door close. I put my hands out as the floor began to move.

Angela sniggered at me. 'Haven't you ever been in a lift before?'

'No,' I whispered. Mostly I was unnerved at being trapped. No windows. No chinks. No keyholes to spy out of. Part of me was also disturbed at my own reflection. There was nothing *wrong* with me, but I didn't look *right*. Stupid skirt. Long black plaits. If Mrs Goose could have produced a pair of scissors from her crocodile bag, I would have happily snipped my hair short there and then.

A bell chimed. The lift doors opened onto a sea of underwear. I shrank away.

'It's all right,' said Angela. 'They're only girdles. They don't bite . . . unless some cheeky boy tries to get inside them!'

'Nothing like the lovely things we had before the war,' sighed Mrs Goose.

'What do you think about Colin Oakley?' Angela asked suddenly. 'He's got a Saturday job and everything. He drives for Gant's, the glove factory. Do you think he's a seven or an eight? Ten is highest. Only Joseph Summer ever got a ten from me, back before . . . you know. The crash.'

'Come here, Angela!' Mrs Goose's voice lowered to a loud whisper. '*Brassières!*'

I followed them through waves of peach, pink and white . . . silk, net, elastic and rubber.

'It's my first fitting,' Angela confided. 'Awfully inconvenient having bosoms, when you're doing sports. They bounce around like little lambs. I'm going to ice-skate in the Olympics one day. Or win the tennis cup at Wimbledon. I can't decide. *You're* all right, you're as flat as an ironing board. Bit of a late starter, are you? I say, how d'you fancy *that*?!' She stopped at a cardboard torso modelling two pointed pads of satin with ribbon straps. 'Spiral stitching. That'd give even a boyish figure like yours a bit of *ooh la la*. Oh, don't worry, you *pad* them. With cotton wool, or socks – or a whole jumper in each cup, in your case, ha ha.'

'An-ge-la *dar*-ling . . .' Mrs Goose's voice was now drawn out in warning. While her mother quibbled over coupons with a shop assistant, Angela picked up various bras. She found a titchy one and pointed to me . . . then a huge

69

double-boulder-shaped bra labelled 'Avro' which she mimed would do nicely for her mum. Finally she put the Avro one on her head like a bonnet.

She was funny. If I'd wanted friends, she might have been one.

I didn't have any coupons to buy clothes. I did have quick fingers though and big coat pockets. I took the plainest bra I could find, guessing the size.

The Gooses shopped for hours. I was summoned to carry things – packages of purchases for the new patient mostly. I shuddered to see Mrs Goose select a set of swirly patterned purple pyjamas and pitied the patient having to wear them. Ditto the matching dressing gown.

'I'm utterly ready for *cake*!' announced Angela eventually. 'I could eat a horse.'

'Horse tastes bad,' I said, remembering starving Berliners scuttling out of air-raid shelters to slice pieces of a horse that had been killed by a bomb.

'Ugh, that's disgusting. Mother, you *promised* we could eat at the Palm Court Cafe. Come on, B, it's on the top floor. We can take the stairs if you'd rather.'

Cake. I hadn't had cake or tarts or ice cream since 1939. No, that wasn't quite right. Mama always tried to find treats, even in the worst times. She'd once found only slightly stale pastries in a bakery bin. They had little raisins in and tiny crystals of sugar. I couldn't believe I was going to have cake now, for real.

The cafe was very elegant, like Vienna before the war. We brushed past potted plants to a room filled with wicker furniture, twee cushions and . . . a *piano*!

70

Mrs Goose pulled me away from it. 'You sit in the corner, Brigitta, behind the pillar. Are you hungry?'

I was ravenous. For *music*.

I think a waitress came. I think there was a pot of tea for Mrs Goose and glasses of something for me and Angela. I think cake appeared – thin wedges of sponge with jam in between the layers and a dusting of icing sugar. I barely noticed. The pianist had arrived, wearing a suit that had been ironed too many times. He had dark hair, a long face and sorrowful eyes. I scanned the cake eaters and tea drinkers. If the pianist was a Jew – and I thought he was – would anyone mind that he was sitting down, or object to him playing? Men had been shot for less in the war. But now, here, nobody seemed to care. Perhaps I could relax just a little?

No. I heard Mama's voice telling me ladies always sat up *straight* and kept their knees together, just so.

The pianist began with a simple, old-fashioned melody. A little tune to lighten a dull afternoon. I recognised it straightaway and played along, inside my head. Mrs Goose's smile softened. '*Moonlight Sonata*,' she sighed. 'This takes me back years.'

'Nostalgia alert,' muttered Angela.

'It was long before the war, when Lord Summer had just brought his new bride back to Summerland, or maybe when Joseph was just a baby. One of Lady Summer's foreign friends from school days came to stay. We were invited to an evening's entertainment. I remember it so well – that girl's piano playing would melt stone.'

Angela yawned and finished her cake. 'B, can I have your slice if you don't want it?'

71

'Angie dear! Don't talk with your mouth full!'

I let Angela take the cake. I was savagely wishing that everyone would just *shut up shut up shut up* so I could listen.

It was the happiest, saddest half-hour I'd known since the war ended.

They wanted to leave before the pianist was done, some nonsense about catching the bus back to the village. And of course I had to go with them. As we left, the pianist happened to look up. He saw my expression – or did he see something else? – and he nodded, just once.

Outside, the lights of Victoria Department Store shone into a twilit world of umbrellas and cars and upturned collars. I touched Mrs Goose's arm. 'Excuse me – you mentioned a girl at Summerland, before the war . . . ?'

Angela interrupted. 'Will you just look at that? Begging in the streets. He should find a job.' She was staring at a man puddled in rags and rain. He had a sign saying: *Can't Work. War Wounded. Can you Help?*

I suddenly remembered the money that Mrs Rover had pressed on me on my way out. It wasn't much – two silver shillings – but it was a fortune to me. All the money I had in the world in fact. I put it into the beggar's bowl.

'He's *sozzled*!' said Angela. 'Drunk and *disgusting*.'

I quoted her earlier words politely: 'Charity begins at home.'

'Oh bother. I suppose so. Mum, have you got any change . . . ?'

The crocodile bag opened, charity was dispensed. The wounded veteran looked up at us with bleary gratitude. I didn't feel good giving my money away, I just knew how it felt to be ignored when you needed help.

72

* * *

The bus home was *jam-packed* – Angela's expression. Rain pounded. The windows were steamed up. This time I sat on the aisle. My lap was loaded with shopping, my head was full of music, one note trickling over another. I didn't know how I'd be able to keep it all in; to keep still till I got home – I meant, to Summerland.

We got to the stop by Gant's factory. Angela wiped condensation off her window. 'Ugh, look!' I thought she was going to comment on some boy and give him a low mark out of ten. Instead she gave an ugly laugh. '*Darkies*. Don't stop for *them*.'

'Gant's girls, I bet,' said Mrs Goose without much interest. 'I hear coloureds make good machinists.'

I didn't think the bus would even slow down, let alone stop. But it did – quite a way from where two wet figures were standing, drenched. The door at the back slid open. A passenger got off. The two girls on the pavement raced up.

'We're full,' said the conductor. 'You'll have to wait for the next one.'

One of the girls backed away. The other wasn't so easily put off. 'Wait longer in this rain? Come on, you can squeeze in two more.'

'I said, *no room*.'

'You're kidding me! We're only little.'

'Go back where you came from!' muttered one of the passengers.

'What, Liverpool?' said the girl with scorn.

'So mouthy,' said Angela.

I stood up. 'Here is a seat.'

Angela tugged at my coat. 'Don't make a scene.'

The conductor ignored me and went to slide the door shut.

'Here is a seat!' I said again more loudly, face flaming, heart pounding. 'There is room for everyone, you stupid people!'

'Oi, I'll have none of your lip on my bus!' objected the conductor.

'I will leave your bus!' I shouted.

I dropped all the parcels and did just that.

The doors slid shut and the bus drove away.

'Well,' said the gutsy girl on the pavement, 'that showed them. Now we'll all three of us get even wetter.'

Fish 'n' Chips

Connie was the bolder of the two, I learned. I could see that, even bedraggled and drenched, she was a force to be reckoned with. A determined expression, bright eyes and shoulders set back, ready to take on the world. She introduced herself, then her companion.

'My pal Val. Say hi, Val.'

'Hi.' Val had a squeaky voice, like a violin tuning up.

'I am Brigitta.'

'You're a fool,' said Connie, laughing and shaking her head. 'Fancy making a fuss on the bus. I love you for it. Mostly people are all right once they get over staring, and wanting to poke your hair to feel how springy it is.'

'People ask me if it's hot in Africa,' said Val.

'It can be hot in the Sahara,' I said, remembering Mama's whispered geography lessons, with a battered old atlas.

'Except I'm from Jamaica. I came over as an ATS girl – that's army. They would've sent me back when they realised I was coloured, but all the paperwork was completed and they needed us recruits when all's said and done. I mopped floors and scrubbed bathrooms for the duration – my bit to beat the bloody Jerries. Oh drat, *you* sound foreign – you're not German, are you?'

'Austrian.'

Val's mouth dropped open. 'Are you really? With convicts and kangaroos and everything?'

Connie gave Val a shove. 'Austrian, not *Australian*. Though they have plenty of criminals in Austria, namely Mr *Heil* Hitler.'

I did not like to see her mock Nazi salute.

Val just shrugged. 'They might have kangaroos in Austria too – you don't know.

Darkies, Angela had called them. Someone else on the bus had called them a word beginning with N that I didn't know.

Vermin, lice, darkies, foreigners, scum. Every language had its own ways to turn people into nothing.

'You said you are from . . . Liverpool?' I didn't know this town.

'That's right,' replied Connie. 'British born and bred. Served in the air force during the war, selling sweets and aspirins to the fly boys at East Summer air base. It was all right when I was in uniform. Back on civvy street you get gumpf from idiots, like those on the bus. All they see is the colour of your skin.'

'Not in the blackout, they didn't!' Val laughed, twirling the horn case in her hand.

'That's right. They shouted, *Put that light out!* when we smiled, and we've got to keep smiling, haven't we, Valerie, my lovely?'

They did both have nice smiles. It made me want to smile

back. They were older by a couple of years. So confident, so full of life.

Connie suddenly clapped her hands. 'Listen, have you got anywhere you need to be?' Before I could answer she carried on. 'Too bad. Ditch your dull plans and come with us. We're talking Saturday night with Lindy Hop, jumpin' jazz and jive alive; hot to trot and heading for Harlem one day, my name in bright lights all over New York – *Live Tonight at the Cotton Club* – the incredible swing sensation Connie Snow, with Ella Fitzgerald and Josephine Butler!' As she spoke her hands conjured up a billboard with her name on it, in the air.

'That is you, Connie Snow?'

'Swing Sensations is the name of our band. I'm Connie Crackerthorpe really, but you got to get the right name, see? Create a *persona*. Give people what they want to see.'

'You are going to New York?'

'In my dreams, and you don't get if you don't try. Ella Fitzgerald is my idol, Josephine Butler too.'

'My Mama went to see Josephine Butler once, before the war.'

'You're kidding? Hey, Val sweetie, that bus goes our way. Wave it down. Come on, you two – *run*.'

It was like being picked up by a whirlwind and dropped in a dream. Somehow I was carrying Val's horn case and Connie's make-up bag and standing at the edge of an abandoned airfield. The sign at the bus stop read: *East Summer*. Rain still sluiced down. We sprinted between empty barrack blocks and almost onto the runway. It was splotched with weeds and puddles.

77

How many hundreds of planes had taken off and landed here during the war? Now it was empty space.

'In here,' said Connie. 'Before we drown.'

The dance hall was an old aircraft hangar and it was enormous. 'Over a thousand couples on a summer Saturday night!' said Connie. 'Hundreds more in the crush outside. Just you wait . . .' She was already snapping fingers and humming. 'You can dance, can't you? Everyone can dance.'

Dance? Did silent shuffling across the Trautweins' hearthrug count? Mama had taught me some steps. Small steps, for fear of knocking over the fire irons. I wouldn't call it *dancing*.

'Hey, Charlie – we made it!'

A tall boy with a halo of frizzy black hair nodded at me. 'Who's that?'

'I'm nobody,' I replied, but he'd already lost interest. Who could blame him when I stood next to Connie?

The rest of the band was setting up on a makeshift stage at one end of the hangar. At the other end there was a bar made of beer crates. Wooden chairs and stained tables lined the walls. I set Val's horn on the stage. Time slowed when I saw the piano. Just a well-used upright, stained on the top with round marks from drinks glasses and a few cigarette burns. Unlike the piano in the Trautwein house, there were no doilies or dark green pot plants or portraits of Hitler. Carefully I lifted the lid. There they were. Eighty-eight notes. My fingers tingled as I let just the tips drift along, feeling the smooth ivory of the white keys and the tantalising lines of the black ones.

'Do you play?' Connie bounced into view.

I nodded. Then shook my head. Yes. No

'You're an odd girl, Brigitta, you know that?'

I knew that.

'Come backstage and tart yourself up a bit.'

Backstage meant a toilet and a cramped room full of coat hangers and dusty light bulbs. Connie went behind a ratty screen to change.

I squinted at myself in a square of mirror. If I just undid my braids and fluffed them up a bit . . . How was that? Not me. Why not? Couldn't I be glamorous too? Blend in, Mama said, well, here blending in meant being bold. And black, like the whole band, but I couldn't do anything about that.

Quickly I unbuttoned my blouse to put my new bra on. Shoulder straps – that was easy – but how to fasten the hooks without dislocating both my arms? I took the whole bra off. Should I do hooks and eyes at the front and swivel it round? That worked. I jerked the straps up, pushed some wads of toilet paper in – nasty flimsy stuff like tracing paper – and soon had my blouse on again. Buttoned up wrong. More fiddling. I borrowed some of Connie's blusher. Looked like a tart. Rubbed the blusher off. Looked like a country cousin. Sat down.

It was either this, or go back to Summerland and be sensible.

Connie appeared again, in a brilliant red spangled sheath that went in and out in all sorts of interesting ways.

'How d'you like the dress? I made it. Sneaked a go on the sewing machines at Gant's. They've no idea I gig on Saturday nights.' She sighed. 'Gant's is a good steady job till you get married – that's what my ma says it is.'

'You like to sing instead?' I stated the obvious.

Connie's answer surprised me. 'What I'd *like* is for someone to look at *me*, past my bonny black skin, and say, Hey, Miss Crackerthorpe, how'd you like to be a bank manager, or a rocket scientist, or a journalist? As if *that's* going to happen. Factory girl or entertainer, that's all a coloured girl's expected to be. Luckily I'm fabulous onstage and a *great* singer, so I'll just have to be famous for my voice.'

I thought about that, about how you couldn't hide being black like you could hide being Jewish. But why should you have to?

Charlie stuck his head round the door. 'Onstage in fifteen!'

Connie tensed. 'Shoot. Nearly time. I get nervous before I go out there. All those people staring.'

We looked at each other in the mirror, each of us dressed up in our own way.

'You have to play a part,' I said carefully. 'People see . . . what you show them.'

'People see what they want to see too. And tonight, they want *Connie Snow*, queen of jump 'n' jive!'

She pulled on a pair of long, red satin gloves.

'Wish me luck!'

Connie didn't need luck; she had talent. Oh my God was she good! The whole band was so . . . *alive*. How did they do it? Piano notes faster than machine-gun fire . . . Drums setting a beat . . . Strings plucking vibrations in my bones . . . Val's horn outrageously saucy – a call to *move move move*.

Move? I could hardly breathe I loved it so much. My mouth

was open to drink the music in. My feet felt every tremor on the dance floor.

Out came Connie, dazzling in a spotlight. She owned that stage. She seized the silver microphone and sang. *Wa-a-ail* went Val's horn.

The hangar had filled while we were backstage. The crowd *heaved*. Girls came running in. Guys gulped down their drinks and went looking for partners. The first couples had room for all sorts of crazy moves. Feet skimming in a blur, skirts swirling, hands clasping, reaching, flinging. Then it was as if the whole town piled in, a big mass of elbows and armpits and energy.

Connie beamed down over them all, belting out a song about jumping, jiving and wailing . . .

My feet were tapping. I couldn't help it. I'd never heard or seen anything even close to this. On to a new song about a sweet little lady up to something shady – same tempo, same magic. Connie was the enchantress and we were all under her red-spangled spell.

'Hey, sweet little woman!' That wasn't Connie's voice. It was a boy. He was talking to me. 'What are you doing with the wallflowers?'

German. What was a German doing here? Had I been followed? My heart beat faster than the music. Which way out? There were too many people, I was jammed in.

'Whoa, calm down, we're just talking. I saw you there. I thought you might want to dance?'

'*Ich kann nicht . . .*' The words came out in the wrong language.

81

'*Bist du ein deutsches Mädchen?*' You're a German girl? 'Wow! Where from? Nice to meet you.' He held out a hand.

I put both mine behind my back.

'Don't be like that . . . Oh, I get it. You're Jewish, right? Relax. I'm not the SS! I was a navy boy. My ship got torpedoed in the Atlantic and I've been a POW ever since.'

'POW?'

'Which rock have you been hiding under for the last six years? POW stands for Prisoner of War. I work on a farm with others like me. A few Italians too and a couple of British girls. How about you?'

If only the music wasn't so good. It made me want to shed my skin and just be *me*. No more secrets. No more hiding.

Trust no one. No one.

'I'm . . .'

Another boy muscled in.

'Beat it, Fritz. She doesn't want to talk to you.'

'Don't flip your wig!' said the German boy, except he pronounced it *vig*.

If I'd had a wig, it'd be well and truly flipped. As if the evening couldn't get more surreal, here was the boy I'd punched in Summer village. 'Colin Oakley?'

'Large as life and twice as natural. You do know they're all going nuts in the village because you scarpered off the bus? I thought you'd be miles away with the family silver, not cutting up a rug at the airfield dance. Hey, are you leaving . . . ?'

Was I?

'Don't go. I like a girl with guts, even if she does have a

82

mean right hook. Plus, you look –' he gave me a once over and whistled – 'pretty good. I reckon you owe me a dance for busting my nose. Come on . . .'

He'd called me pretty, so like any dumb girl I let him pull me through the crowd. Next thing I knew, he had hands on my shoulder, waist, wrist . . . turning my body . . . making my feet step to the beat.

'That's it! You've got it!' Colin grinned. Val's horn crowed triumphantly.

Slowly, clumsily, I started to dance. My skirt swirled round like those of the girls around me. My socks fell down. My new bra straps just about stayed up. At the final piano chord everyone cheered, me included.

'I haf never danced like that before,' I said, laughing.

Colin slicked his hair back. 'Not bad for a beginner. Want to practise some more?' Snapping his fingers, he sang along with Connie's next song, then we were dancing again, faster and faster, so full of energy.

'So how come you're here?' he shouted over the music.

'I came with Connie,' I shouted back.

'Connie Snow? Seriously? You're not pulling my leg? Wow!'

'I must pull your leg?'

'I mean, you're not kidding me?'

I jumped up and waved at Connie. She spotted me in the mayhem and blew me a kiss back. Colin sent me spinning out and spinning back. I let him.

'Had enough?'

Two dances later Colin pushed me towards bar end of the

83

hangar. I was hot and thirsty. I thought I should go to the bathroom and check my bosoms were still straight.

'I'll wait for you,' he said.

The mirror in the ladies' room was plastered with girls. In one tiny inch I saw my hair was a hay bale and my eyes were bright as twin full moons.

'Careful, Brigitta,' I told my reflection. 'This is wrong and you know it.'

Oh, but it felt so *right*.

A couple of burly girls came barging in. One with a mountain of red hair shrieked, 'You've lost *what*, Doris?'

'Only my ruddy knickers!' her friend shrieked back. 'The button popped off right before I shimmied. Next thing I know, one pair of peachy passion-killers are puddled on the floor.'

'No!'

'Yes! So what does my Romeo do? Scoops 'em up, and puts 'em in his pocket, cool as a cucumber, then carries on dancing.'

'With a pocketful of *bulge*!'

'Oooh, Peggy, you're so naughty!'

'And you're knickerless! Go ask for them back. We've got to scoot. Have you seen the time? They'll be locking up at the hostel.'

Cackling like lunatics, Doris and Peggy reeled out again.

'Land Army lasses,' said a girl next to me, as if that explained everything.

It was another world. Another universe.

* * *

'I have to go home,' I told Colin who was standing outside like a guard.

'OK. I borrowed the work van. I'll give you a lift. Do you want to grab a bite to eat first?'

I dashed backstage for my coat. The music was still throbbing and wailing, but Connie was at an open fire door, having a cigarette break. The rain had finally stopped.

'Brigitta!' she exclaimed. 'You are one dark horse hepcat!'

I laughed. 'I have no idea what you mean.'

'Leaving already?'

'Going home. After a *bite to eat*.'

'You've clicked!'

'Clicked?'

'Got yourself a fella!'

She blew out a stream of smoke. 'Have fun, sweetheart, but not *too much* fun. One girl to another, no guy is worth the trouble. And come see us again.'

'You . . . You were . . .' I spread my arms wide. I couldn't think of a word big or brilliant enough.

As I left with Colin, Connie's voice was once again filling the hangar, this time a slower song with the words *I just want to be loved* . . . Girls were shivering and giggling on one side of the open hangar door, boys postured and smoked on the other. Some had already coupled up in alleyways. A few ghosts had drifted into view – more airmen. When they were alive, the hangar would have been full of aircraft and engineers, fuel hoses and bombs. Something to take to Germany on their next mission . . .

'You coming?' Colin steered me towards his van. The writing

on the side read *Gant's for Gloves*. I thought of my one grey glove, back at Summerland. It could wait.

'Where are we going?' I asked.

'D'you fancy fish 'n' chips?'

'What is it?'

'You've never had fish 'n' chips? No wonder you lot bloody lost the war: nothing worth fighting for. The chippie it is then . . .'

He drove me to a shop on the outskirts of town called The Happy Cod. It smelled of fat and fish. 'Fish and chips twice,' he told the big man behind the counter. The man shovelled long chunks of potato onto a square of newspaper, then set a piece of something orange and crusty on top. Colin handed over some money.

'Salt and vinegar?' Without waiting for an answer, Colin squirted a dark liquid onto the potatoes and then sprinkled on lots of salt. Angela Goose was right – Colin Oakley was a nice-looking boy. If I wanted a date – which I didn't – he wouldn't be so bad. As we ate, he kept flicking looks at me. The chips were hot. The fish batter looked disgusting but it actually crunched then melted beautifully. The fish inside was a bit dry. So what? I wolfed it all down, then remembered *Nice girls don't gobble*. Nice girls probably didn't lick salty grease off their fingers either.

Who said I was a nice girl?

We went to sit on the empty stalls of a marketplace. Other kids and couples were loafing there too. I watched some girls do acrobatics over the metal rails. They shrieked and pretended to be shocked that their skirts flopped open to show their underwear, while boys pretended not to be impressed. Stupid skirts. Why did girls have to wear them? If I had trousers on, I'd be flipping round and round and dangling from my knees too. From my ankles even.

'So. I know you're called Brigitta, and Mum told me you're working at Summerland, right? Are you really a German?'

'Austrian. From Vienna. A seamstress.'

He wasn't really listening. He had his own stuff to say.

'I wish I hadn't missed the war. I mean, I was alive and I did air-raid drills, collecting scrap to make into Spitfires and bomber planes, all that stuff. But it's not fair I didn't get to *fight*, you know? Bloody Joseph Summer at the big house, he was the *hero*, coming home from training in his swanky uniform, showing us his pilot-officer stripes. I was just a stupid kid to him.'

'Joseph Summer. He was shot down –'

'You're a girl,' he went on. 'You're lucky. You don't have my father telling you over and over again that the best generation fought in the war and boys nowadays are all pansies. *Big girl's blouses*, he calls us.'

'Blouses?'

'Timid. Soft. Like a girl.'

'Girls are soft?'

'Only in the right places.' Colin moved closer. Ah – *the look*. I inched away. He said, 'I like you, Brigitta. You're different.'

You have no idea.

He crumpled up his chip wrapper and reached for mine.

87

'I don't mind that you're German, or Austrian. As long as you're not a . . .'

'*Nazi* . . .' I read the word on my greasy newspaper. There was no escaping the news. More war trials in Germany. More criminals hanged.

Colin read over my shoulder. 'Bloody hell, are you Jewish? You weren't in one o' them camps, were you?'

'Auschwitz,' I said automatically.

'Wow. That's . . . I'm so . . .'

'It's all right.'

'No, it's not! But you're safe now. This is England. We're decent people. Civilised. All that violence and murder, it couldn't happen here.'

He dropped me off at the village green, saying, 'Lady Summer will go bananas if I drive up and wake her. Are you OK to walk the rest?' He leaned over the gear stick for a kiss . . . and caught the edge of my ear.

'Goodnight.'

I waited until the van drove off belching fumes, then I ran.

I ran, ran, ran, danced, and ran, all the way to Summerland. I'd been out! I'd had *fun*! Who cared about stupid Lady Summer? Who cared about policemen? Who cared about anything?

My feet danced onto the terrace at the side of the house. Eyes closed, I swirled to my own secret, silent music – piano notes rippling up and down my spine, into my toes and fingertips. I wanted to dance forever, just spinning round and round and round and until everything except the stars disappeared.

'I don't care!' I whispered. 'Don't care, don't care, don't care . . .'

Ivy rustled. I heard a polite cough in the darkness. I stopped dead, breathing hard.

Rice Pudding

'Is this a private dance or can anyone join in?' said a voice, sounding amused.

It was just a ghost, barely visible through the curtains of ivy sweeping down the side of the house. Had I seen him before?

'Good evening,' I replied. I gave a deep curtsy, followed by a bow for extra politeness. Then I carried on remembering dance steps. I didn't mind a dead audience. Ghosts didn't count. Why should anyone care what a ghost thinks? It's the living that judge and hate and kill. Ghosts were the only things you could trust. They couldn't do anything or change anything. If they could, they'd be alive still.

Hold my hand . . . came a whisper in my mind.

I shook it out and jumped up onto the stone balustrade edging the terrace. Behind me, the lake showed little dots of starlight. The moon was thin, lost beyond Summerland's chimney-pots.

I hummed one of Connie's boogie-woogie songs as I danced along the balustrade like a trapeze artist.

'Imagine I'm clapping,' said the ghost. One transparent hand against another would hardly make a good round of applause.

He'd made the point, not me. I don't go around telling ghosts they're dead. It's not polite.

'I am not good at dancing. Tonight is my first time.'

'You've never danced before?'

'Only quiet steps, on a carpet. Like this . . .' I showed the ghost how I had marked out the basics of a waltz with Mama tapping the rhythm with her fingers against my arm.

'That was one crazy waltz you just did.'

'*That* was jump and jive.'

'Not bad.'

'Connie Snow was singing. She is *nicht von dieser Welt*.'

Out of this world. A ghost would know all about that. He must be one of the air force boys, drifted back to a place that had been familiar before death. Now he'd haunt Summerland like the others – nights, months, years, decades, until he was as fine as dust motes in a sunbeam, then . . . gone.

'I must have missed hearing Connie Snow. I've missed . . . a lot,' the ghost said. Then, 'You're not scared of me?'

'Of course not. I don't care how you are.'

Did I imagine a ghostly smile at that?

'That was your mantra just then. *I don't care, don't care, don't care.*'

'Always I have to be careful,' I explained, now feeling anything but. 'Always I have to remember what to say, what not to say. Keep quiet. Be still. Be a good girl. Tonight there was music and . . .'

'And suddenly you felt free.'

'Yes. Free. You understand.'

'Not really. I'll never feel free. Never!'

There was no echo. The word hung in the air then drifted into silence. I was alone.

Bad luck follows good, as surely as day follows night.

My mama didn't like me thinking that way. *It's all good really*, she'd say, each time a fresh disaster overtook us. *We just don't know it yet. We need to wait until we can see it differently.* 'It's a Lovely Day Tomorrow', Liebling.

I crept round to the back of the house and let myself into the kitchen with the key Sophie Rover kept hidden under the boot scraper at the back door. Unfortunately Mrs Rover herself was waiting in the kitchen, frying pan at the ready.

'What the bloody hell, Brigitta! I thought you were a burglar. Do you have *any* idea what time it is? Where have you *been*? I had Angela here in a right pother because you'd done a runner, and Mrs Goose on the blower to Lady S. And Ribble came round to make a missing persons report. Even Colin Oakley turned up saying he'd go drag the lake for your body . . . looking like he wouldn't mind if he found one at that.'

I heard a torrent of words and names. It seemed best to say nothing. Eventually she ran out of anger and put the frying pan down.

'Well? Where have you been?' she said finally. Then, because she was Sophie Rover she had to ask, 'Have you eaten?'

'I had fish and chips,' I announced with pride. 'With salt and winegar.'

'I'll salt and winegar – *vinegar* – you! What were you thinking, jumping off the bus like that, not a word to any of us?'

The music and the magic trickled out of me. I hadn't been thinking, that was the whole point. I'd been *living*.

'Oh, don't look like that, you big sausage. You're young, you're supposed to be stupid. I should know – I got put on jankers so many times in the army, for coming back to base after curfew, not wearing my hat straight, not saluting an officer . . .'

'Jankers?'

'When you're in trouble. There are punishment duties. Maybe a spell in the clink – that's a prison cell.'

Now I was fearful. 'I can go to prison for fish and chips?'

Mrs Rover laughed. 'You might wish you were locked up safe in the police cell when Lady Summer has a go at you. She wants to see you in the morning, *first thing*. Now get upstairs *quietly*. We've the patient to consider now, asleep in his own bed for the first time in forever.' She shivered. 'They reckon he's recuperating. Looks half dead to me.'

I knew all about being half dead. My night in the dance hall was a taste of life. I couldn't let it happen again. I had things to do.

Even so, I went to bed happy.

Autumn sun pushed through a gap in my bedroom curtains the next morning. I dressed quickly, putting on my new bra, with only a minimal bit of padding in each cup. I didn't want people commenting that I'd sprouted bosoms overnight.

Lady Summer wasn't in her study, and for once the door was partly open. I knocked quietly then slipped inside. How long did I have before she returned? I went straight to the telephone on the desk, lifted the receiver and dialled '0' for the operator, as I'd seen people do.

'Number, please?' came a clipped voice.

'I . . .' My voice came out all croaky.

'Hello. Number, please?'

'I do not haf – *have* – the number. It is a name.'

'Oh. What's the name you want, miss?'

'Not miss. Mister. He is . . .'

I couldn't do it. I couldn't say the name out loud. It was too dangerous. Someone could be listening. What if . . . ?

'What are you doing?' Lady Summer was in the doorway.

Slowly I slipped the receiver back into the cradle. Should I tell her? *Trust no one.*

'The telephone. It was ringing. I answer it. Wrong number.'

Her eyes narrowed. 'I should dismiss you immediately. Leaving all my parcels on the bus! Running away goodness only knows where, to do goodness knows what with God knows *whom*! No decent girl would behave in such a way. I should have known you'd bring disgrace on yourself. I only let you stay here because I felt pity for you, a foreign girl from . . . from one of those places.'

Something made me lift my gaze from the carpet. Some defiance that training should have buried far deeper. I looked Lady Summer straight in her immaculately made-up face.

'You have no pity. You want me to stay here because your house is old and dirty. Because I clean for no money.'

'How dare you! You work for your bed and board, and by the way you're filling out, I can tell you're eating plenty. Food's not *free*, you know, whatever handouts you may have had from

94

the Red Cross, merely because your parents were too careless or stupid to look after you themselves.'

How *dare* she talk about my parents? She knew nothing about it, the spiteful old witch.

'As you have looked after your son?' I spat out, gloriously rebellious in my anger. 'I am not your prisoner. I am prisoner of no one, never again! I go now!'

And I went. Trembling. Nails digging into my palms. A crescendo of drum beats and cymbal crashes playing in my head.

Church bells were ringing for the Christian Sunday service. In the kitchen Mrs Rover was hard at work preparing a big dinner. There were smells of her signature dish, *meatuntooveg*, but I was angry, not hungry. Mrs Rover took one look at my face and said, 'I know what you need. Follow me.'

But before she'd gone more than a step, another woman burst into the kitchen. She was wearing a nurse's white cap, a blue uniform and a crisp white apron. Something slimy and cream-coloured was spattered over her clothes and sliding down her face. Bits dropped in spots on the kitchen floor.

'Forget this for a lark!' the nurse bellowed. 'I took our patient a nice bowl of rice pudding and the little sod threw the whole lot back at me! Said he didn't need a nanny or a nurse and I was to get out and stop staring at him like he was in a circus freak show. The cheek of it! I was told this would be an easy job with a poor cripple boy, not some violent *maniac*!'

Mrs Rover drew herself up tall. I could picture her as a

sergeant major on a parade ground, or marching at the head of a military band. '*We* were told the agency would be sending a professional nurse, not someone who's put out by a bit of pudding.'

'Well!' said the nurse. 'If that's the way of it, I resign!' She turned on her heel, skidded on cream and slammed the door behind her.

'Lightweight,' muttered Mrs Rover.

I fetched a rag and wiped up the mess. Once I'd been so hungry I would have licked the whole lot off the floor.

'Leave that. Come with me. Sunday roast can wait.'

She took me to a room called the drawing room, though I couldn't see any paper or pencils. Together we rolled up a carpet, dragging it from under a lovely Bechstein upright. So Summerland had two pianos that nobody played. During the war there were times when I would have killed to play a piano. For our first years in hiding, Mama and I had done silent fingering of notes and chords on keys scratched on wood or in the dirt, humming the notes since we couldn't actually play them. Then we snatched hours at night, stroking the keys of the well-polished piano at the Trautwein house – every note in silence, matching hand movements to imagined music. All those nights barely daring to breathe in case the Trautweins woke up from their bed. All those beautiful unplayed tunes.

Mrs Rover hoisted one end of the rolled carpet onto her shoulder. I got the other end and we processed past the fifteen military toilets, out to the yard.

'The rain's just mizzling – perfect. Help me hoist it over the washing line, that's right. Now for the fun part.' She grinned. 'Tell me who you want to murder!'

I was reaching for my knife just as Mrs Rover waggled a carpet beater at me instead.

'Set the beater flat side to the carpet and *whack* it like this, like *this*, like *this*!' With each stroke the twisted cane walloped clouds of dust from the carpet. 'Go on, you try. You look like you need to let loose a bit. Not like that! Not little fairy taps ... *Hit it!* That's it. Harder!'

I did as she said, whacking the carpet harder and harder in my fury.

'Whoa – steady, steady, don't bring the whole washing line down. Brigitta! Stop now – enough!'

She wrested the carpet beater from me. I couldn't wiggle out of her arms. She had me pinned. For some reason tears were running down my face. I was shaking with emotion. Anger. Grief. More anger. How awful, that once you let one bit of emotion out more came cascading after it, far messier than one thrown bowl of rice pudding.

Slowly Mrs Rover loosened her grip. 'You poor beggar,' she murmured. 'What's been done to you?'

It was raining hard when Lady Summer came to my bedroom.

Knock knock.

'Come in,' I said.

She paused in the doorway, fiddling with the single strand of pearls at her throat. 'I have never been to the servants' floor. It is ... bare.'

I shrugged. What did it matter to me? My suitcase was packed; I was ready to leave. I'd been busy with my dictionary, prepping a speech that would strip that smug expression from Barbara Summer's face. It was time to tell her why I'd come to Summerland.

She got in first. 'I may be that I was a little harsh to you earlier. I have since been informed that you were at least in decent company last night. Colin Oakley from the village said he found you safe at the Salvation Army taking Bible lessons. Girls your age can't be too careful in town after dark. Didn't your mother teach you that?'

Ha! That was almost funny, given the lessons I'd learned from my mama. Once Berlin fell to rampaging Russians, she wasn't around to teach me any more, but she'd drummed enough skills into me to survive in daylight or after dark.

'I knew a girl,' Lady Summer continued, 'good-looking like you – very like you in fact. She gave up so much for love, or whatever she thought it was, that she lost her family, her reputation, her money. Such a waste.'

Now I paid attention. 'What happened to her?'

The pearl-twisting became a little more agitated. 'What do you think? She got saddled with a wishy-washy pauper husband and a brat of a son.'

'And then . . . ?'

The necklace snapped. Pearls sprayed all around. She watched them bounce and skitter across the floorboards. I dropped to my knees and began picking them up one by one, pouring them – dust and all – into her cold hands.

'Never mind about that – the girl. It was all a long time ago.

98

I only speak of it as a warning to behave more appropriately. As your employer, I feel a certain responsibility.'

'My employer?' My face must have shown surprise.

'I have decided you may stay. You will have wages, and I will arrange for ration books. Summerland has been neglected too long. I am determined to return it to its former glory, albeit on a budget.' I truly couldn't speak, it was so unexpected.

After she'd gone I flipped through my dictionary again, looking up *wishy-washy* and *pauper*. Oh. Now I didn't know whether to be grateful or furious.

Stay or go? Go or stay? It wasn't as if Summerland was home or anything. No one would miss me. On the other hand, I had nowhere else to live, and Summerland was the only place I knew.

I wished there was someone I could talk to. Perhaps one of the ghosts – that wistful one from the terrace? I waited until midnight before creeping out of my bed to find him. He wasn't out on the terrace, or with the other ghosts in the ballroom. He hadn't joined the gang silently sliding on a tea tray down the main stairs. Ursula wasn't mopping round his spectral feet on the backstairs. He surely wouldn't be haunting Mrs Rover, Miss Baggs or Lady Summer? I paused outside the closed door to the patient's rooms. No sounds from within. I'd yet to see the legendary Joseph Summer, shot down over Germany and returned to his stately home mashed up and bad-tempered. Now that he'd seen off one nurse with a bowl of rice pudding, would they get him another? None of my business. He could rot for all I cared.

99

I was just about to tiptoe into the blue guest bedroom – empty, because Lady Summer was too haughty to have guests – when I sensed something behind me. There he was. My ghost. Not in uniform like the other airmen, just wrapped in a dark robe. He beckoned me to follow him, so I did, through an unlocked door, up a spiral of stone steps and onto the Summerland roof. He lingered in the moon-shadow of a chimney-stack while I roamed around turrets and crenellations admiring the view. It was so beautiful.

'Beautiful, isn't it?' he said in his soft voice. 'Everything you see belongs to the Summer family. Land, cattle, church, pub. Every fish in the river, every rabbit in the woods. None of that seems relevant now.'

'Summerland is special. It must be nice to belong.' The dead haunted places that mattered to them after all. 'I have no home. I belong nowhere.'

'Rubbish. You belong wherever you are. You're like a snail – you carry your home with you.'

'A *snail*?'

'You know . . . What is it in German?'

'You know German?'

'A few words. You are German, aren't you? That's what they said.'

Ghosts gossiped? It felt strangely nice to think of this one talking about me.

He snapped his fingers. 'Got it! Snail is *escargot* in French.'

'*Schnecke?!* You are not eating me with garlic!'

'Too bad,' he said, laughing. 'You look tasty.'

Suddenly awkward, I set off, practising my dance steps as

well as I could remember them from last night. When memory failed, I made up my own. Why not?

'I like it up here,' I said eventually, heading back to look for patterns in the stars. 'The air is free. There are no walls and no eyes.'

'Except that owl . . .'

Something wide and white-winged flew past. I didn't hear so much as a feather frond.

'Like a ghost,' I said.

The ghost sighed. 'I miss flying. Not that it was anything like as graceful as that owl. Bloody noisy in fact. Pretty smelly too, when you factor in seven men in a Halifax bomber, the stink of fuel and Pongo's cheesy feet. Pongo was the navigator. Daft as a brush, but damned good at his job.'

'You were the pilot?'

'Nothing so heroic. Bomb aimer. A bit of brain work and a lot of lying down staring into darkness.'

'Bombs?' I echoed.

He didn't notice my tension. 'I flew over Summerland in a Halifax once, from RAF East Summer. What a racket a low-flying heavy bomber makes! I swear the roof tiles rattled. I suppose was proving I was a man or something. I was just a kid really.' His voice trailed off a little. 'That was only last year.'

'What is it like, to fly?'

'Flying? Magic! From up in the air everything's in miniature. Ribbon roads and toy railways.'

'What about houses and people?'

'Rooftops are like postage stamps. People are invisible.'

'That is good for you,' I snapped. 'You don't see where the bombs fall or what they hit!' I marched off towards the door back into the house, angry and upset.

'Hey, don't go . . .'

Of course I went. It was that or stay and try punching a ghost.

Yorkshire Parkin

Out came my knife. I stabbed hard but the flesh was tougher than I expected. Once I'd gouged out as much of the innards as I could, I carved eyes and a jagged mouth on the turnip front.

Mrs Rover took the entrails saying, 'This'll do nicely in tomorrow's beef stew.' She swapped them for a stub of candle, which I set inside the excavated turnip. Then she put a match to the candle and the lantern was complete. When she switched off the room light, flame flickered through the gruesome face, casting strange shadows around the kitchen. Two other turnip lanterns were lit beside it.

'Yours is the worst,' said Andrew Goose, his four-year-old eyes full of admiration for my handiwork.

'Mine's bigger,' said Angela Goose. She wrapped her arms around her turnip in a sulk. The shadows it cast made her face look gruesome.

'They're all terrifying,' said Mrs Rover soothingly. 'I shan't sleep a wink tonight I'm so frit.'

'And we make these because . . . ?' I was lost for words.

Angela sighed. 'I *told* you – it's All Hallow's Eve. Don't you know *anything*? The spirits of the dead come out tonight!

Ghosts and ghoulies and things that go bump! This is what we do at Halloween. We make lanterns and tell ghost stories.'

She had been glaring at me since she arrived at Summerland with her brother. As soon as Mrs Rover left the room, Angela pinched my arm hard. '*That's* for leaving us in the lurch the other day. You're crazy, you know that? Jumping off the bus to make room for coloureds! I told my dad and, well, he stuck up for you, which was really annoying, because he's *my* father not yours. Anyway, he said it's important to speak out about things you believe in, even if that sometimes means you're thrown to the lions.'

'I thought she went to a dance, not to see lions?' said Andrew, frowning.

'He meant the first Christians, stupid. They were always getting eaten alive. Anyway, I told Dad I didn't see what the problem was, calling those girls darkies. They *are* dark.'

Angela really had no clue why that scene on the bus had been so horrible. If you're used to throwing stones, you don't stop to think how it feels to be hit by one.

'They are people,' I pointed out.

'That's what Dad said, except he phrased it more like, *They're all God's children* and then he went on about loving everyone equally.'

Andrew giggled. 'Angie loves Colin Oakley. She drew a heart with his name on it.'

'Shut up, you little twerp, or I'll pinch you too!' she threatened.

Andrew scooted out of his sister's reach. 'He likes Brigitta best anyway.'

'He does not! Does he? Did he tell you that? Stupid boy. Doesn't know what he's talking about. Anyway, that's not why I'm cross with you, Brigitta. I'm mad because I had to carry all your parcels when you ditched us.' Angela lowered her voice. 'They were for Joseph Summer, weren't they, those things we bought in town? Have you seen him? What does he look like? Miss Baggs was in the shop talking about *scars* and *bits missing*. He must be hideous or he wouldn't hide away all the time. Baggs says the door is kept locked *from the inside*. That's so weird.'

'What's weird?' Mrs Rover came bustling into the kitchen with a dinner tray. The patient had barely touched his supper. What was so wrong with him he didn't eat food when it was offered, and he kept himself hidden on purpose even when it was safe to come out? I took his breakfast up every morning. I'd put the tray on the floor and knock. After about a minute the bolt would slide back, the door would open and a hand would emerge to pull the tray inside.

Mrs Rover repeated her question. 'What are you calling weird?'

'Brigitta,' said Angela quickly. 'Don't you think she's odd? She's never done Halloween. She doesn't know what Harvest Festival is either. How about Christmas, B?'

'I am Jewish.'

Had there been something like a harvest festival back home when I was small? I remembered rustling leaves and fat fruit decorations. It suddenly hit me hard how much I'd lost during the war. Not only my parents and relatives, also my roots. My heritage. All those things that add into the mix of making us who we are. Now I was slowly getting used to the fact that it was safe to be Jewish in England. In fact I was getting used to a lot of things. The turnip lanterns lit the faces of three people who knew me. Who maybe liked me.

They didn't know me of course.

I checked the clock and put on oven mitts. When I opened the oven door a waft of gingery heaven filled the room.

Andrew squealed. 'Parkin! Parkin!'

'Specially for Halloween,' beamed Mrs Rover. She slapped his hand away. 'Wait till it cools. Brigitta, cut it into squares and leave it on the rack.'

I breathed in the amazing aroma. It was called Yorkshire parkin and it tasted like gingerbread. I knew that because I had licked the bowl out. Before the war we'd been at something Christmassy. I forget which town or country. A market, I think. There were glass baubles and spiced wine . . . and iced gingerbread stars. Mama gave me a star all for myself. I'd nibbled the icing off first.

When the parkin wasn't so hot I eased squares of it out of the tray and onto the cooling rack. Andrew raced past and snatched two, one for him and one for Angela.

With her mouth full Angela cried, 'Can we tell ghost stories now?'

'Let me get a cushion to hide behind first,' said Mrs Rover, who didn't look like someone who'd hide even if a Tiger tank was bearing down on her.

'Just so you know, Auntie Sophie, I've decided I'm going to be a bestselling author. I've started a story already. It's

106

going to be three books long and feature a beautiful schoolgirl hockey player who outwits evil Nazis hiding in the Peruvian jungle.'

'Are there Nazis in the jungle?'

'Bound to be. They're everywhere – I heard it on the radio. Spies and war criminals. Come on, B, leave the washing-up. Prepare to be thrilled, chilled and spooked out of your skin! Gather round, gather round,' she went on, a little pointlessly since we were all at the table already. 'Midnight, the witching hour draws near . . .'

'It's only six o'clock,' piped up Andrew. He showed me his wristwatch. 'I can tell the time.'

'Shut up!' hissed Angela. 'We've got to be home by seven, so it's as close as we can get to midnight. Anyway, as I was *saying* . . . The witching hour draws near, and the chill of Halloween enters our bones! 'Tis a night to test our courage. Ghosts of the graves all around, I summon you now –'

'*Woe, woe, woe* . . .' A dismal voice made us all jump.

'Who goes there?' challenged Andrew. 'Friend or foe?'

'Mrs Rover, oh my poor head!' A creature pushed open the door from the main house. It was a hideous apparition: Vera Baggs in a fluffy yellow bed-jacket, a frilled net nightcap and a flower-sprigged nightgown down to her ankles. She spluttered into a handkerchief. 'If I didn't have such an iron constitution I would surely be in my grave by now.'

'Cold still making you poorly?' Mrs Rover asked politely.

'It's not a cold!' Miss Baggs sneezed again. 'It's the *flu*. I've only left my sick bed to request a little glass of your ginger wine, for medicinal purposes.'

Mrs Rover fetched a bottle from the scullery and passed Miss Baggs a glass.

'Not *that* little!'

Mrs Rover poured some more. 'And how is Lady Summer?'

'Nothing like as bad as I am. The aches! Oh – is that fresh parkin? No, no, I've no appetite at all . . . Far too poorly. I'll, er, just take a few pieces back to bed with me . . .'

She wasn't long gone when we all started to laugh.

We sat in the kitchen until the candles guttered, the wicks were snuffed and Mrs Rover switched the lights on again. 'Home time for you two little terrors,' she announced, giving Angela and Andrew a hug.

'Can't Brigitta have a cuddle too?' asked Andrew.

'Don't be stupid,' scoffed Angela. 'Sophie's *our* aunt. Brigitta's got her own.'

Did I have aunts? Was there anyone from my family left alive? How could I know? I had to forget all those names and faces. They belonged to before the war.

When they'd gone, Sophie Rover patted my shoulder. 'Don't mind Angie, she's got a good heart. She gets lumbered with baby Daisy and little Andrew all the time.'

I thought about that. Had my mother felt lumbered with me? She could have survived so much more easily without a child. Unlike me, she 'passed' as non-Jewish, which meant she was acceptable to the Nazis. Otherwise she'd never have been able to work for the Trautweins, who had a photograph of the Führer in their bedroom. Did they say, *Night night, Hitler*, as they snuggled into bed?

Mama had to dust that picture, and the one on the piano.

'Our Führer will see us through,' Frau Trautwein used to say, when it was clear that Allied bombers would soon reach Berlin, despite her husband's continued denials that a single bomb would ever fall. 'Our leader has all sorts of secret weapons ready to win the war. Ray guns and radio-controlled flying bombs that can wipe out whole cities at a time.'

'Won't that be nice,' Mama replied. The old Traut didn't understand sarcasm.

Would my mama have abandoned me to save herself?

Never.

Did my papa?

Absolutely.

I'll find you, he called out.

Here I am. No sign of you, was my answer.

There was no sign of life in Summerland at midnight. The ghosts, on the other hand, were gathered around the ballroom piano. Judging by their winks and nudges, it was just as well there was no sound because the song was definitely rude.

I went softly, softly along the first-floor landing. Vera Baggs had a little room off the main bedroom, where Lady Summer slept. The only sound I heard was a series of wet snores and snuffles from Miss Baggs. Right at the end of the corridor, was a room I'd only seen in daylight. It was called the Blue Room, because it had lovely blue Chinese wallpaper and faded silk curtains. My mama would have loved it. Blue was her favourite colour, especially when matched with grey.

There was a wardrobe in the Blue Room. I'd had to clean

a mouse nest from under its clawed feet. There were mirrors on the wardrobe doors. When I pulled the curtains open I saw a ghostly image. Was that me or Mama haunting the glass?

'It's the guest-room,' came a quiet voice. 'Or it was when guests actually came here.'

I turned. The dead bomb aimer was in the doorway, in the shadows. I said nothing. I was still churned up at the thought that he'd lost his life helping others lose theirs.

'I'm glad I found you,' he went on.

'You want to talk about bombing people?' came my angry whisper.

'I want to apologise. You were right, what you said before. On missions, we never did worry about what happened on the ground. We were there to deliver our payload and get home safely. As far as we were concerned, the more dead Germans the better. We didn't think of them as people. We couldn't. We just wanted to win the war.'

He shocked me into silence He wasn't done. 'That doesn't mean I'm not sorry for what I did. What we all did. I've thought about it ever since, wondering how many houses I flattened, how many innocent people I killed.'

I went to perch on the window seat, away from the wardrobe and the mirror. Night enveloped us both. Darkness was familiar. I imagined the airman was haunting the wardrobe I once lived in. A friend I could talk to about anything I liked.

'It's Halloween,' I began, unable to just blurt my story out cold. 'We made Yorkshire parkin.'

'I used to love Halloween! We did apple bobbing . . .'

'What is that?'

'You put apples in a barrel or bowl of water and have to catch one in your mouth – no hands – if you want to eat one.'

I smiled. 'We made turnip lanterns today. Then we told ghost stories . . .' I let the words linger. 'In the kitchen earlier, Angela talked of a woman called Lettuce, but I thought that was a salad.'

'Lettice! It's a name,' he laughed. 'She must have meant Lettice Varley, the gamekeeper's wife, killed in the cottage. I knew about that. Do you suppose she haunts the Bomb House now?'

He didn't seem to mind talking about ghostliness, so I went on, marking time while I gathered up all my courage and all my English words. I would tell this dead boy what had happened. I couldn't keep everything squashed inside me any longer. My hopes, my plans, they burned inside me like a candle in a lantern. The dead could keep secrets, even if I couldn't trust anyone living.

'I don't know ghost stories; I only know real ghosts. In all places, there are the dead. In all houses, all seas, all rivers. In the sky and the ground. Peacetime ghosts, and millions more from the war. Sometimes, if the love is strong, ghosts can help you.' My voice was so low I almost hypnotised myself. 'One night in Berlin, the bomber planes flew. The – how do you call it? – air-raid *noise* . . .'

'Siren?'

'Yes. The air-raid siren, it was loud. People ran downstairs to the *Kellar* . . . the cellar, you say? With babies, and food and warm clothes. One girl, she couldn't go down to the cellar because she would be arrested, so she stayed in the house and

111

her mama stayed to keep her company. The bombs falling . . . explosions all over the city. Louder and louder the aeroplanes. Closer and closer the bombs, then BOOM! The house was hit. Top floor went to ground floor. Bedroom to cellar – all gone flat.'

'And the girl?'

'Dead, in the ruins. Lying in a broken piano, next to a broken Adolf Hitler picture and a broken wardrobe, and her broken mama.'

'Her mother was dead?'

'Like dust in the wind, a soul with no body. Then the girl moved. She breathed.' I took a deep breath in, as if coming back to life. 'She moved. She was . . . *gefangen* . . .' I mimed it.

'Trapped?' he suggested.

'Yes, trapped. No help. No people. Fires were burning, close and hot. Suddenly the girl hears a voice. *Hold my hand*, says the voice. *Don't let go*. There is a hand, a grey hand, reaching. The girl takes it and climbs out of the fire and bricks and broken piano bits. She is escaped. She looks for the lady who helped her – it was her mama. Her mama's ghost helped the girl out.'

'The girl – that was you?'

'When the daylight came, in the smoke and dust the girl had one thing in her hand, from the ghost helping. It was one grey glove.' I pulled the grey glove out and laid it flat on my palm. In the wardrobe mirrors, my reflection held out a glove too. Almost a matching pair.

'I have not shown this before. It is my secret. I am come to Summerland to find the other glove. I know who had it. A man. His name . . .'

* * *

His name.

Something clicked in my mind. I was an idiot. A stupid potato-headed *idiot*. I pointed at the ghost. 'You ... *Wie hießt du?* What is your name?'

'What ... what do you mean?'

'Who are you?'

'Don't you know? Who do you think I am?'

Delusions came crashing down inside me, like the Trautweins' obliterated house. 'You're Joseph Summer, *ja?* Not a ghost. I cannot tell you things.' I covered the grey glove quickly. 'Come closer, where I can see you. Why do you hide?'

'No – I ...' His shadow shifted.

'Wait! Don't go. Please, tell me ... Do you remember, before the war, a man ... name Golanski ... ?'

The corridor was empty. The patient's door clicked shut. The bolt slid home.

Toad in the Hole

Summerland was a fridge. Only the kitchen was snug. There were no fires in the bedrooms. Lady Summer permitted herself a small amount of coal in the study, where she worked sorting bills and harassing men at the ministry who still hadn't managed to remove the fifteen military toilets.

One of my jobs was to fill stone bottles with hot water at bedtime. These were wrapped in towels to warm the beds. I had one myself, and an extra blanket in my little attic room. It was starting to look quite homey up there. Sophie Rover showed me how to crochet strips of old stockings into a rug so the floor wasn't bare. I had a picture too.

I'd been in other attic rooms for Lady Summer, searching through the cobwebs and clutter for things to bring out of storage. I liked it up in the eaves. There were chinks in the roof where sun-fingers poked through. Among the lumber I searched for photographs from when Lady Summer was a girl. No luck. I found a lot of Joseph's things. Cricket bats riddled with woodworm. Tennis rackets with saggy strings. Tarnished trophies for sporting wins. All the things a normal boy might have in a normal life.

When I was done fetching down boxes of old books and crockery sets and clocks that didn't tick, I smuggled the picture I wanted into my room. It was quite small, with a wooden frame carved into oak-leaf shapes. The colours were mostly dark – smudges of brown and black – but in the middle of the murk there was a half-peeled orange and a knife. You could see every dimple on the peel, almost smell it. I wanted to bite into the juicy segments and taste how sweet it was. I set the picture on the chest of drawers in my room so I could admire it from my bed.

I ran down the frosty avenue to the village, with letters to post. My own envelopes were mixed with the rest. I'd written to the Jewish Agency and to the Red Cross. It was a huge risk of course. If they had any news of a Golanski, they'd have to write back to me at Summerland, which meant the authorities would know where I was. Not good. The other problem was Vera Baggs. She liked to collect the post as soon as it arrived. How would I explain away letters addressed to me? *Who've you got to write to? You're nobody*, she'd say.

I could see the Goose children were in the village, bundled in warm woollies. Angela was pushing baby Daisy in a giant pram. Andrew pushed a doll of a man in a wheelbarrow. The man had bulbous arms, straw coming out of his trousers and a crayoned face. His hat looked very much like Miss Baggs' best hat. In fact, it *was* Miss Baggs' best hat. It suited him better.

Andrew waved me over and held out an empty jam jar. 'Penny for the guy!'

'What are you doing?'

115

'We're going to burn him,' Andrew said.

Angela butted in. 'Once we've taken him round the village and cadged enough money to buy firecrackers at Oakleys'. Come with us.'

'I don't want to burn anyone.'

'It's an English tradition,' said Angela. 'You have to learn our culture if you're going to live here. This is the first Summerland bonfire since before the war. The whole village is invited.'

'We've got two pennies now,' Andrew boasted. 'One's from Mum. Dad says we shouldn't be such . . . what was the word, Angie?'

'Heathens.'

'That's it. Heathens don't believe in God, except we do – we just want to have a big fire, don't we?'

'Why do you burn the guy?'

'Guy Fawkes blew up the Houses of Parliament,' said Angela. 'Or tried to. They caught him, tortured him and burned him for treason.'

'In the war?' I asked, confused.

'No, centuries ago. I can never remember dates. That's why we have Bonfire Night, with fireworks. *Remember, remember the fifth of November, gunpowder, treason and plot.*'

Later I looked up the word *plot* in my dictionary.

The last plot I remembered was when someone tried to blow up Hitler. When the news leaked out the Trautweins could talk about little else. I crouched in the wardrobe, listening for details. Eventually I heard the Führer's voice on the wireless, crackling and weak. It took more than a bomb to blow up Adolf. When he killed himself at the end of the war, his corpse was doused in petrol and burned outside his bunker – that's what I heard.

Somebody should draw a Hitler moustache on the bonfire guy, I thought. Later, I saw that somebody had.

'Hey! Wait for us!' Colin and Poppy Oakley spilled out of the shop. I went to post the letters, whispering *good luck* to mine as I dropped them into the red pillar box. Colin showed Angela something wrapped in brown paper. She whistled.

'Catherine wheels! Look, Brigitta – you hammer these on a fence and light them, and they spin round and round with sparks.'

'Named after some stroppy woman who didn't behave nicely so got tortured on a wheel,' said Colin with enthusiasm. 'Come on, let's get some more pennies.'

'Don't ask our mum,' said Poppy. 'She's got crab apples ready instead of pennies.'

Angela said Andrew could go knock on village doors to ask. 'Because he's soft in the head so people feel sorry for him.'

Andrew said *I* should go. 'Because she's pretty.'

Colin snorted but he didn't argue. In fact he winked at me. I remembered how it had felt to dance to Connie Snow's amazing music with him. My fingers tried out jazz-rhythm notes against the side of my leg. I suddenly felt very alive.

It was a fine, cold evening, so Sophie Rover said we could carry a table outside for the bonfire-party food. 'I reckon the whole village will turn up to have a nosy how things are in Summerland now the young master's back and my lady's fixing

117

the place up. We've apples to dip in toffee, potatoes to bake, onions to fry and toad-in-the-hole to mix.'

I had a quick scan of my dictionary. Toad. *Kröte?* For tea? Never in all our wanderings had Mama caught *toad* for us to eat. The English were mad. There was no other explanation.

The bonfire was at the side of the house, not far from the terrace. It was built of junk wood dragged down from the attic, all laced with cobwebs, as well as garden rubbish and moth-eaten curtains. I'd enjoyed piling it up over the last few days.

Sophie Rover had said, 'You'll have muscles on your muscles at this rate, Brigitta, and nothing wrong with that.'

'A waste of fuel,' was all Miss Baggs had to say. 'We'll regret burning that wood come winter, mark my words. It's going to be a bitter cold one.'

Twilight thickened to full dark, with dots of stars tufted by cloud. Lady Summer came out to watch us light the bonfire, wrapped in a glossy fur coat, with fur-lined boots and a silky scarf. Her face was utterly expressionless when the guy on top of the bonfire began to smoulder.

Villagers walked up to the house, slicing the avenue with flashlight beams. Mr Oakley from the shop nodded hello as I carried out trays of something called bonfire toffee. Mrs Oakley sniffed at me, especially when Colin smiled and waved my way. I recognised Mrs and Reverend Goose, Old Rory the farmer, a couple of his Land Girls, and Tim Rover, Sophie's husband. He had quite a collection of empty beer bottles around him. A friendly drunk, but drunk all the same. He looked up like a hopeful puppy every time he

118

saw his wife. I could tell she liked him. She was friendly with him. But it was different from how my parents had been – or at least how they were in my wispy memories of before the war. Mama and Papa adored each other – that's how I remember it. Then he left us. Then she died. Then there was just me left.

There were lots of other people at the bonfire that I didn't recognise. They all knew each other. They belonged.

Vera Baggs oozed around everyone, soaking up gossip. Quite a few people had asked about the Master Joseph. *That poor boy*, as they called him. He didn't appear. I looked up at his windows a few times, wondering if we'd ever get the chance to speak again.

Constable Ribble was chatting with Mrs Rover. He had a newspaper in his hand. He saw me and tapped the side of his nose. What did that mean? A secret? A warning? I kept out of his way.

Flames leaped high on the bonfire. Children began to dance round it, dodging in as close as they dared, then darting away. I did not join them. I remembered the smell of charred flesh and singed hair after the bombs on Berlin, when the wreckage burned people trapped inside. Just beyond the circle of light, a row of eyes twinkled. When I went to investigate, the eyes blinked and little figures skittered off into the woods.

'Varleys,' said Mrs Rover, as if that explained everything. I remembered the gypsy girl on the bicycle when I first came to the village. Weren't they invited to the bonfire?

Out came trays of hot toad-in-the-hole. It wasn't baked green amphibians after all, just fat sausages in lovely crispy batter.

Colin nailed a Catherine wheel to a gate-post and lit it. It fizzed once and fell off.

Then – a *bang*!

I crouched down, arms over my head, but everyone else was saying, 'Oooh!' and clapping. I slowly uncurled. It wasn't Russian rockets or British bombs. Not gunshots even.

'Rockets!' shrieked the children.

After that came firecrackers, squibs and fizzing sticks called *sparklers*. 'Make your name, like this,' said Angela, scrolling her spitting stick into a pattern of light.

I hesitated, then wrote *Brigitta* in the air.

Angela dragged me away. 'Oh that's disgusting, did you see? Colin's just drawn a kiss with his sparkler and he was looking right at us! Come on, let's play games. Anyone for Hide and Seek?'

I nearly laughed out loud at that. I was a world-class winner in hiding and seeking.

'I've got a better idea,' shouted Colin. 'Who wants to play Murder in the Dark?'

Murder in the Dark

The words were ominous, but in England, it seemed *murder in the dark* didn't mean watching your neighbours getting dragged out of bed and shot at three in the morning. Colin explained the rules. All players were to draw a card from a pack. The cards tagged you as detective, murderer or victim. The detective – in this case, Poppy Oakley – stayed in place. All the other players then scattered and hid . . . or hunted, if they were the murderer.

Could I just stay gazing into the glowing heart of the bonfire?

Should I escape to the kitchen to do the washing-up? I felt eyes on me. It was Lady Summer, staring through the heat of the fire.

Best to blend in. Be like normal people. 'I will play too,' I said. I took a card and saw my role: victim.

'Ready everyone?' said Angela. 'One, two, three – *go!*'

Where to run? Most players had scattered among the statues and potting sheds of the garden. Someone rattled at the locked door of the garage. Outside was safer because you were less likely to be trapped. Inside was warmer. I ran inside. It was strange hearing living people in the house after dark. There were echoes of running feet and slamming doors. Rugs were rucked up. Curtains shivered.

My heart was pounding.

'Think of it like a game,' Mama had said, when we first went on the run. That was before we hid in the convent but after Papa was arrested. 'Just a game. You don't need to be frightened. Hold my hand. Let's see if we can find somewhere so safe no one will ever find us . . .'

Colin and Angela went straight behind a sofa together – both victims, I presumed, from the way that they were giggling, not killing each other. Andrew and some others thundered towards the ballroom. I knew of hundreds of hiding places in the house; I just couldn't bring myself to fold up small into any of them – not wardrobes, cupboards or even attics. For a while I just stood in the centre of the Blue Room, watching a pale ghost sway like spider silk in the breeze of my breath.

Footsteps. I hid behind the door. A girl I didn't know came in. While she looked in the mirrored wardrobe I slipped into the corridor, meaning to nip down the servants' stairs and

121

along to the kitchen. Down on the ground floor I could hear the doors of fifteen military toilets being flung open.

My feet didn't move. What was wrong with me? There was someone coming up the main stairs. Fear had me gripped. At the far end of the dark corridor I heard a bolt click and a door handle turning.

'Brigitta? Is that you? Ow!' It was Colin on the stairs. He'd reached the first-floor landing and stumbled into the table with the bowl of glass oranges.

As he crashed about, cursing, I heard a another voice whisper, 'Brigitta? Is that you?' This one was faint, familiar. The patient's door opened a sliver.

I took a deep breath and slipped inside.

The room was dark, with just a square of dim orange light at one end, where the window looked out on the bonfire. The patient was on the other side of the door. He drew the bolt as soon as I got inside. We both stood with our backs to the door, just breathing.

Eventually he said, 'I was watching you at the bonfire. It's all I see when I close my eyes. Fire and smoke and the sky spinning round. The same dream of burning and falling over and over.'

'Brigitta?' Colin tried the door handle. I think he stayed there a while then moved away. I was alone with . . .

. . . with Joseph Summer. Not a ghost. A warm body. Someone who breathed like me. Someone who was ever so slightly trembling.

'Brigitta?'

I couldn't look at him. I inched nearer. Our shoulders were

close. I felt his warmth even through our clothes. My right hand almost touched his left hand. Our fingers were almost laced.

I swallowed. 'Joseph?'

Could a smile be heard? If so, he was smiling. 'Call me Joe. My friends used to.' His mouth was next to my ear, lips almost brushing my skin. My hair felt electrified. I closed my eyes. There was a blood-boiling scream.

'*Murder in the dark! Murder in the dark!*'

Andrew discovered the body. His sister Angela had been killed. Interrogation of all players – with threats of tickling torture – revealed that Colin had been the murderer. We celebrated with chunks of Mrs Rover's bonfire toffee, a dark, sweet mass that stuck your teeth together and made you wish it was 5th November every night of your life.

The bonfire dwindled. The night grew colder. Inside Summerland, ghostly airmen settled down to read in ratty armchairs, or to smoke and chew pencil stubs over faint crossword clues. When I eventually lay in bed to try to sleep, it was with the knowledge that in a bed on the floor below was living, breathing Joe. Was he as restless as I was?

Lemon-Curd Tarts

I fell in love with winter.

Living in a wardrobe, I hadn't savoured seasons so much. It was cold and cramped or hot and cramped. Now, at Summerland, I had so much fun kicking up dead leaves, crunching the ice on frozen puddles and studying ice patterns on the inside of my bedroom window.

There were days when I forgot about my one grey glove, because I now had a pair of my own gloves, knitted and gifted by Mrs Goose. They were the first thing I'd ever had new, since the war at least.

'That's a fine, warm coat you've got,' commented Sophie Rover one day, as I came in with a pile of logs. 'One of the first things I noticed about you, your coat. It's so distinctive.'

There was more to her words than she was letting on. I said nothing, just set the wood in the log basket and went to hang the coat up. I thought about the secrets that crackled inside the coat lining. Were they safe? Should I put them on the fire along with other waste paper? I'd carried them with me all the way from Berlin. Was it time to let go?

We were silent for a while as I helped her make pastry for

lemon-curd tarts. Apparently these had been one of Master Joseph's favourites before he went away and Mrs Rover's husband had managed to acquire a couple of lemons from a mate at the pub. 'All very under-the-counter,' said Mrs Rover, 'What with lemons being rarer than hen's teeth.' I planned to take a tray of the tarts up, to see if Joe would open his door to me again.

'Anything to get that boy eating again,' Mrs Rover sighed. 'I wish you'd known him before the crash. A proper daredevil he was. He climbed the clock tower once, to see if he could touch the sky. Now he won't even leave his rooms.'

It was a bittersweet recipe. After squeezing lemons, I stupidly rubbed my eye and nearly blinded myself. After measuring the sugar, I licked a finger and let a few crystals sparkle on my tongue.

'What's that tune you're whistling?'

I stopped cutting pastry rounds. 'I was whistling?'

'It was nice.'

'It is a song my mama liked – "It's a Lovely Day Tomorrow".' As soon as I said the words I wanted to bite them back.

'Of course! I recognise it now. Your mum was a Vera Lynn fan then?'

I hesitated. What harm was there in revealing a few innocent things? This was Sophie Rover after all, not the Gestapo. 'We heard Vera Lynn sing it on the BBC, when we listened to the radio in secret. Mama loved music. Piano mostly.'

'Can you sing?'

Sing? I wouldn't know. For years I'd barely spoken above a whisper.

'Only whistle,' I said. I began the song again.

125

Mrs Rover began to sing along, awfully out of tune. Maybe it was her singing that soured the tarts. Maybe it was my secrets. Either way, the lemon curd was too bitter to eat. We had a funeral procession and buried the first batch in the back garden. Even the chickens wouldn't touch it.

'Cheer up,' said Mrs Rover. 'We'll make some more.'

What a nice idea: move on from past mistakes. If only it was that easy.

Sophie Rover's main philosophy in life was that everyone should be well fed and comfortable. If only *she* had been leader of the Third Reich, not Adolf Hitler. *Meatuntooveg* instead of mass murder, misery and world war. *Heil Rover!*

So much food was making me bigger. Mrs Rover said I must be getting stretched on a rack each night, I was growing so much. I felt it too, all the unwelcome changes – taller, wider, with hair in strange places. Not good. The worst embarrassment was when she collared me washing my smalls in the laundry. *Smalls* was her word for underwear.

'D'you need anything for your monthlies, Brigitta?' she asked. 'You know – rags, pads, whatever you use? Oh, your face is a picture! Haven't you started yet? You're a late bloomer then.'

'Mrs Rover, I haf . . . *have* no idea what you are talking about.'

'Bless. You will soon enough. The curse comes to all girls in time. Come and see me when it does – let's just say it's red and it's messy, since you've no mother to explain your body plumbing.'

She was right there. No mother could explain how my body felt these days. Like my skin was too tight and my limbs were too loose. As if I could kill the world or dance around it or throw it high in the air like a balloon. I'd had a balloon once, before the war. Had there been a birthday? I remembered a boy cried when the balloon popped unexpectedly.

I knocked at Joe's door, holding a plate piled high with lemon-curd tarts. When the door stayed locked, I got so mad I kicked it hard – stupid stuck-up toff, skulking in his rooms as if that would solve everything! – and stormed down the main staircase instead of the backstairs –

Vera Baggs was in the entrance hall, snooping through the post as usual. She jumped when she heard me and quickly set the letters down on a sideboard. 'What do you mean, creeping up on me like that? I may look the picture of health but my heart isn't what it ought to be, you know. No wonder, when the world's gone so mad servants forget which stairs to use! Don't think I don't know about you, sneaking about the place, little Miss Foreign Muck. One word to Lady Summer and I could have you booted out like *that*!' She snapped her fingers.

I eyed the letters. 'There is something for me?'

'Expecting something, are you?' She made a big play of sorting through the envelopes again. 'No, nothing. How disappointing for you.'

I should have had a reply to my enquiries by now. I stormed back to the kitchen and began banging pans around, swearing in German under my breath. Stupid woman, stupid house, stupid country, stupid everything.

Mrs Rover lost her temper too. 'Brigitta, you're a nightmare. Clear off outside. You've been cooped up for far too long.'

'Cooped?' The word came out as a bit of a squeak. My voice

kept doing that, or going gruff. I swallowed and tried again. 'Cooped?'

'Like a chicken. Shut indoors.'

For more years than she could possibly know. 'What shall I do?'

'I don't know. You're young. Go play.'

'Play?'

'*Play*. Run around. Climb trees. Have fun.'

I thought about that. I had climbed trees before, once, in a winter forest when there was a search party out looking for us. It had been cold and we worried about wolves as well as police. Winter is a problem – snow shows your tracks. Sounds carry further on a chill, still day. Water freezes. The ground's too hard for digging roots to eat or a hole to hide in. There were no wolves on the Summerland estate at least. No dogs or hunters with guns and farm tools. *It couldn't happen here*, people said.

'I will go and chop wood.'

'You'll do no such thing! I'm not letting you loose with an axe, the mood you're in.'

'Then I will go and *play* if you like.'

I marched out in such a temper I forgot my coat and my gloves. It felt good to slam the back door. I tried doing the same to the garden gate, but the hinges were rusty and it just squeaked at me. I took off across the lawn, past the lake and into the woods, not bothering to look up at Joe's window. Who cared about him? Who cared about any of them?

By the time I noticed how horribly cold it was, I was in the thick of tangled trees. High branches patterned the sky like brown lace. I trod carefully, suddenly mindful of the jagged mantraps set to catch Jews on the run in Poland. A few minutes further on I came to a clearing near a snowy mound of tumbled stones – a house of sorts. There were three walls standing, more or less, with half a roof balanced across and one glassless window. This had to be the haunted house the village kids talked about, the one hit by bombs, where Lettice Varley died. I suddenly became aware of how silent the woods were; a strange sadness drenched the whole clearing. Then sun broke through cloud and I remembered what Mama used to say about not being lost: I was exactly where I was on the surface of the planet.

I found myself humming the tune of "It's a Lovely Day Tomorrow". When we were together, it was always going to be a lovely day . . . tomorrow. Now, in the peace of this English winter, I realised it was a lovely day today.

Wood snapped.

I went absolutely still.

I heard the breathing next.

Slowly I turned my head towards the sound.

A collection of rags with bright eyes and a rosy nose was standing on the edge of the clearing. It held a bundle of twigs and small branches. The creature looked ready to run, and then we recognised each other. It was Nellie Varley. *A dirty, flea-ridden gypsy*, Angela had called her.

'I am Brigitta.'

'I'm Nellie. You stopped them kids throwing stones at me when I wus on me bike. You live at the big 'ouse . . .' Nellie jerked her head in the general direction of Summerland.

'For now.'

'I wa'n't nicking the bike, you know. That Joseph Summer, he dun't need it now he's a cripple, so I took it fair 'n' square. Mi dad, he used ter work fer 'Er Ladyship. Then we got bombed and he hit the bottle 'n' she give 'im the old heave-ho. That there –' she nodded at the ruined shell – 'that used ter be our 'ouse. Our mam were killed by a stray bomb.'

'Where is your father now?'

'Gone. He'll be back soon, wi' food and money. Where's your dad?'

'Gone.'

'Is 'e coming back?'

'No. Never.'

'Huh. Are you a furriner?'

Furriner? Oh. Foreigner. 'Yes.'

She eyed me more warily. 'How furrin? Scotland?'

'Austria.'

'Nivver 'eard of it. Near Scotland?'

'In Europe.'

'Huh.' She thought about that. 'Where the Nazis are?'

'Yes.'

'They 'ang Nazis now, our dad says. Hang 'em by a rope till they twitch and their tongues come out like this.' She stuck her head on one side and her tongue down to her chin.

I shuddered. In the final days of street fighting in Berlin they'd hanged men and boys who'd tried to lie low instead of defending Hitler in his bunker to the very last second. Strung them from lamp posts. Thanks to the war trials, it was now the Nazis who were dancing on air.

Nellie nodded her approval. 'I'd 'ang 'em, me, if I ever met

130

a Nazi. 'Ang 'em dead for bombing our mam.'

I looked at her pinched, pale face and had a thought. 'Are you hungry, Nellie Varley?'

Hungry? She had a wolf in her stomach, I could tell. She also had a brother, two sisters and a dog. I invited them back to Summerland too, and took them all to the dining room. This was a long, gloomy space, watched over by portraits of equally miserable Summerland ancestors. I'd polished the enormous table. It could seat twenty people on the spindly chairs, even if they stuck their elbows out when they ate. At night the ghosts used it for ping-pong. For the Varleys I spread one end of the table with a red chequered cloth and matching crockery. Then I fetched out every bit of food in the scullery and set it before them. They didn't waste time with cutlery.

Sophie Rover found me pouring tea into gold-edged cups and saucers. Nellie Varley smiled and waved, which wasn't such a good idea when she had a mouthful of sandwich and a fistful of very crumbly cake. Unfortunately, Lady Summer and Vera Baggs also arrived home at the same time. They might not have realised I had guests if the Varley mutt hadn't run into the hall to find a safe place to eat its bone.

'A rabid dog! Get it away from me!' shrieked Miss Baggs.

The Varleys were still giggling when Lady Summer appeared, framed in the doorway like a dramatic portrait of some vengeful goddess.

'What is the meaning of this?'

For once Mrs Rover was speechless.

'They came to tea,' I said.

Every drop of blood drained from Lady Summer's face.

'You let Varleys sit on the Chippendale dining chairs? You served them food on my best Royal Doulton?'

I looked at the gold-rimmed plates and shrugged. Let her hang me from a lamp post. 'You do not use them. You have no friends for tea. The children were hungry. There is enough here to share.'

'Insolent girl!'

'I am not!' At least, I didn't think I was. It wasn't a good time to be looking up words in my dictionary.

Lady Summer went from smouldering to blazing. 'Get out! Get out at once – all of you! Dirty little vermin!'

That did it for me. I took one of those fancy-pants plates, held it high and smashed it onto the dining-room floor. I loved how it made Lady Summer gasp.

'Yes, I break it! I will break it all! You care more for things than people. You live in this big house with many rooms and these children are in a . . .' I didn't know the word in English – small, cold, broken . . .

'Hovel,' said Mrs Rover helpfully.

'. . . and you powder your face and paint your nails, and your door is shut to those who need help.'

'The misfortunes of others are not of my making,' said Lady Summer, while Miss Baggs swept Varleys out of the dining room and into the entrance hall. 'I fired Roman Varley from the estate because he was – and is – an irresponsible drunk.'

Nellie flared up. 'That's mi dad yer talkin' about!'

Another little Varley piped up, 'Our Nellie, Dad *is* a drunk – you's always saying so.'

'He's my dad. I can say it. *She* can't. At least 'e loves us, s'more than anyone does 'er.'

Lady Summer recoiled as if she'd been slapped. 'I will not tolerate this any longer. This is my house, and . . .'

'Actually,' came a new, deeper voice, 'it's *my* house, as you so often remind me, telling me to *be a man* and face up to my responsibilities.'

Finally, visibly, Lord Summer had come out of hiding. We all turned to look at him as he stood on the great stairs. He wore the hideous purple dressing gown and pyjamas we'd bought in town. One of the sleeves was empty, tucked into a pocket. His hair was uncombed. It hung over the rumpled scar tissue of his face.

'Joseph, dear, don't let us disturb you. I'll sort this little fracas out. Mrs Rover . . . where are you going?'

'To the pub, to give that Rom Varley a good talking-to. He is a drunk and a derelict, as no father should be. Him and my husband are as bad as each other, boozing all their money away. Can I suggest Brigitta sees these kids safely home . . . with whatever leftovers the little mites need? Best you close your mouth, Miss Baggs, or something might fly in.'

And off she went – magnificent.

That wasn't the end of it. More had broken than just a plate. The spell that had kept everyone at Summerland apart had somehow splintered too. Joe went into the study with his mother and they had a long, long talk, which resulted in plans to clear the chauffeur's flat above the garage, for the Varleys to move into.

The next morning I found a pair of rabbits strung over the kitchen door handle. They were still warm.

For the furrin girl, said a note, in dark lead pencil.

After breakfast, someone took an axe to the ivy that was slowly strangling the orchard apple trees. Miraculously, the rusty garden gate got oiled hinges. The chicken run had extra wire put round, against foxes. Tiles were straightened on the coal-shed roof and someone raked the gravel forecourt. There was even a ladder up to the clock tower. I caught glimpses of a dark man with a bag of tools and a wheelbarrow moving around the estate.

Mrs Rover marvelled. 'Will wonders never cease? Rom Varley off the drink and working his old job again? There's some deep magic at work there . . .' She looked at me as if I'd lifted a curse. I didn't see what the fuss was about. Anyone who's ever needed help knows the magic of simple kindness.

Constable Ribble came by the kitchen for a *cuppa*, as it was called.

'That Lady Summer, she must be off her rocker,' he said. 'Taking Varley back again.'

'Don't you believe in second chances?' asked Mrs Rover.

'I believe in these lemon tarts,' he answered, helping himself to a second one. 'Ruddy lovely they are.'

I smiled. At least someone appreciated them.

Ribble went on. 'The Varleys have gypsy blood in 'em and no good comes of that. Mind you, they say Hitler murdered half the gypsies in Europe and he was definitely off his rocker, so maybe Lady Summer's has got it right after all, giving the kiddies a home till they get proper sorted.'

Lady Summer was avoiding me. I had good reason to know she'd no history of hospitality, not even when dear friends needed it the most. If I ever forgot that, the faint ghost in the Blue Room reminded me each time she wafted past on the edge of after-dark awareness.

I took a plate of the tarts to Joe's room, with a note that Sophie Rover helped me draft: *Compliments of the chef.* This time when I knocked he slid the bolt back and invited me in.

His room was dark. He went to huddle in an armchair, an island in a sea of books. One small lamp was lit. I sat opposite. We ate lemon-curd tarts.

'My God,' he said suddenly, 'this reminds me how hungry I am. I haven't felt like eating for ever. Since . . .' He turned his face away.

'Look at me,' I said.

He wouldn't.

'Please?'

He couldn't. I knew that need to hide.

Picking crumbs off the plate, he said, 'We should be enemies, shouldn't we? English and Austrians – opposite sides of the war. Did you know it was a family of Germans who took me in after the crash? They found me half-drowned, half-burnt and all tangled in parachute. They were munitions workers from the very kind of factory we'd have bombed if it had been our mission target. They slathered me with ointments for the burns. Paid for a doctor to come for this.' With his one hand, he indicated where the other arm had been. 'Held me down when I was delirious. Cleaned up when I spewed, and worse.

Later, in the military hospital, it was German doctors who carried out the skin grafts. I wish they hadn't bothered. I'm good for nothing now.'

'You're alive. You have a home. Family. And Vera Lynn.'

'Vera Lynn? What's she got to do with it?' Now he did look up.

I shrugged and smiled. 'You know – "It's a Lovely Day Tomorrow".'

Liver and Onions

I took a deep breath. 'This is a bad idea.'

'It's a great idea,' said Angela Goose. 'Here, don't you know how to tie a tie? Stand still, I'll do it.'

'I have never worn a tie before.'

'Never worn a tie, never been to school. What *have* you done?'

As if I could tell her that.

We were behind a hedge, on the road heading out of Summer village towards town. I'd already layered up with my disguise – a blouse, a gymslip, gym knickers and a blazer, all in the most disgusting shade of dark cabbage green. Angela was adding the finishing touches. A wool hat with a badge, and a striped green and yellow tie.

She stepped back to examine her work.

'Brilliant! You look just as awful as the rest of us now, though prettier than most, I'll give you that. I couldn't blag a spare satchel off anyone, so just stuff things in your blazer pocket or give them to me to carry.'

'What things?'

'Pens, books, homework . . . Oh. I suppose you don't really have anything like that.'

I had nothing. Not even my knife. I was planning to spend the day as a normal English girl, and I guessed they weren't usually armed. My own clothes would be wrapped in an old mackintosh and hidden in the hedge until school was over.

Yes, school.

Angela gave me one final, critical look-over. 'You're too smart. Loosen your tie, shove your socks down so they're a bit wrinkled and, whatever you do, *don't* wear your hat straight.'

Colin and Poppy Oakley were some way ahead on the road. As we walked we were joined by other cabbage-green pupils heading the same way. Mostly they ignored me. I was happy just to watch and listen and learn what normal girls were like. They giggled, they gossiped, they moaned about homework and mooned over boys, marking them out of ten on their looks. I thought about Joseph Summer. What would they mark him now?

A high brick wall surrounded the even higher brick school. 'It looks like a prison,' I said, wary.

'It is,' groaned Angela. 'We're sentenced to boredom till three thirty this afternoon.'

She didn't look so bored. She talked non-stop and said hello to everyone.

'Hey, who's your friend?' asked one of the boys. He pulled one of my braids. Without thinking I shoved him away, hard, and clenched my fists, ready to defend myself. No knife, but that was all right. I knew where to hit first to bring a boy down.

The other pupils smelled a scrap brewing. By some

unconscious, savage choreography they gathered round and, at the same time, left a space like a boxing ring. Next thing, a chant started.

'*Fight fight fight fight . . . !*'

'Girls versus boys!' whooped Angela. Fuel on a fire. How quickly people turn against each other.

The boy looked bewildered, tried to back away. 'I were just being friendly . . .'

'Is that the girl you told us about, the one who floored Colin Oakley?' asked one of Angela's friends.

A collective murmur rippled across the playground.

That's her – knocked Colin Oakley unconscious – nearly killed him . . .

A black-gowned gargoyle appeared and blew a whistle.

The potential for violence seeped away. Teachers were in charge now.

We had to make two separate lines to go into the building, facing two doors with stone labels marked for girls and boys. The oldest kids, me and Angela included, were at the back of the lines, looking down at the younger ones in front. She said lots of her friends had left school at fourteen to work, but she was staying on for exams. I felt ancient compared to everyone else.

When the whistle blew once more we shuffled forward. I kept my head down. Once we'd gone through the girls' entrance, everyone mingled together again. The older girls were noisy and sweaty and friendly and fun. I quickly figured out who was the leader in the group (Angela), who were the hangers-on, the odd girls in orbit and the solitary girls in their own private universe. We jostled along corridors to a classroom. Angela made sure I was in a seat near the back, behind a big lad with broad shoulders.

Bells rang. The first lesson was history. I was stupid. Knew nothing. Bells rang. A scrum in the corridor, a new classroom, and English. I was stupid. Knew nothing. More bells, more bashing and bruising, another room. Maths. Mostly stupid. I knew more than lots of the other kids though. Didn't put my hand up. Bells. Break time.

It was chaos out in the yard. So much yelling, screaming, running, shrieking. Child-size monsters in green going wild. I loved it.

'Aren't you playing?' Angela asked. 'There's two-ball, French skipping, rope skipping . . . It's OK, even us older girls do it. Some of us barge in on the boys' football. You've got to be tough, but it's fun.'

Football looked strange. One skilful player had the ball and the other boys trailed after him. French skipping was strange too, but addictive. Two girls stood with a loop of elastic – a prized possession – around their ankles, making two taut strands. Another girl did twists and tricks with the elastic, creating patterns while they all chanted. The bell for lessons rang far too soon.

By dinnertime at noon I'd been labelled deaf, dumb *and* stupid by harassed teachers in black gowns who happened to pick me out to answer questions. One made me come to the front of the classroom and stand by the blackboard in a cloud of chalk as an example, because I couldn't label the parts of a dissected apple correctly. Mama hadn't thought to teach me that as we crossed Europe looking for a safe haven. Whenever we got apples we ate them, or traded them for a night's shelter.

Few of the other kids on our table would eat the hot school dinner provided, which was liver and onions. The liver was like leather with bits of rubber piping in. I'd had worse. The onions looked like beige phlegm. Pudding was a square of fruit-dotted yellow sponge, with more yellow poured over it. I ate that too. Nowhere near as good as Sophie Rover's.

'Spotted Dick!' giggled the other kids, picking out the sultanas and calling them squashed flies.

Afterwards I had a go at skipping. Two girls held a long rope, turning it in a great loop while everyone chanted songs. I liked the song called 'Nancy Went to War'. According to the rhyme, while Nancy was at war she lost one arm (it went behind the back) then the other (ditto), then one leg – this meant hopping – then she lost both legs and dropped down dead. I thought Nancy was a good, resilient role model but ultimately unlucky.

'Not bad,' said Angela, when I had completed all the skipping challenges. 'I'd like to see the boys try our games instead of laughing at them. All they do is kick a ball around and tear their trousers.'

Bells rang again.

Angela groaned. '*French*. Why didn't I eat the liver at dinner and die from indigestion first?'

During the French lesson I daydreamed about running away to Paris to play at a conservatoire like Mama. Or running away to New York with Connie Snow to play in a Harlem

141

jazz club. Or just running away anywhere, because I was sick of jamming my long legs under a wooden bench.

Suddenly a piece of chalk hit me on the ear.

'*Attention!*' shouted the French teacher. 'You, girl, stand up.'

All eyes turned to me. Slowly I rose. The teacher said something in French. I stared at her. She repeated it, much more loudly. Her fingers gripped a board rubber, as if ready to throw that next. Then she said, in English, 'Answer me, girl!'

I blinked and replied, in fluent French, 'I'm sorry, *madame*, but with all respect I cannot answer as I did not understand the question, since your French accent and grammar are so bad.'

It took a while for her to translate my words. When she did, her face went as white as chalk. She slammed down the board rubber and rushed from the room. The class erupted, banging desk lids and spilling little pots of ink as they cheered.

Angela stared at me in amazement. 'I think we must now elevate you to the status of a god, Brigitta.'

The final lesson of the day was hardest. It wasn't even because I was stupid. I just couldn't do it. Needlework.

'You'll be great at this,' said Angela, prodding me in the ribs. 'You were a seamstress in the war, in that prison camp – Auschwitz – right? Can you just run up a gorgeous dress and humiliate this teacher too?'

I looked at the scraps of gingham cotton everyone was labouring over, some with tongues stuck out, some with eyes crossed.

I folded my arms.

'I will not sew.'

'Why not? Look sharp – Miss is coming over . . .'

Miss was indeed coming over, an angry pucker between her eyes. I knew that expression. It meant interrogation. How far to the door? The window was closer . . .

'Miss, can you help me?' One of Angela's friends waved her hand for attention. 'I think I've just stitched this to my school skirt by accident.'

'Miss . . . can you thread my needle?' wailed another friend.

'Miss, I'm in a right tangle, can you do it for me . . . ?'

I smiled. How quickly people rally round each other.

When the final bell rang children exploded out of the school and spilled into the streets all around. I got a few friendly slaps on the back and an invitation to try out for the hockey team – *What was hockey?*

I couldn't wait to tell Joe all about it. It was too windy to go up on the roof so we met in the conservatory – a room called the Winter Garden, full of unhappy spider plants. It overlooked the terrace and had wicker chairs with bits that stuck in you when you sat down.

'School's hell,' was Joe's verdict.

'It was also fun.'

'Yeah, it was fun too, except I was sent to a stuffy boarding school. I miss it, sort of – the pals, not school. It nearly cured me of loving books, we were fed such stodgy texts. Now reading's about all I do. I used to love sports! Cricket was wizard. Rowing was all right. Some of the rags we got up to!'

'Rags?'

He grinned. 'Messing about. Playing jokes.'

'Like the airmen at Summerland who put underpants on the *shandy*— what do you call it?'

'A chandelier. Did they do that? Excellent fellows. Are you shocked? Boys will be boys . . .'

'Boys can behave badly. Girls have to be good.' One of many sex differences I was puzzling over. What made a boy a boy, or a girl a girl?

'Yeah, I suppose,' said Joe. 'We maybe got up to a few tricks in the RAF too. We burned a piano one night, when we got our wings. Don't hit me! It's air force tradition. There was also something going on with toilet seats, but I don't remember that bit. Too much beer.'

'Why don't you see your friends now?'

'Who'd want to see me?' He turned a bit savage. 'One old chum came to the hospital when I was convalescing. The *pity* on his face . . . I promised myself no one would look at me like that again.'

'I look at you.'

'You don't mind what I'm like.'

That was true.

He shifted a little closer. I didn't move away. How close could I let him get? He didn't know me. He didn't know the worst of me. There was still such a lot I had to find out; I couldn't lose sight of why I'd come to Summerland in the first place.

'Joe, do you know a name . . . Golanski?'

'You asked me this before. Golanski? Sounds Russian, or Polish.'

'Polish. Do you know of him?'

'Was it one of the airmen stationed here? I know a lot of Poles

144

came over to do their bit after Hitler invaded Poland. There were a few in my squadron. Decent chaps. But, no – Golanski doesn't ring a bell.'

I wasn't sure why bell-ringing was relevant, but it was another setback. Time to try something else.

'I am interested in, er, local history. Your mother – does she have photographs of before the war? Perhaps of her time in school . . . her schoolfriends . . . ?'

'Probably. I'll get her to dig some out if you're that keen, no problem.'

As easy as that! So why did I feel so nervous about uncovering the past? Was it because I was somehow enjoying the present so much? The wind outside made the glass panes of the Winter Garden rattle. I shivered.

Violet Creams

It was not my fault the trip to the cinema turned into one of the worst days of my life.

I bumped into Colin while he was helping out in the shop one day after school. It was icy, but the river still tumbled unfrozen under the bridge, and it wasn't the sort of cold that ate into your bones. I'd known winters where the breath inside your lungs seemed to freeze.

Colin bagged up all the things on my list, then said, 'Hey, I'm off on Saturday afternoon. Do you want to come to the pictures?'

I was so surprised I said yes.

Later, I met Joe on the moonlit roof. I'd fetched up hot water bottles and we both had blankets.

'Getting a bit nippy,' he said. 'Are you all right to stay up here for a bit? Not too cold?'

'I'm freezing!'

He offered me space under his blanket. Like a coward, I just stayed huddled in my coat.

'It is mad, meeting up outside, but the house is so dreary.

Mother's obsessed with restoring it all for my *inheritance*, even though we've barely got two shillings to rub together. I couldn't give a monkey's about living here. I'd be off like a shot if it wasn't for . . .' He grimaced and flapped his empty sleeve.

'Where would you go?'

'Anywhere. Everywhere. Pointless talking about it. I can't fly any more, so what would I do?'

'What do you like to do?'

'Flying. Sport. Messing about. Drawing, I suppose. I used to sketch a lot before I joined the RAF. Even in briefings, I always had a pencil to doodle. What about you?'

'I can't do anything.'

'Oh, come off it. You must have talents. And you're whole and healthy, aren't you? Me, I'm washed up before I hardly got started. Crashed and crippled and too scared to leave my room except to talk to you. Maybe I should join a circus, as a freak.'

'I will come too. We will ride elephants and swing on the . . . what do you call it?'

'Trapeze? Sure, why not? I'll be a one-armed trapeze artist. In the meanwhile, what would you like to do? You can't clean toilets for the rest of your life.'

'Will you clean your own, Lord Summer?'

'Fat chance. That's not the point.'

'I need a job.'

'You could get a better one.'

'Do you want me to leave?'

'No!'

The word came out like a bullet. He lowered his voice to a whisper. It lured me closer.

147

'No, I definitely don't want you to go. You're the only thing that makes this place bearable.'

'You can't hide forever . . .'

'I can do what a bloody well like! I mean . . . Sorry. I'm just so messed up. I should just pull myself together. Snap out of it. *Be a man*, they say.'

I sometimes felt the same way.

'Here I am,' he continued, 'moping around in the dark like a ghost, good for nothing. Don't laugh, but I thought you were a ghost when I first saw you that time, dancing on the terrace.'

'I thought you were a ghost also. There are many in Summerland.'

'Really? That old yarn about the drowned maid?'

'Her name is Ursula. She has a mop and bucket.'

Joe did a double take. 'You've seen her?'

'Yes. Many times. Also, the airmen, from the war.'

Now he did pay attention. 'Ghosts of the guys who were stationed here? That's incredible. Are you pulling my leg?'

I wanted to touch his leg. Was that bad?

'I am serious. The ghosts are in all the house. Sometimes in uniform. They read books, play games. They don't know they are dead.'

Joe was silent for a while. 'I never thought about it before, whether people really haunt places. It's . . . hard . . . to think my crew, my friends, might be ghosts somewhere, wafting around our old airbase, or up in the clouds above Germany.'

I had a vision of ghosts raining down from those clouds and the dead soaking into our skin.

'War's not as exciting as you think it's going to be, is it?' he said finally.

That's when I decided Lady Summer had been right, the day we first met. We had to pretend there'd never been a war. We had to enjoy ourselves today and have fun and adventures and *live*. Enough worrying about what might happen.

'We could dance!' I said, leaping up. 'I'll teach you the steps I know. I'll hum the music. You could come out with me to the airfield on Saturday nights. They have a band there – Connie Snow. The music is sensational.'

He backed away from me – 'No!'

So I told him I was going to the pictures with Colin and he said fine and I said fine and it was all *fine*, goodnight, thank you very much.

The Picture Palace in town was dazzling – bright lights and glam film posters. The pavement was jammed with young people queuing for tickets. I loved how everyone was laughing and flirting and messing about. Colin had slicked his hair back, and he wore a tie. He kept looking around proudly as if to say, *Hey, this is my girl*. I wasn't anyone's girl. I saw my reflection in the glass of the poster cases, wearing my red check coat. Did I look pretty? Did I want to look pretty?

Colin talked non-stop about his job, his friends, his favourite films and anything else that came into his head. I hoped he'd shut up once the film started.

'I used to come to the cinema loads with Joseph Summer and other lads from the village,' he said. 'Then Joe joined the RAF and thought he was better than the rest of us, swanning around in his uniform and jawing about his training. I could have been a hero too, if the war hadn't ended so soon.'

I'd been to the cinema before, during the war. I can't remember which city it was, or even what language – somewhere on the way to Berlin. Mama used to buy one ticket and sneak me in. I had to hide at her feet in case the police came, and we'd stay and watch the same film over and over. Jews weren't allowed in cinemas, but it was warm in there and better than being on the streets all day.

'Chocolate?' Colin shoved something at me – a blue box wrapped in a white ribbon. 'They're almost impossible to get,' he boasted, 'what with rationing. I saved up from my Saturday job at Gant's. Go on, they're for eating, not just for looking at.'

I pulled the ribbon bow and lifted the lid of the box. Fat, round chocolates nestled in crinkled paper cups. My mouth watered just looking at them. I picked one out and nibbled a tiny bit from the edge. Heaven!

Colin got a funny expression. *The look.* He was watching my lips. I stopped savouring the chocolate and chomped the whole lot . . . and had to resist spitting it out. It was disgusting!

'They're violet creams,' he said proudly. 'Only the best.'

They tasted like old ladies. Not that I'd ever eaten old lady. I remembered Frau Trautwein had a precious glass jar of something perfumed called talcum powder. She dabbed it on after a bath. Afterwards the apartment would be haunted by the smell of dead flowers.

Colin steered me through the crush towards a shell-shaped double seat at the back of the auditorium. I was amazed at how grand everything was – red velvet and gold scrolling, with just a few scuffs and sweet wrappers. In the gallery above, younger kids were dangling over the barrier dropping spitballs. The couple in the next double seat along were already plastered together, nuzzling each other's necks.

I took off my coat and put it between me and Colin.

He must have been tired, because as the lights dimmed he yawned and stretched an arm out along the back of the seat.

First up was a comedy show about a fat man and a thin man who just couldn't help bashing each other with ladders, stepping on garden rakes and falling in pots of paint. The fat man got so exasperated and the thin man was so feeble . . . I laughed so hard I thought I'd crack a couple of ribs. They were called Laurel and Hardy and they were the best thing I'd ever seen in my entire life. The whole cinema – hundreds of us – were lifted up with that laughter.

The lights came on and Colin moved his arm, cracking his shoulder back into place. I don't know why he sat like that if it made him sore.

'Would you like an ice cream?'

I was still sunny with laughter. 'Yes, please!'

As vanilla cooled my mouth, I thought how generous Colin was. I'd been with him on the dance floor. He wasn't afraid of life. When the lights went down again I moved my coat so it wasn't between us.

When I asked, 'What is next?' it took him a moment to realise I was talking about the pictures, not where his hand could settle.

'Usually a couple of short newsreels, then the main feature,' he answered. We were shoulder to shoulder.

The big screen flickered. There were white scratches running down the title of the next film: *A Defeated People*.

Colin never saw a single scene. He seemed to be trying to lick me. He kept getting hair stuck on his lips, but I never felt a single one of his kisses. The film was so real I thought they must have pulled memories out of my head and wound them onto a reel to project. Germany: vanquished. A camera panning over flattened cities and rubble mountains. Hard-faced survivors tasting the ashes of humiliation. Mixed with the film soundtrack, I could hear English voices in the cinema – *They got what was coming to them . . . No more than they deserve . . . Poor beggars. Not so Sieg Heil now, are they?* On the screen a German housewife poured out her bitterness by a pump that wouldn't pour water: *Alles ist kaput*, she moaned. It's all ruined.

That was the past, I told myself. Houses could be rebuilt; pumps could be mended. I wasn't going to think about war any more.

Colin had a hand on my leg. I moved it off. The first news film ended. A new one began. This one was footage of the Nuremberg trials. Newspaper headlines made real by cinema. Scenes of liberated Horror Camps interspersed with shots of Hitler's henchmen awaiting judgement.

Colin was breathing heavily. I couldn't hear the commentary. I pushed him away. They were filming in the courtroom. The faces were a black-and-white blur – judges, lawyers, Nazi criminals – oh no, not *him*, not that face from so long ago, not now, not here, not several feet high on a screen for all the world to see . . .

I rose from the seat, not knowing if I should fly into the screen or pull my eyes from their sockets.

I called out one word.

'Papa!'

My papa. Alive and he hadn't come for me. Alive and he didn't want me.

In Nuremberg, in the courtroom, a judge was reading out verdicts . . .

Death by hanging . . . Death by hanging . . . Death by hanging . . .

Colin pulled me down into the seat. 'Are you all right?'

Shh, said the crowd. The main feature was starting, to a ghastly wail of violins. It was called *A Matter of Life and Death* and it was about an English bomber pilot and the girl he loved. I knew this because Colin had told me when he invited me to come. I saw nothing of the film, nothing of the actors. The music was a soundtrack to my own emotions, which I was desperately folding up and putting away in the deepest hidey-hole of my mind.

'Did you have a good time?'

Somehow I was home. Sophie Rover had kept *meatuntooveg* warm in the oven for me, but I wasn't hungry.

'Enjoy your day off?' sneered Miss Baggs, when we passed in a corridor.

I did not go to see Joe at midnight. I did not even undress and go to bed. I stood in the dark in my room, holding the one grey glove, trying to understand everything I had seen. Then, distraught, I walked through the house.

No clocks ticked. The ghosts had scattered . . . all except one, waiting for me on the first-floor landing. I knew her already. She was the wisp of sunshine ghost I'd seen briefly while cleaning Joe's rooms all those weeks ago. The spider-thread ghost glimpsed in the mirror of the Blue Room. At night she drifted beyond the clusters of airmen, too faint to make out clearly, too persistent to ignore.

The Blue Room was more grey than blue tonight. The ghost was standing with her back to me at the unshuttered window and the bright crescent moon shone through her body. When I blinked she was gone. Behind me. At the bottom of the stairs. Pausing while I caught up.

Wait for me.

As if in a trance, I pushed open the ballroom doors. I needed more light – even pale moonlight would do. The ghost didn't move as I opened the curtains and shutters. She sat on the piano stool, her face still turned away. My feet moved so I went with them. To the piano. To the stool. I sat down also, enveloped in memory. She was with me as I straightened my back.

Hours we'd practised together before the war, me as a child in her lap, my small hands on top of her supple ones. Her breath warm on my hair. Her love wrapped round me. Since the war I had never coaxed a sound from a piano.

Now I lifted the lid of the Summerland grand piano. Set my feet to the golden pedals. With reverence I let my fingertips graze the keys. They were cold. I shivered.

I took a deep breath. With my eyes closed I let my finger push down on a black key. C sharp. The vibration was pure ecstasy. My whole body thrummed. I played the note again, picturing the felted hammer touching wire. One note rippled into many. Beethoven. It had to be him. A German composer for German memories. I began with the low G of sonata No. 14 – the *Moonlight*.

One note rippled into many. The sound spread and filled the room. I could have been anywhere or nowhere. All I knew was that my papa was alive, and I was finally, utterly playing music.

The ghost played with me. A duet of living and dead.

The last note died and the ghost vanished with it. An audience had gathered. Airmen around the ballroom walls, like grey flock wallpaper. Joe, more solid, was there too. Two women in the doorway, hair clamped in clips, faces white with night cream.

'How dare you touch that piano!' hissed Miss Baggs.

'Who . . . ? Who taught you to play like that?' whispered Lady Summer.

I bowed my head over the keys.

'My mama taught me. She is dead now. I wish I was too.'

Christmas Pudding

Summerland in the snow. Is there anything more beautiful than fresh snowflakes falling softly on your face?

'Get a shift on,' called Sophie Rover through the kitchen window. 'I need a hand with the sprouts!'

I loaded up the coal shovel and lugged it back into the house.

It took seven of us to get the Christmas tree in. Three to lift it – me, Mrs Rover and Mr Varley – and four little Varleys to dance around in excitement until Miss Baggs threatened to sweep them out with a broom, and she wasn't joking.

The tree was freshly cut from a grove in the woods. We heaved it into a giant pot of gravel and set it in the ballroom. There was to be a New Year party to celebrate Summerland's revival: builders were arriving in January and the fifteen military toilets would finally be removed. Until then the ballroom was like a Siberian wasteland, because what little coal there was available had to be saved for special occasions only. The thing that warmed me was Joe.

'My father planted the saplings when he was a boy,' he told

me. 'Christmas at Summerland was always magical. Before the war.'

His papa had died in a traffic accident. That was why his car – a Rolls-Royce – was kept locked in the garage and never driven. Joe said it was hard to miss his father. He hardly knew him. 'He never did anything like this – decorating the tree. He was all about the house, the prestige, being a *lord*. I've no idea why Mother married him.'

'Because she is the same?'

'She never used to be. From what I can tell, she got up to all sorts of tricks when she was at school. That reminds me – you asked about her photographs from back then. She's got an album . . .'

'No. Thank you. Let's do the tree.' I'd lugged a box of decorations down from the attic. Joe dived in, finding long-forgotten treasures nestled in the tissue paper. I watched him fumble, clumsy with one hand. What would that be like?

'Brigitta!' Lady Summer appeared in the ballroom.

I sprang to my feet. Things had been strange since I came back from the pictures and played *Moonlight Sonata*. Joe had mumbled something about *the music – so beautiful*. That embarrassed me. I hadn't done it for him, though I danced inside to know he was impressed. Mama always said that in dangerous times it was best not to draw attention to yourself. *Girls in particular have to pretend they know nothing*, she warned. *Otherwise men see them as a threat. We can't afford to be noticed, or to be memorable – remember that.*

I'd drawn attention to myself at the cinema, which was worrying. I dreaded meeting Colin Oakley again. I kept

157

seeing the film clip of the courtroom in my mind. *Hanged by the neck until dead.* That face, grey and grainy on the big screen. It probably wasn't him. After six years, how could I even know what he looked like? Best not dwell on it. Be alive now.

'Yes, Lady Summer?'

She was distracted for a moment, watching Joe fiddle with the ribbons on the baubles. He was trying to tie loops so he could hang them on the tree. Wisely she didn't offer to help. It was enough that he had come out of his rooms. She turned to me, holding out a sheaf of papers.

'I found these. They may be of interest.'

Music! My hands trembled as I leafed through the scores. Satie, Debussy, Chopin . . . I *loved* all these! 'And Germaine Tailleferre,' I said in wonder, recognising a composer my mama admired.

'Indeed. Not as well-known as she should be. Madame Tailleferre taught at a conservatoire in Paris where a dear friend of mine studied.'

That was when I noticed a name in faint pencil at the top of one page: *Hélène Jacobs.*

The room stilled. Through sudden tears I saw single green needles on the fir tree and light sparkle on a glass snowflake. Hélène Jacobs. My mama.

'A . . . a dear friend?'

'A foolish girl who wasted her youth, her education, her talent, on a poor law student. I begged her to continue her studies, but she claimed to be deliriously happy. There was a child – a boy, I think. Perhaps they married, I don't know.'

158

'What . . . what happened to her . . . and the child?'

'Enough interrogation! The war happened. Play these if you wish. You have talent, that is clear, beyond cleaning and a tendency to adopt stray gypsy children. Perhaps in the New Year we can see about finding a piano teacher for you. Goodness knows, we'll need a distraction once the builders start work. First we have the New Year's Eve party to look forward to, a fine Summerland tradition, made all the more special now my son is home. Perhaps you'll play for us then, to accompany the string quartet. Go on, play something now.'

Joe gave his mother a look. Her face softened just a little.

'If you please,' she added.

I could tell her things about her old schoolfriend – my mama Hélène. Wipe that haughty look from her face. Rub her snooty nose in the filth of my history. Or I could keep my secrets. Keep living at Summerland. Keep Joe.

I went to the grand piano and lifted the lid. I took Hélène Jacobs's score and placed it in front of me. It was a lovely piece called *Impromptu*, one that she'd played for me on imaginary piano keys, humming the tune as her fingers showed me the pace and patterning. It would be difficult. Would I even remember how to read music? My eyes hurt. I realised they were filled with tears. I couldn't do it – couldn't bear to bring this piece of music back to life when she was so very dead.

Mama, you taught me everything beautiful and you never gave up on me, not when we were all alone, not when we crouched in a pigsty, or suffocated under floorboards, or dodged

159

along trains. Always you gave me music.

Idiot! I told myself. You owe it to her. You have to play something. And so, wrapped in an old cardigan, with my fingers stiff and awkward from the cold, I began to play.

On Christmas Eve Lady Summer, Miss Baggs and Mrs Rover went to church. Lady Summer said she'd make enquiries about the nearest synagogue in the new year, saying it was important I rediscovered my Jewish faith. Her interest surprised me. God, Jesus, prayers – none of it had meant anything to me during the war. I'd just wanted to get out and run free, and my religion made that impossible, thanks to the foul Nazi laws. Could I be Jewish again? Had I ever stopped? How did anyone ever know *what* they were? I was so messed up now.

I spent the evening practising at the piano while Joe read by the light of the Christmas-tree candles. Always he kept the scarred side of his face away from me. When my fingers became too tangled and the notes jumped around like tadpoles on the paper, I lowered the piano lid. The ballroom was still. The ghosts were fainter than they used to be.

'Are you happy that Summerland will be made beautiful again?'

Joe looked up from his book. 'This old junk-yard? It's the past and I'm done with that, like my old cricket bats and tennis rackets. We should sell the place. Sell *me* why you're at it – I'm old and useless.'

'I will buy you. How much?'

'How much have you got?'

I thought of the money I'd saved so far. It wasn't anywhere near enough to get me to Nuremberg in Germany, so why was I hoarding it? 'What can I get for a penny? Penny for the guy?'

His answer came back too quick for thought. 'A kiss.'

I couldn't answer, except for a clumsy *goodnight*. Once out of the ballroom, I ran down the corridor past one, two, three, four, fifteen military toilets. I was slower up the stairs to bed. Kissing Joe was out of the question, even if I wanted to.

Which I did.

Very much.

I fell asleep holding my one grey glove.

Movement woke me. A shadow in the dark. Ursula? No. This was no ghost. The shadow moved to the chest of drawers. An inch at a time I reached under the pillow for my knife. It was possible to slow the heart rate and the breathing down to a silent stillness; I knew that from experience. Through slitted eyes I played dead and kept watch. The shadow came towards the bed. I gripped the handle of the knife hard. A second later, the figure was gone and the door clicked shut. I was still holding the knife when I fell back to sleep.

Knock knock.

'Who's there? Is it morning?'

'Christmas morning – Merry Christmas!'

It was Joe. Joe in my room. Luckily I was bundled in nightshirt and blankets. He was in slippers and dressing gown. 'What are you doing?'

161

'Have you opened your stocking already?'

'Stocking?'

'If you're good all year, Father Christmas comes down the chimney and fills a stocking –'

'I have not been good. And the chimney is blocked.'

'And yet . . .' Striding to the window, he jerked the curtains open, one at a time. It was still dark, so he switched the light on. The only spots of colour were the painting of the orange and a lumpy khaki sock hanging off a drawer knob. 'You see?'

The figure in the dark.

'Did you . . . ?'

Joe laughed. 'It wasn't me.'

'F-Father Christmas?'

'Do you think he has an army green sock? Go on, open it. I've got one too . . .'

Sophie Rover had made me a Christmas stocking.

Joe sat on the end of my bed to open his. He quickly tore off bits of ribbon and brown paper. I took my time. Every little gift was a treasure. There was a rolled-up scarf to match my gloves – I put this on at once because the bedroom was freezing and it helped me to feel less undressed. There was a little metal biscuit cutter in the shape of a star. A toothbrush. A few twists of barley sugar. Homemade toffee and . . . I had to stick my hand right to the toe of the sock for the final present . . . an orange.

My very own orange.

'Your face!' said Joe. 'Haven't you ever seen an orange before?'

Yes, I had. I'd eaten one. A gift. The first year we hid at the Trautweins' my mother stole an orange from the fruit bowl at Christmas. That was also the last Christmas anyone saw oranges, thanks to the war going badly for Germany. Mama sneaked it to me in the wardrobe. I was cramped and bored and cross. Our hands touched briefly as she passed it to me. Can't stay, *Liebling*, I have to go join the Trauts for compulsory carol singing. This is for you.'

I ate that orange in the dark, every last juicy segment. The Summerland orange I peeled with my knife and I shared it with Joe.

'I have a gift for you,' I said shyly.

'Don't need any more than this,' he said, grinning, but he took the little parcel I had ready for him. It was a pencil set, bought from Oakleys' shop.

He waggled his empty sleeve. 'What am I supposed to do with pencils?'

'Draw, you idiot.'

'With my elbow?'

'With your left hand.'

'I'm right-handed.'

'Not any more.'

How had my mother put it . . . ? *Adapt or go under*.

'Merry Christmas!' cried Sophie Rover when I got to the kitchen. She gathered me up in a big hug despite her handfuls of spoon and tea towel. 'Grab yourself a Christmas breakfast if you can find a free space at the table. Here, have a festive sprig.' She tucked a little twig of holly into my hair.

'Thank you for the sock, Mrs Rover.'

'Don't know what you're talking about. Pass me that skillet, pet.'

'What can I do?'

'Nothing, my lovely . . . Unless . . . Could you just . . .'

Christmas dinner on rations was an art. Mrs Rover was in her element. She chopped veg, boiled endless pans and kept opening the oven to check on the most delicious-smelling tray of dressed meat. Her face was pink and her hair was steamed to a frizz. She was beautiful.

'Hand me that colander . . . Stir this . . . Before the war, when there were servants, and *food* in the shops, Summerland would have twenty or thirty guests for Christmas dinner,' she said, juggling pans on the range. 'Mind you, back in '44 I did Christmas goose with all the trimmings for two hundred maniacs from the Army Air Corps. What a hoot that was. Bless 'em, they *all* thought they could fly by the time they'd had my boozy pudding.'

'What's *boozy*?'

'You'll find out at dinner. I've made two puddings – one for the fine folk and one just for you. Right. Let's put the festive kettle on. Dig out my boots, will you, and my mackintosh.'

'You're going out? Aren't you having dinner with us?'

'Sit down with the missus? I don't think so! I'm meeting Mr Rover today – yes, I forget I have a husband too sometimes. I'm quite fond of him, as long as we don't see each other too often. He's taking me for dinner at a hotel in town – fancy that. I shall have to mind my manners, won't I, pet?'

I hoped she didn't. I liked her just the way she was.

***

The dinner guests were all ancient and awful. I served them tea in the drawing room. One prehistoric relative was going on about how dreadful it was that Gant's employed so many foreign workers. She sounded like a damp oboe – badly tuned and reedy. She didn't even wait until I was out of the room before saying, 'So *that's* the Jew girl? It's above and beyond the call of duty, my dear, taking on a charity case like that. I wouldn't be so imposed on.'

I would've spat in her tea, only I was on my best behaviour because Joe had agreed to show himself in public. He was dressed in proper clothes, with only one shirt button in the wrong hole. I itched to fasten it right, and to straighten his tie and to smooth back his lovely tufted hair, and . . . and then my thoughts took me to so many dangerous places.

'Marvellous to see you up and about!' coughed an elderly man in a bow tie when he spotted Joe. 'Horrible . . . you know . . . being maimed so badly. But where there's life there's hope.'

Joe said, 'How very cheering.' He endured an embrace from his mother, then used her as a human shield to avoid the same from Vera Baggs.

Miss Baggs wanted to hold his saucer while he drank tea. 'Your poor arm,' she said, oozing with pity. I was just happy to catch his eye. To feel his gaze on me. To be in the same room.

'Joe's in the drawing room,' I sang to Mrs Rover back in the kitchen.

She gave me a funny look, but her eyes lit up. 'Master Joseph, what a surprise! Go set another place at the table.'

The dining room was swathed in holly and ivy. Cutting the branches had been tricky: little Varleys had appeared out of nowhere and quickly got stuck to holly prickles. I had set the table with silver cutlery and the Royal Doulton dinner service, and Mrs Rover had showed me how to fold the linen napkins into peacock tails.

Roast beef was carved and lavished with meat gravy. Potatoes came out of the pan crispy on the outside and fluffy as cotton inside. There were mounds of vegetables and a tongue-biting sauce called horseradish. The taste of it folded time for me, back to a strange and sombre meal with Papa and lots of grown-ups I didn't know who told me to sit still and gave me . . . *maror*, that was it The bitter herbs for Passover. I reeled at the memory. How much had I buried along with my old name and identity? How much had I lost? All those people at the table, where were they now? Had they hidden and survived, or . . . ?

Suddenly the family Christmas at Summerland seemed like a fairy tale, something I was just reading about, that happened to other people. My story was darker.

'Penny for your thoughts?' sang Mrs Rover. She took up a big pan of round green things called Brussels sprouts, tipped them in a sieve and squashed them flat with a plate.

'Vegetables must be cooked until they're properly dead,' she explained.

Perhaps the servings were scant compared to pre-war. Perhaps there was a bit of tension every time Miss Baggs offered to cut Joe's food into smaller pieces. Perhaps the quality of the beef was not what Lady Summer was used to. Even so, there was magic in that meal, especially when the pudding appeared. Sophie Rover had instructed me how to serve it. I'd stared at the bottle of brandy and the box of matches.

'Are you sure?'

'Bless you, you little innocent. Do it as I've told you, then tuck in to your own pudding. And watch your teeth . . .' With that mysterious advice she was bundled in layers and out of the door, calling one last, 'Ho! Ho! Ho!'

So in the dining room I poured the brandy over the big round pudding and set it on fire. How it flamed! Blue and purple and orange! Joe broke into a pudding song – 'For we all like figgy pudding' – and even Bossy Baggs clapped her hands with delight. There was a jug of plum sauce and enough pudding for everyone ten times over. The guests found tiny charms hidden inside – some mad English tradition designed to break people's teeth.

As promised, there was another tiny pudding for me. Partway through my teeth cracked on something hard. I pulled out a silver coin – an English sixpence.

Next it was drinks in the drawing room. Miss Baggs asked for a teensy-weensy sherry. I filled her glass to the brim so she couldn't drink without spilling it.

'Gifts!' said Joe suddenly. He leaped up – how had I ever thought him ghostly, he was so pulsing with life! – and left the room, returning with a gift for Miss Baggs, and a few neat parcels for his mother. Nothing for me.

'Sorry, Brigitta, there wasn't enough time –'

I cut him off. 'That's all right.'

It wasn't of course. I still handed over my second gift to him.

Lady Summer was curious. 'What is it, darling?'

Joe had fallen silent. Had I done something wrong? Why did he look almost tearful? He walked to the upright piano on the far side of the drawing room and set his gift there. 'Will you play it for me?' he said quietly.

'Is it music?' asked Lady Summer. 'Play it for all of us.'

So I did. I sat and played a melody that had begun in my head as a few simple notes and grown into a wordless song. Sitting at the kitchen table, I'd drawn lines to score the music. It had no title. To me it meant friendship. A reprieve from solitude. A call to dance freely and fly high. To the listeners, who knows? They were all quiet as I finished.

I turned on the piano stool, heart banging like a hammer. 'Lady Summer. You had a friend at school. She visited Summerland when Joe was a baby. Her name was . . .'

'Heavens, what *is* that awful caterwauling?' cried Miss Baggs, leaping to her feet.

The moment was lost. Miss Baggs was at the window making hand-flappy shooing gestures to a group of carol singers on the front steps. During the war I'd heard the Trautwein tone-deaf rendition of *Stille Nacht*, and a post-war Russian army improvisation too rude and rowdy to repeat, but I'd never had my ears assaulted so badly as when the Varleys caroused outside Summerland with their robust English version of *Silent Night*.

Lady Summer went to pay them to cease immediately.

* * *

168

It was late when the washing-up was done and the guests ejected. Late when I trudged upstairs.

I reached my bedroom, weaving around ghosts who were dancing some kind of reel in tartan skirts. There was a faint light under the door. I opened the door slowly. Ursula was standing in the middle of the room, entranced by the glow of tiny candles that burned on the drawers and on the windowsill, some shining through her grey body. Magical.

On the bed there was a sheet of art paper and a written note. The paper was a sketch. A face. It was me.

Me, regardless of how long my hair, what I wore, what language I spoke, where I came from. Me, captured in confident pencil strokes and shadings.

I picked up the note.

Sorry this took so long and wasn't ready before. I couldn't quite capture what makes you so beautiful. Yours, Joseph.

Down I flew to his room, hoping no one would spot me.

Knock, knock.

'Door's open – I was hoping you'd come by,' he whispered. 'Do you like it? I mean, the sketch was rubbish, I know. My left hand isn't so good, but I'll get better . . . What is it?'

I passed him a penny.

He looked at the penny. Looked at me. Remembered what he'd offered for that price.

Then I panicked. Snatched back the penny. Made for the door. He caught up with me.

'Keep the money,' he whispered. 'This one is for free.'

It was just a light brush of his lips against my cheek.

Ursula winked at me when I got back to my own room. 'Mind your own business,' I said in German. I spotted the grey glove abandoned on the chest of drawers. I didn't pick it up. I didn't want it. The past was past. I wanted to live *now*. Why shouldn't I stay in Summerland and be happy?

Sherry Trifle

It snowed.

On 26th December, a day called Boxing Day for no understandable reason, the local hunt gathered outside Summerland. Lady Summer went out in her furs to patronise the riders in their red jackets and to get jumped at by hounds with wagging tails. I had no wish to see horses go galloping across the white fields. I had been a fox, streaking away from pursuers. We ran across an icy city bridge one time, chased by braying thugs from the Hitler Youth, after easy prey. That was early on in the war, when we still thought things couldn't really get so bad. I was hit by a stone on the back of my head. Mama turned on those boys in their fascist uniforms and screamed, 'Stop right now or I'll rip your scrawny little heads off with my bare hands and throw them in the river for the ducks!' Some sense of shame made them drop their missiles and let us limp away. We were lucky that time.

It snowed.

Drifts up to the windowsills, ice thick on the lake. The water in my bedside mug had a film of ice on it when I woke.

It snowed.

I went out to shovel the paths and doorsteps, working till my muscles ached and I was too tired to stay up late with the ghosts. Mr Varley worked with me. We fought back when the little Varleys ambushed us with snowballs.

It snowed.

The Land Girls from Old Rory's farm came with their red tractor to clear the avenue, ready for guests at the New Year's party.

''Tis the season to be jolly . . .' sang Sophie Rover as she upended a bottle of alcohol into a mix-up of sponge cake, tinned fruit and jelly, dolloping custard and cream on top. *Trifle*, she called it. An English thing. 'There, that's enough sherry to get even the near-dead relatives singing *ta-ra-ra-boom-de-ay* on the tables as the clock chimes midnight.'

'The clock is broken,' I said.

'Good news for Cinderella. She won't turn into a pumpkin, or a frog, or whatever's supposed to happen when the clock strikes twelve. That said, I did spot Rom Varley lugging ladders to the roof for a tinker with the clock tower. But talking of Cinderella, when's your fairy godmother coming over to help with your fancy dress? Angie's a dab hand with crêpe paper and scissors. She does the school-play costumes every year. What's that face for? Every girl likes a bit of a twirl in a fancy frock.'

'Even you?'

'I've been known to cut a rug! Get Glenn Miller on the radio and I'll show you how army lasses get in the mood.' She grabbed my hand in one meaty paw and began to Lindy Hop, steps that Colin Oakley had taught me at the airbase

172

dance. She was pretty nifty too, although we didn't get as far as cutting rugs up, whatever that was all about. She had just spun me out towards the pan rack when Vera Baggs came through to the kitchen.

'I see I'm not interrupting anything *worthwhile*,' she said sarcastically. 'I hardly think *that* sort of gyration will suit the evening's music. We have a very elegant string quartet booked,' she announced with a smirk.

'Haven't you heard?' replied Mrs Rover. 'Lady Summer is being unusually jolly in her invitations this year – she's invited local children to join the toffs, and you're to supervise their party games.'

'That . . . That cannot be true. Lord knows I adore children – dear little cherubs – but *here*? In Summerland? Party games? Oh dear, I shall speak with her at once . . . There must be some mistake . . .'

No mistake.

'I told you Mother was human,' said Joe, when I quizzed him about it. 'It makes her feel like Lady Bountiful to let the commoners come and romp around Summerland every once in a while.

'Have you told her about the string quartet yet?'

He grinned. 'Cancelled them yesterday as we agreed, and informed dear old Ma that they're stuck in snowdrifts up in Scotland. She called them snivelling buffoons and almost postponed the start of 1947, saying there simply had to be music. Then yours truly –' he bowed – 'informed her that he knew of a rather marvellous band, which should be arriving to set up any time . . . now!'

A crashing knock on the front door. I scooted off to open it. And it did open, thanks to Roman Varley's handiwork – swinging wide to reveal Connie Crackerthorpe, Val, Charlie and the other members of the band. Perhaps Lady Summer would kill me for setting this all up, but it would be worth it.

Connie gave me a crushing hug.

'Nice pad!' she whistled, gazing at the chandelier. 'Thanks for getting us the gig, Brigitta – you're a star. How've you been?'

'All right.' This was how northern people answered enquiries about their well-being, whether they were exploding with happiness or facing certain death. 'How about you?'

'Same old, same old. No nearer to New York, more's the pity, and Val reckons she'll jack in the horn playing so she can take evening classes and become an accountant, or something serious. Wowser, that's one hell of a piano – Charlie, Charlie, come and tinkle these ivories!'

I hovered by the piano. 'I . . . I have been playing . . .'

'You *do* play – thought so. Go on then.'

I was paralysed. *Come on come on come on*, I told myself. You can't live your life in fear. I gave them a few bars of Debussy's 'The Snow Is Dancing'.

Charlie came over. 'Nice. Duet? Squish up . . .'

'I can't . . .'

He made me. He took the lead, improvising runs of notes. As soon as I realised it was just a matter of taking the tune and messing around with it, I was away. It all came so naturally. I felt as if gravity had been switched off and I was floating into the fun.

'You should play more,' Charlie said eventually. 'Seriously, try this . . .'

As soon as she heard us playing what she snortingly called *honky-tonk*, Vera Baggs ran, arms flapping, to fetch Lady Summer, escorting her to the ballroom.

'The band are here, my lady. Not at all suitable, my lady. They are *Negroes*, my lady.'

'I am Connie Snow. We are Swing Sensations,' said Connie with a flourish. I burned inside at Baggs's bigotry.

'They're *black*,' said Miss Baggs.

'How very observant.' Lady Summer was as cool as ever. 'Haven't you an urgent matter to attend to elsewhere in the house, Vera? Miss Snow . . .' She extended a hand.

Connie took it and lightly shook it.

'Tell Brigitta what you require, Miss Snow. You know, Vera and I, along with our friend Hélène, had the honour of seeing Miss Josephine Baker perform in Paris once, at the Folies Bergère. We were just schoolgirls. It was the first time we had seen a black woman, believe it or not. Perhaps we lived sheltered lives. She had remarkable talent.'

'That Baker woman should have stayed in Africa,' muttered Miss Baggs from the safety of the corridor.

'She's *American*,' came a chorus from me and Connie and Lady Summer.

'French now,' added Connie.

'Is that so . . . ?' said Lady Summer. 'Brigitta, when Miss Snow and her friends are settled, come and see me in the dining room. I wish to speak with you before guests begin arriving.'

The dining room was decorated for the party in paper chains, lovingly and messily stuck together by little Varleys. Lady Summer shuddered at how gaudy it was.

'Come here. I have something for you.' She went to a sideboard and fetched out a box and a packet. 'These are best kid leather,' she said, passing me the packet. 'You wear them in the evening.'

'When I am drying dishes after tea?'

'Tonight, at the party. I understand Reverend Goose's daughter will dress you in something more suitable.'

I stroked the backs of the soft white gloves. My mother would have loved them. Inside they had the Gant's label.

Next Lady Summer opened the box. A string of creamy-white pearls nestled on the velvet.

'You may wear these also – a loan only. I never had a daughter to pass them on to, nor do you have a mother to lend you hers.'

'My mother sold her pearls to pay for protection.'

'How disagreeable.'

'It was when the landlady took her money but turned us out into the street in winter anyway because we were Jews.'

She slammed the box down. 'Did I not tell you, we do *not* speak of the past? There is too much to lament. I lost my husband, remember, and my beautiful boy.'

'Joe is alive.'

'Joseph will never be the same again. You did not know him when he was whole and handsome and king of the world.' Even though she turned away I still saw her face in the mirror above the fireplace. 'I lost a dear friend to the nightmare in Europe also.'

'Hélène Jacobs.'

'Yes.'

My voice was rough as a cheese grater. 'Perhaps she had no one who would take her in and protect her.' I stopped. I would not speak of the war with Barbara Summer. I would play her fancy pianos and eat her sherry trifle and enjoy myself.

Angela climbed up the stairs to my attic room, armed with packets of blue crêpe paper, sewing gear and a pot of glue. She was in fancy dress as Joan of Arc, complete with painted cardboard breastplate. 'Trust me,' she said. 'I'll have you looking amazing in no time. I'm going to pin your hair up and make the dress around you.'

'I don't want to undress.' I folded my hands across my chest.

'Silly, I've brought an old slip. Put that on first.'

'Go outside.'

'God, B, it's just us two girls. Fine, I'm going. Yell when you're ready.'

I yelled as instructed. It was still excruciating to stand there and have someone so near to my body. She quickly covered me in sweeps of blue, splodged with glue and stitched with great lengths of thread.

'Hey, B, are you joining the rest of the children in the dining room? We're having party games – musical bumps, musical statues, musical squares, musical chairs . . .'

'I would like to see the band.'

'Oh yeah, me too, yeah. Games are for kids, right? I suppose you'll want to dance with Colin Oakley again . . .'

I wanted to dance all right. With Joe.

177

Angela laid one more dab of glue and I was ready.

'Ta da! You look . . .' She stepped back for a full view. 'You actually look beautiful.' Her admiration was genuine. I hated myself for hating the dress. I knew it was lovely, I just didn't want to wear it. I was conscious of wood-chopping muscles, and floor-scrubbing hands. My legs were bare – too downy, I thought, but I had no stockings.

'A proper blooming flower. Oh, I *love* your gloves, so elegant. And you're wearing *pearls*? Mum said I was too young. She didn't even want me to stay up till midnight, can you believe it? As if I'd miss the countdown to the new year and 'Auld Lang Syne'. Come on, you can't hide in the bedroom forever. Let's go downstairs and dazzle!'

Colin Oakley stood among the crowd of guests at the bottom of the main staircase, looking smart in a black beret, a striped top and a black leather jacket.

'He's dressed as a French resistance fighter!' sighed Angela.

For a moment I remembered the horror of the cinema trip. Would Colin pester me about it? Luckily he had other things on his mind.

He whistled. 'You look absolutely smashing!'

'I made her outfit!' said Angela, pushing in front of me. 'Brigitta's a flower – a forget-me-not.'

'I wouldn't bloody forget her in a hurry, looking that gorgeous.'

Angela's face soured. 'As if it matters what *you* think. Girls waste too much time on boys. *I'm* going to pass my A levels with triple distinctions and go to university and be a professor and give lectures which change the course of history.'

'Good idea,' he said. 'Fancy a dance, Brigitta?'

What a moment, when Charlie stepped out onto the makeshift stage in the ballroom to announce the Swing Sensations. Mr Varley had made the stage that morning by nailing wooden blocks together, and the little Varleys had decorated it with paper streamers and ribbon rosettes. Next Val blew her horn like a huntsman calling the hounds. I wish I could have photographed the faces of all the guests when Connie Snow appeared, dressed in the royal robes of a Snow Queen. How dark her skin looked against her white dress. How powerful her stage presence.

She'd been nervous backstage, otherwise known as the butler's pantry.

'They'll hate me, Brigitta. They were born with silver spoons rammed up their pasty behinds. When they see this . . . me . . .'

'You have to go out and show them what you are. What you can do. You are amazing, Connie Crackerthorpe. One day you will have your name in lights, and your songs on the wireless. I will come to New York to hear you sing.'

'Will you come to Harlem, you little flatterer? If you learn how to play jazz piano, we can perform together.'

'It's a deal.'

We shook hands, neither of us believing it could ever really happen.

'Good evening, ladies and gentlemen, guys and gals. Welcome to Summerland on the last day of 1946. Let's see out the old year in style, starting with this little gem, often sung by the great black lady Adelaide Hall, who entertained us all during the war . . .'

Connie didn't kill them with swing, not at first. She took up a ukulele and drew them in with 'I Can't Give You Anything But Love, Baby', for a touch of old-fashioned romance.

It was pitched perfectly. By the time she began to notch up the rhythm, everyone's feet were tapping, even the grisly aristocrats. The first couple started dancing and others were keen to move. Connie winked down at me and called to the crowd, 'Don't be shy, grab a girl or guy, and come move your feet to the snappy new beat known as Shim Sham and a song called "T'ain't What You Do (It's the Way That You Do It)!"'

Colin grabbed my hand. 'This is magic – come do the Shim Sham with me, B! Here, let me show you how . . .'

He was definitely a great dancer. So light on his feet . . . sending me out, sending me back, then leading the way with a slower Shim Sham step. My feet couldn't help moving too, usually in the wrong places, though I had the beat right at least.

Val's horn was glorious, as was the chorus that Connie belted out. Summerland had never seen or heard anything like it.

Angela pounced. 'Teach me!'

Colin wiped his face with a hanky. 'Come here, Miss Goose, and learn to swing . . .'

His face. Joe's. I saw him through the crowds in the ballroom. Val was playing a solo horn piece called 'I Need That Man' when the elusive Lord Summer arrived. He wore a blue cap and uniform with a pair of wings on his chest and one blue band at the sleeve cuff. At first he went unnoticed, apart from a few people nudging and pointing. Quickly his mother was at his side. Her ice cool melted with pleasure that he'd chosen to appear. Other relatives and aristocrats soon swarmed.

For her sake he stood there to be congratulated and commiserated. For her sake he was paraded before them all.

'So brave. So handsome. Such a shame . . .'

Connie finished the first set of songs with a flourish and went off for a nip of sherry with the band. The fizz went out of the party. I looked over at Joe, then at the grand piano. If he could come out of hiding, perhaps I could too.

My dress rustled as I sat down. The seat was warm from Charlie. I couldn't follow his fabulous fingering. I riffled through his music until I found a piece we'd been playing earlier. With any luck everyone would be too busy talking to listen.

'Could everyone be quiet, please! We have our very own piano virtuoso here in Summerland.'

I whipped round. That was Joe calling attention to me. Fine. I'd show him.

'*Guten Abend, meine Damen und Herren* . . . Good evening, ladies and gentlemen. Tonight I am going to play for you. It is a song by a man I don't know in a film I have not seen.'

For some reason, they all laughed. I tinkled out the opening bars of Fats Waller's 'Ain't Misbehavin'', feeling more and more fabulous as the song played on.

Someone started singing. Unbelievably, it was Joe. I stopped dead in the middle of a chord. He was draped over the piano with his empty sleeve looking nicely nonchalant.

'Nice uniform,' I said.

'Ma said it was fancy dress tonight, so I'm disguised as a war hero.'

'No bomb dropping,' I warned.

'You're the bombshell,' he teased. 'I can't keep my eyes off you.'

'It's not right . . . It's not me . . .'

'Whatever you do is *you*. Now keep playing . . . I'm making my musical debut here. Ahem.' He gave a little cough, let me begin the song again, and happily murdered the first verse, which was all about being happy alone because he was saving all his love for me.

They were just song lyrics. I knew that. They were very convincing though.

It was so much fun that other guests began to join in. Joe looked so happy, so alive, I suddenly got an idea of what he must have been like before the war . It made me wonder, what would we both have been like without a war? Him without his scars inside and out; me . . . No time to think about that now! The band jumped onto the stage and the drummer began a stormy beat. Colin took Angela through the steps and before we knew it the party was back in full swing.

My face! I must have been lobster red. Too much fun, too much attention. I couldn't speak to Joe any more. Couldn't look at anyone. I jostled through the crowds to get out on the terrace and breathed in great lungfuls of cold air. It was snowing still, melting in dark spots on my paper skirts.

Someone began to croon behind me. It was Colin, warbling about a pale moon and starry eyes.

I didn't turn around. 'Aren't you dancing?'

'Are you avoiding me? I haven't seen you properly since our date. I notice His Lordship has crawled out of his cave. We could ask the band to play something for him. Perhaps the hokey-cokey. Do you know that one? *"You put your right arm in, your right arm out. In, out, in, out. You shake it all about . . ."* Oh, he can't, can he? No right arm.'

'You're drunk.'

'With love.'

My lip curled. 'Don't be silly.'

'Oh, come on, don't be so standoffish. You've been leading me on for ages now, Brigitta, with your moody behaviour and your *touch me not* looks.'

'*Don't* touch me.'

'Girls like you can't help yourselves, blowing hot and cold, all wrapped in mystery. I'd like to unwrap you . . .'

'Get off me!'

His breath was sharp with alcohol and his lips were wet. 'C'mon, this is what you like, isn't it? Someone to be strong and masterful. A real man. I've never been with a Jewish girl before . . .'

And you won't now, you creep.

I was backed up against the stone wall of the terrace, slipping on drifts of snow. He was like an octopus, hands everywhere at once.

'Shall I take these off?' he mumbled, fingers going up my skirt to my underwear.

From inside I heard Connie singing about love and I thought I'd be sick.

'No, no, no! *Hände weg, du dreckiges Schwein!*'

I knew where to knee him all right. Down he dropped with his hands at his groin, so I kicked him again, and because my hands weren't doing anything, I punched him too, right on the eye, and I wasn't sorry, and I had my fist up to swing again, the dirty pig, who did he think he was, I'd beat him to a pulp, except . . .

Except I heard my name.

'Brigitta! Where's Brigitta? There's someone to see her . . .'

My white kid glove had blood on it. My dress was crumpled and my hair was limp from melting snowflakes. I spat on Colin and left him crying.

'Where's the piano girl? Tell her to go to the front door . . . here she is! Brigitta, you've got a visitor.'

I steadied my breath. A visitor? 'Who?'

Angela got to me through the crowd. 'A foreigner . . .'

Golanski? My heart fluttered.

'. . . called Francine or something. She worked with you in the war, she says. She's tracked you halfway across Europe. Come on, hurry up, it's about to strike midnight.'

Joe waved at me over a sea of faces. I was carried along, like a leaf on a stream. I couldn't go back, only forward, into the Summerland entrance hall.

'Here she is!' cried Lady Summer. 'Brigitta, what a marvellous surprise. Oh, it's time! Midnight!'

All around me people started counting. *Ten, nine, eight, seven* . . .

They had drinks and paper hooters. A squat woman in scarf, coat and shawl stood dripping snow on the hall's chequered floor.

184

'Here she is!' said Lady Summer again. 'Here's Brigitta!'

. . . six, five, four . . .

The woman looked me up and down.

. . . three, two, one!

'Happy New Year! Happy New Year!'

The giant clock on the rooftop began to ring midnight. The first chimes of 1947. People linked arms and began to sing, *'Should auld acquaintance be forgot . . .'*

The woman looked me up and down and, in a strong Eastern European accent said, 'She is not Brigitta Igeul. I have never seen this girl before in my life.'

Hard Cheese

I stopped breathing. Heard my mother's voice pulsing in my head.

If we are found, you know what to do, don't you? Run and hide, and don't look back. Do not look back.

So I ran.

'Oh no, you don't,' wheezed the woman. She tackled me like a rugby player. Down I went crashing onto the hallway floor.

'Get off me, get off me!' I shouted in German. 'You don't understand – let me go.'

'Like hell,' she shouted, also in German. 'You shite-bag imposter. Where is she? What have you done with her? *Where's my friend Brigitta?*' With each word she banged my head onto the black and white floor. I had the vague thought that it would be my job to wipe the blood up.

'Not Brigitta?' cried Lady Summer. 'What do you mean, not Brigitta?'

Somebody hauled the woman off me. It was Joe, still strong even with one arm. I didn't stop to thank him. I ran. What else could I do? I didn't want to see their faces when the chimes stopped and the truth sank in.

I dashed out of the front door and into the snow. Motor cars were parked everywhere. Where now? Who was she? Where had she come from? How did she know Brigitta? How had she found me?

I ran fast, vaulting the fence, sprinting past the house, around the lake, into the woods. Which way was best? Didn't matter. They'd track my footprints in the snow.

Mama had said, *If you have to run, dodge side to side if they're shooting. Go through water if they have dogs. Get as much distance on them as you can. You must stay alive, Liebling, you must!*

They wouldn't have guns, not yet. Would they follow? Perhaps they'd let me go. Why should they care anyway? But no – Joe cared. Joe would follow. Joe mustn't find me; mustn't see me now . . .

My thoughts were faster than my legs.

Lights were slashing the night. Car headlamps? Guests leaving the party? Quick as a squirrel I chose a tree that looked easy to climb and scrambled up. Minutes, days, hours passed and I heard voices, faint through the woods. I shivered, sending snow flurrying down. They were looking for me.

What could I do?

Wait it out.

Stay hidden.

Keep alive.

Someone with a flashlight passed about fifty paces from my tree, then moved on. Darkness closed in again. How long should I wait? Until everyone had gone? Until daylight revealed my hiding place? Until I froze to death?

I could hear no music. No jazz, no jive, no swing. Not even the blues. I was too far away. And it was too cold. I would truly die if I didn't move soon. I blew on my fingers, just enough to get them to uncurl and grasp branches again. With as little sound as possible I slid down the tree trunk. Which way now? Where could I go, dressed in paper, pearls and kid gloves? I'd no money, no food, no knife . . . and no grey glove.

The English had an expression – *hard cheese*. I'd heard Mrs Rover use it to mean tough luck. That's what this was. The hardest cheese in the history of yellow dairy products.

Hello, 1947.

The woods were still. No owls, no foxes, no hunters. I took one step in the snow. *Whack!* Something hard cracked the back of my head. I pitched forward onto the snow.

'Got her!' came a savage cry.

'Pile on!' shouted a host of voices, coming closer. Before I could twist and run again, I was weighted down by heavy bodies. My arms were jerked back and tied. Something wet and woollen went over my head.

They had me. Not the Gestapo. Not the SS. Not even Jew-hunting peasants in a Polish forest. My predators were the children of Summer village.

Who was there, hustling and prodding me along? Nellie, I thought. She had a slingshot capable of bringing down rabbits or fleeing refugees. It could have been her stone smacking into my skull. From various muted words, I guessed at Colin and Poppy Oakley, Angela Goose . . . and others I didn't recognise.

They must have formed a posse to seek me out. What a great game to play at a New Year's party.

When I stumbled over snow and roots I was hauled upright. Where were they taking me? Not Summerland – I would have heard people or music. We were deep in woods still.

'In here . . .'

That was Colin. I should have knocked all his teeth out back on the terrace, and his brains too, such as they were.

Where had they brought me?

A hand yanked the cloth off my head.

Oh.

Not good at all.

It was cold in the Bomb House. Snow had fallen through the wrecked roof, blown into banks up against the walls, and settled into neat white lines along the ceiling rafters. The floor was soon scuffed up by many pairs of boots, and by the marks of my feet being dragged to the middle of the ruin.

The hunters circled me with a ring of blinding torch beams.

'Light a fire,' said Colin.

'There's nothing to burn,' said Angela.

'Her dress is paper – that's flammable.' Colin laughed, like he was joking, except I could tell by the sudden silence that the other kids were wondering, *Can we burn it? Shall we burn it?* One little match of a bad idea is all it takes to set violence flaring. This was not going to end well for me.

The more I struggled, the more the crêpe paper ripped. Off came one sleeve. Down fell my bra strap.

'Look at that!' said Colin, with a funny catch in his voice.

'Her bosom's fallen out! She pads her bra with socks! She's such a fraud, even her titties are fake!'

My face burned hot. 'Let me go!'

'Not a cat in hell's chance, you *fake*. Not till we know who you really are. Hold her, Angie.' Colin unknotted his tie and used it to bind my wrists even more tightly behind my back while Angela gripped my ankles.

'Stop kicking!'

'Please let me go! You don't understand –'

Slap! Colin's hand left my cheek stinging.

'Easy to hit someone when they can't hit back,' I taunted.

Slap! Blood filled my mouth as my head snapped sideways.

'You shouldn't hit girls,' said Andrew, hiding behind his sister. What was *he* doing here? He shouldn't have to see this, shouldn't have to be part of it.

Colin jumped up on a fallen block of masonry, immediately putting himself in charge. 'It doesn't count when she's a *Nazi*.'

There. The word was said. Lines were being crossed, one after another. The circle round me widened as all the kids took a step back.

Colin loomed above everyone, arms folded. 'She ran. That proves she's guilty, right? She said she was a prisoner in Auschwitz. Look at her arms. Show them, Angela – no tattooed number like real prisoners in the Horror Camps had.'

Angela pulled my wet gloves down and twisted the skin on my arms. She frowned. 'Weren't you in that place?'

'I don't like this,' wailed Andrew.

'I asked you a question! Were you in Auschwitz?'

I spat blood into the snow. 'No. I was not in Auschwitz.'

'Is your name Brigitta?'

'No.'

The other kids gasped. It was like they were an audience – no, a jury, in a courtroom, Angela as prosecutor and Colin . . . Colin was puffing himself up to be judge.

'What *is* your name?' asked Angela.

I was silent.

'Why isn't she Brigitta?' cried Andrew.

Angela burst out, 'She must be a spy! They said Nazis are hiding in England. I read a story about it in *Girl's Adventure* magazine, where the gym teacher is sending coded messages back to Hitler and only the girls of the Lower Fourth could stop her plans to kill the king.'

'Hitler's dead,' scoffed Colin. 'I don't think she's a spy.'

'I am not a spy,' I said.

'As if you'd admit it if you were. No, I think I know your secret.' Colin jumped down off his rock and began to circle me. 'It was at the cinema that I first had my suspicions –'

'You never suspected her!' interrupted Angela. 'You fancied her and you took her on a date.'

'Never mind about that. I was right next to her when a film came on about the Nuremberg trials. She stood up, pointed to the screen and shouted, '*Papa!*' when she saw the Nazis all lined up. Prisoner in the dock, do you deny it?'

'I saw the film, but it was . . .'

'Oh, put a sock in it.' He stuffed the sock fallen from my chest into my mouth. I choked on wet wool and outrage.

You can't just do this. You can't just turn on me. Except I knew

191

they could. This was how it went, from *It couldn't happen here*, to, *It is happening here, right now.*

Colin jumped back to his vantage point. 'The military call this kind of set-up a kangaroo court. Evidence is presented, the jury decide on a verdict and a sentence is pronounced.'

'I want to go home,' said Andrew.

'Silence in court!'

I wanted to go home too. I wanted to go back in time to the life we had before the war, when Papa came in singing and Mama had a piano. When life was full of picnic meals and glasses chinking and big people talking all at once. When I didn't have to hide.

They wouldn't really take this all the way to the end, would they? No matter how many times Mama told me to *trust no one*, she also impressed on me, *The world has good people and bad. Some don't know which way to swing, but they're mostly good most of the time.*

Right now, here, they were mostly bad.

Colin had everyone's attention. 'We know she's a Nazi. We know what the Nazis did in the war. Nellie, they bombed your mum to death in this very house. They shot our Joseph down and left him a wreck . . .' I squirmed at that. Joe was not a wreck! 'They tried to starve us all to death and take over the world. We all know what the punishment for being a Nazi is.'

'We could give her to the police,' said Angela.

'We are *not* going to the police. She'll just spin some story and bat her eyelashes at Ribble to fool him . . .'

'Like she fooled you?'

'*Who* just revealed her true evil identity? *I'm* in charge here, and I say she's guilty. Guilty. Guilty!'

All the others joined in – *guilty, guilty, guilty*. All of them except Nellie and Andrew. Andrew began to snuffle. 'I don't like this. Is Brigitta in trouble because she killed Jesus?'

'Go home,' said his sister. 'You're too young.'

Andrew clung to her leg. 'Daddy said in church the Jews killed Jesus, and Brigitta's a Jew.'

'Shut up, Andrew!' Colin gestured for Angela to remove the sock from my mouth. 'Has the prisoner got anything to say in her defence?'

I retched and gasped and spat into the snow.

'Don't do this . . .' was all I managed before Angela shoved the sock back in.

'I thought you were my friend,' she said angrily.

Colin was taking his jacket off. Unbuttoning his braces. Snapping his fingers for Angela to hand over her belt. Fastening belt and braces together. Looping them over a low beam of the Bomb House roof.

'This court pronounces the imposter shall be hung by the neck, like her Nazi scum dad.'

In the torchlight I saw the slanted ghost of Nellie's mama, Lettice Varley, standing next to her daughter. Her face was expressionless. Was she waiting for me to join her, to keep her company with the other dead?

They wouldn't do this. Couldn't do this. This was England. These were my friends.

Having gone so far, they didn't stop to think.

I resisted as hard as I could, with my hands and feet tied. They held my legs until the noose was round my neck. They heaved. The beam creaked. I was stretched onto tiptoes. I heard a horrible choking sound. Me. My neck was on fire. The noose pulled higher. I was dangling.

'Kill her, the Nazi!' hissed Colin. 'No, Andrew! Get out of the way!'

Andrew was kneeling on the floor. He had hold of my kicking legs, but not to pull them down, to hold them up. I just flailed, desperate to get another breath, another breath, a last breath . . .

My toes found Andrew's back.

'Don't be stupid,' Colin shouted.

'No, *you're* stupid,' Andrew shouted back. 'Killing people is *wrong*.'

My feet slipped off. I swung round. Fought to find something solid again. Another body, trying to support me. Nellie this time.

Colin screamed, 'She's a liar! She's a Nazi!'

'Angie, I don't like this,' Andrew keened.

Angela was whiter than the snow. 'Oh God,' she whispered. 'Stop it, Colin, just stop it . . . Stop it!'

Perhaps they would have slipped the noose free. Perhaps they would have let me go. Perhaps I would have escaped.

We'll never know.

The wooden beam cracked and broke. We were all thrown to the ground. I covered the children as best I could when the roof caved in. Then I think I died.

Sweet Cocoa

I died for a while. It wasn't so bad. Mrs Varley's ghost looked on, neither happy nor sad.

Nellie Varley was somewhere underneath my corpse; Andrew too. They were wriggling like puppies. I strained hard to shift the wooden beam off of us. Eventually it moved. Hands reached in. Andrew and Nellie were pulled out. Hands came back, stretched the noose away from my neck. Angela.

'Come on, Brigitta.'

'Not. Brigitta.' I mouthed the words. My throat was too raw for sound.

'All right, but come on. It's freezing.'

That it was. Somehow I crawled from under the beam, half paralysed with cold and shock.

Colin, Poppy, the others, they had gone. Just Angela and the littlies remained.

'T-take them home,' I rasped. 'Too cold. Go home.'

'What about you?'

I shook my head. 'Go. Shoo.' I flapped my kid-gloved hand at them like they were chickens. They shooed.

* * *

How beautiful the woods were. Night-dark and silent. No people, no horror, no history. Snow and trees.

The lake. Frosted snow on the ice, like glitter. Magic. In my flower dress I could be an ice skater, gliding around, carefree and graceful. I took a step onto the ice. It held. Had we skated once? Mama, Papa and me? Couldn't remember. There'd been ice. A river. Crossing along the girders of a bombed bridge. *Hold my hand*, Mama said. *Just let go*. No, that was wrong. *Don't let go*. I walked further onto the ice. Why not? Ursula had done it, decades before. *Just let go*. Let it all go. Past, present, future. People, places, none of it mattered. The stars shone and the ice crackled . . .

Crackled, cracked and tipped me in, God in heaven that was cold so cold clamped on my chest freezing brain stabbing glass shards so God devil swear-words cold floundering for solid, floundering on ice, holding, slipping, slipping, *Mama* where's your hand where's your hand where's . . . ?

A hand.

Strong. Bones, sinews, skin, nails. Holding. Pulling.

'Don't let go!'

Two of us in the water, swimming, gasping, pushing through ice, on snow, burning cold snow, out of the water, snow, land, fall, safe. Joe.

Joe, putting a jacket round my shoulders, leading me past stone statues, whispering ivy, the terrace, the gateway, the kitchen door.

Sophie Rover, a warm giant in a blinding bright kitchen. 'You found her, thank goodness.'

'Shh,' said Joe.

'What's happened? Her neck . . .'

'Shh,' said Joe. 'Not now.'

'Right. Kettle's on. You're both soaked. Towels. Out of those wet things.'

'No no no no no no,' I said, somewhere deep behind the fire in my throat.

'Shh,' said Joe. To Mrs Rover, 'I've got this. Honestly, I'll take care of her. We'll deal with the rest tomorrow. Please.'

Tomorrow. That was my mama's song – 'It's a Lovely Day Tomorrow'. Was it tomorrow already? Mrs Rover left. Joe helped me to a chair near the range, clothes plastered to my body, dripping on the clean floor. I watched him move. Getting a silver pan. Pouring white milk and sugar. Whisking in brown cocoa. Two blue-and-white striped mugs on the kitchen table. Sweet hot cocoa for us both.

'I'm s-sorry, Joe . . .'

'Shh. Let's just get warm.'

I cupped my hands around my mug. He cupped one hand. Through his wet shirt I saw the puckering of his shoulder stump for the first time. We drank.

'Good,' he said. 'That'll warm your inside.'

My teeth had stopped chattering but my voice was still hoarse. 'You jumped in the lake for me.'

'Of course I did. Come on, we have to get out of these wet clothes. There's no one here, and I don't care anyway I want you to see this, everything I've been hiding. Here I am. This is me.'

He tore the wet shirt up and over his head. I saw all the ridges of scarred flesh on his chest and the empty air where an arm had been. When he turned there were more burns on his back.

197

'I had a ton of grafts,' he said. 'Skin from my legs.' He peeled off his wet trousers too and draped them over the towel rack. 'See, where it's smooth here. They took it from my thighs for my face and chest. Luckily they left my nipples in the right places.'

I was wondering what the English word for those brown dots was. I didn't have vocabulary for private parts of the body or for all these new sensations.

Joe wrapped a towel round his shoulders and a tablecloth around his middle.

My turn.

I set my mug down and peeled off the kid gloves, letting them splat to the floor. Never taking my eyes from Joe's, I tore off the limp sheets of the paper dress. My skin was stained blue in places and water ran down from my hair, over my flat chest. I took my underwear off too and became painfully naked. What was the point of hiding any more? Someone had to know. Someone had to see me as me.

He saw. His face showed a swirl of different emotions. Surprise. Realisation. Something else – something warmer.

He swung the towel from his shoulders and stepped forward. Gently he smoothed it over my hair. Patted my face. Tenderly touched the towel to my neck, each moment acknowledging who I was. He kissed my forehead, my cheeks . . . looked for permission . . . then kissed my lips, his mouth warm, his tongue tasting of chocolate, his arm around me, holding me close so his heat passed to me and I was dying again, a different kind of death where everything was light and amazing.

Eventually I had to breathe.

'You don't care?' I asked, meaning me, my body, my secrets.

'Oh, I care,' he smiled. 'I don't think you realise quite how much I care . . . about you.'

We couldn't keep kissing forever. The sun would come up and the spell would break. Until then he was mine and I was his.

Wrapped in towels and tablecloths we crept through the silent house to his room. He made me put on his purple pyjamas because it was bitterly cold now the fires were out. He wore a vest and shorts. I loved looking at him. Loved being in his room, this sanctuary of books and sketches and peace.

We bundled into the single bed, still kissing, still in wonder. I was *me* – me, myself, accepted! Joe piled blankets over us and held me.

I thought how close I'd come to death, and how life still claimed me. Joe understood. He'd half died himself once.

I had to ask, 'What . . . what was it like? The crash? The end?'

He went very still, but he didn't pull away. 'You really want to know? Funny – no one else has even asked me that. They all tiptoe around, pretending it never happened.' He paused, unable to find the words to start.

'What's your last memory from before it happened?' I prompted, thinking of the moment when I'd been in the Trautwein apartment, about to sit at their piano and play the damn thing – who cared about being caught and killed – and that's when the bomb hit.

Joe took a breath and started speaking.

'We'd taken a fair bit of flak, nothing major. Then we got caught in a searchlight. We were like fish in a barrel – an easy target. After that . . . noise, confusion, smoke. Skipper said to bail. I couldn't really believe it was all happening. One minute flying high, the next . . . I was hit on the arm. Shrapnel. Didn't hardly feel it at first. The fire was worst – so hot, and the smell! Pongo was . . . gone. I thought, Should I jump, should I stay on the plane? It was whirling down like a banshee, and all the while the stupidest things going through my head, like, *Will it hurt?*'

'Did it?' I couldn't bear the idea of him in pain.

'I blacked out before I hit the water. I think I remember drowning. Being tangled in the parachute. I was pulled onto land by some farm girls on their way to work and pummelled till I breathed again. It was hell – hearing nothing but German words, thinking I'd be a prisoner, ashamed I'd been caught, afraid for my pals. The rest . . .' He sighed and I sighed with him.

'Joe, about that woman who came to the party. What she said. I should explain . . .' I rasped.

'Shh. Tomorrow.'

He was more interested in making sure we were as close as we possibly could be. I buried myself in his nearness.

'I have to tell you – they wanted to hang me. Colin and Angela.'

He swore fluently. 'Hang you?'

'As a Nazi. I am not a Nazi. I promise.'

'Of course you aren't, idiot. Oh God, wait till I get my hands – my hand – on them.'

'Tomorrow,' I said.

'Tomorrow.' Then, as an afterthought, Joe asked, 'What *is* your name?'

When I told him, he just hummed it quietly back to me.

Hungarian Goulash

It was so easy to sleep in Joe's arms. I didn't mean to. I should've gone back to my own room, instead of snuggling into his embrace. Did that make me *no better than I ought to be*? I didn't care. I felt warm and loved. Enchanted.

The spell was smashed a short sleep later. Morning. A hammering on the door.

Knock knock knock!

'Who's there?' mumbled Joe sleepily. My heart flooded just to hear his voice and to wake so close to him. Then my heart squeezed tight and small. It was happening. The moment I'd feared. The pounding on the door.

They were coming for me.

A voice demanded, 'Where is she? Is she there? Joseph Summer, open this door at once!'

Joe swore, then muttered, 'It's Mother. No – don't hide. We've done nothing wrong.'

She wouldn't think so when she saw me in her son's purple pyjamas, and him just in shorts and vest.

'Just a moment, Ma,' he called out.

'I will not wait an instant longer!'

Bang bang bang on the door.

Joe slipped out of bed. An ice age of cold invaded me. As soon as he pulled back the bolt, the door crashed open.

'She's here, isn't she? Mrs Rover said she'd come back with you last night.'

'Mother, calm down.'

'Don't tell me to be calm . . . *You!*' Lady Summer saw me and went rigid with anger. 'Was it not enough that you lied to us all from the first? Now to find you here, like this, with my son! My *son!*'

'It's not what you think, Mother.'

'Cover yourself up, Joseph! No need to flaunt your injuries.'

Joe flinched but did as he was told. His shame was easily triggered.

Vera Baggs appeared behind Lady Summer, bundled in a fleecy dressing gown and hair net.

'Thief!' she shrieked. 'Imposter! Hussy!'

Joe retaliated. 'Mind your own business, you nosy old harpy.'

'Oh! I am a civilised *gentlewoman* and deserve your respect, young man. And I'll have you know, it *is* my business not to be murdered in my bed by foreigners. See what your kindness and generosity have led to, my lady. You've nursed a viper in your bosom!'

Lady Summer's eyes scraped my skin. 'You are in very serious trouble, Brigitta, or whoever you are. Not just with me. The police have been called.'

Vera Baggs was jubilant as she pulled objects out of her dressing-gown pocket one by one. First a book.

I gasped. 'Give me that. It is mine!'

'I don't doubt it. How do you explain a German dictionary scribbled with codes? For *spying*.'

Joe defended me. 'For learning English, you ignorant witch.'

'What else did I find in her room? *Money*, that's what.'

'Which she has earned, scrubbing this rotting old pile of bricks!'

Baggs went on, not noticing Lady Summer's reaction to Joe's last comment. 'A *knife* – for murdering us all in our beds, I expect. Newspaper clippings about Nazi criminals – her heroes, no doubt. And last but not least, a dirty old glove stolen from Gant's.'

That was the last straw. Like a wolf I sprang at her.

'Murder! Help!' she screamed.

I screamed back, '*Es steht dir nicht zu, das zu berühren!*'

She dangled the glove high. 'You can curse me all you like. I'm a God-fearing woman and I'll see you punished for your crimes.'

Lady Summer took a deep breath. 'She said, *It is not yours to touch*.'

'Touching her things contaminates me!' Miss Baggs threw the glove away from her. I dived but Lady Summer scooped it up first.

'It is mine!'

'Mother, give it back,' said Joe.

Lady Summer stared at the glove. 'Where did you get this?'

A heavy voice sounded from the corridor. It was Mrs Rover. 'My lady, the police are here.'

Straight away Miss Baggs babbled, 'Arrest her! She attacked me! She's a spy and we found her *in bed*.'

'We weren't *in bed* like that, and even if we were –' began Joe.

'Now then,' said Constable Ribble, setting Miss Baggs to one side. 'What seems to be the trouble here?'

Joe was first to speak. 'It's Bossy Baggs you should be arresting, for being a big sack of unpleasantness. Then round up Colin Oakley, Angela Goose and the others who carried out a *hanging* last night! That's attempted murder.'

Miss Baggs muttered something that sounded like, *They had the right idea.*

I put my hand to my throat, and all that horror overwhelmed me again. It didn't matter what I said or didn't say. People had already made up their minds. Might as well get the end over and done with.

'I will fetch my coat,' I said.

'Oh, please allow me the honour,' answered Miss Baggs with succulent sarcasm. 'What a pleasure it will be to see you off the premises. You can get out of His Lordship's pyjamas first – stealing the very clothes off his back! Cheek of it!'

'You do *not* have to go,' Joe told me.

'Be quiet,' snapped Lady Summer.

'I'll be right behind you . . .' He was one-handedly pulling on trousers, struggling with the button fly.

Miss Baggs stared open-mouthed, probably repelled by the sight of his disfigurement in the flesh. I wondered whether I might as well murder her on my way out, since I was heading to prison anyway.

'Where do you think you're going?' Lady Summer asked Joe, in her most chilling voice.

'To stand by my friend. Where do you think?'

'She is not who you thought she was. I know you must feel betrayed, as I do.'

He laughed. 'You know nothing. Nothing.'

As he stood there, skin puckered, arm amputated, half-dressed I saw only his courage and loyalty. Did I deserve him?

'Stay here, Joe. I will be fine. I don't want you to come.'

Constable Ribble coughed. 'Begging your pardon, Your Lordship. No one's going anywhere fast. I barely got through to the house meself. It's like the ruddy Antarctic out there, with snowdrifts up to your armpits.'

Miss Baggs collapsed into an armchair. 'God help us all – we are snowed in with a crazed Nazi killer! For God's sake don't leave us now, Constable! You're the only thing standing between us and Hitler's spawn!'

They let me go back to my room. Not my room. Brigitta's room. I put on clothes. Brigitta's clothes. I folded Joe's pyjamas on the bed. He'd worn them while alone at night, reading his books, dreaming his dreams and perhaps even thinking of me. He knew me. My name, who I really was. He had still wrapped his arm around me.

You can never, never show or tell, Mama said. *No matter who asks. Do you understand, Liebling? Do you understand?*

Even so young, I'd understood: I had to be so ashamed of myself I'd stay hidden. Was it time now to come out of hiding?

Vera Baggs lamented there was no dungeon to lock me in. Joe said no one had any right to hold me. Lady Summer said, 'Put her in the butler's pantry. There's a lock on the door.'

'This will all come right,' Mrs Rover said to me over and over as I was escorted downstairs, past the debris of last night's party, past the fifteen toilet cubicles, through the kitchen and into a small room, empty save for a table and two chairs – just like an interrogation cell. It was the butler's pantry, where only last night Connie Crackerthorpe had transformed into Connie Snow. Now she was gone, and my own transformation was infinitely less glorious. 'It will all come right somehow, you'll see,' Mrs Rover repeated.

'I'm sorry,' I said, so ashamed.

'You've nothing to be sorry for!'

'This is *jankers*,' I said with a wobbly laugh, remembering her word for army punishment.

'Something like that.'

Constable Ribble sat with me first, having told everyone else to go about their business.

'Now then. You haven't been formally charged with anything, whatever that Baggs woman squawks about. To be fair, I'm not quite sure what crimes you've committed. Seems you're an imposter, a murderer and a Nazi spy.'

'Who did I murder?'

'Nobody, yet, to my knowledge. Anything you want to tell me now? Your real name, for example?'

I shook my head. English interrogations were strange. Ribble didn't look like he relished torture. Did the English have secret police like the Nazi Gestapo? They had people who spat at foreigners and tried to hang them after all.

I stared out of the window. The sill was loaded with snow. Above that the sky was grey. Was that a robin fluttering past?

Thick snowflakes still fell, muffling the outside world. What now? They'd taken my knife, my money, even my precious grey glove. Slowly I shut down all senses and emotions until I was left with music – the horrifying scene from Mozart's *Don Giovanni* where death draws close. It seemed appropriate. I played a few jumbled notes against my leg.

Seeing that I wouldn't talk, Ribble let out a big sigh, then left me alone. A key turned in the lock.

The first thing to break into my melancholy recital of Mozart was a tea-cup. It was a tiny little thing with dots of painted forget-me-nots. The tea-cup appeared as a hand swiped the snow off the windowsill. It was followed by a tiny saucer and a tiny teapot, each pushed into place by tiny, grubby fingers.

The music stopped. I clambered up on the table and saw the sill was set for tea. Tea for two. Nellie Varley was standing on tiptoe to pour the pot and push the cup closer to me. Dear, silly girl. She saved my life last night, her and Andrew. They held me up when I was being strangled, before Joe pulled me from the dark lake waters. This was her way of making things right again – with a *brew*.

The next bit of magic for the senses was far more punchy than forget-me-not crockery. Towards noon – the Summerland clock could be heard dimly chiming each hour – I smelled spices.

Paprika. The scent conjured up wild, joyful Hungarian dances by Brahms. It stirred memories of Mama and – was this real? – my papa, dancing around a room to gramophone music while I stood looking through the bars of a cot.

Paprika was the hot, rich orange spice of a home I'd once had, one of many homes before there was no such place. I remembered sausages and stews and . . . *goulash*. That was what I could smell.

Knock knock. Another visitor.

'Good morning,' said the woman who had appeared so disastrously on New Year's Eve – Francine.

Wide, low and frog-like, the woman who'd blown my world apart was nothing very extraordinary. Even so, she filled the room as she entered, with Ribble a silent mountain range behind her.

'How shall we talk? I am tired of English already and I will not speak the language of the Nazis. Do you know Hungarian?'

'Just *Helló* and *Szeretlek*.' I dragged the words from a time before the war. Where had we been? Budapest?

'Hmm. *Hello* and *I love you*. That won't do. How about Polish? Czech?'

'I speak Czech. Polish also. My French is good.'

'Ah, we'll settle on French. I like the French. They make beautiful clothes. Eh, Monsieur Police, you can go.'

Ribble folded his arms. Francine shrugged and set a basket down. The chair creaked as she sat.

I noticed one of Sophie Rover's tea towels in the basket. It brought back memories of Joe draped in a red check cloth and not much else.

'She is a good cook, Madame Sophie,' said Francine, all in rough-cut French. 'Her kitchen is clean and she has sharp knives. Spices – *meh*, not so many. Strong onions and a little paprika. We cooked together. We understand each other. She says you are a good girl. Is that true?'

No. 'Why are you here?'

'To feed you goulash if you like. When you have answered my questions.'

Constable Ribble shifted uneasily. 'It's all very well for you two to *parley-vooz*. I can't *comprendy* a word of it, unless *goulash* is that stinky stew.'

Francine wrinkled her nose at him. 'I ask about Brigitta Igeul. *D'accord?*'

'Ask away. You're not the only one wants to know. I've had a queue of people pestering all morning, half asking if she's Hitler's long-lost daughter, the other half – including His Lordship – demanding she gets released with balloons and a marching band.'

Francine unbuttoned her coat and spread herself wider. I moved away, standing under the window, where I hoped the cold would stop me feeling anything.

Francine said, 'Miss Brigitta Igeul, she was my friend, do you understand? I went through hell with her, literally. Into Auschwitz and back out again, and then lost her somewhere on the other side. My Brigitta, she was a sweet little thing – Hedgehog, we called her. Always curling up and putting prickles out. Sewed like she had a spell on her fingers. Not a mean bone in her body. Now what I want to know is this . . .' She jabbed a finger at me as she asked her question: '*What have you done with her . . . ?*'

What had I done with Brigitta?

I had hidden her. Kept her safe.

'Do you have scissors?'

Francine stared at me. 'Do I look like someone who just carries scissors around with me?'

'Yes.'

'As a matter of fact, I do. Once a dressmaker, always a dressmaker. You won't get very far stabbing me with these dinky things, not with all my rolls of blubber, ha ha. It doesn't matter how much I eat, I never feel full after years of starvation in the war.'

I had no intention of stabbing her, certainly not with the little shears she fished out of a felt sewing kit. As calmly as I could, I asked Constable Ribble for my coat.

He left and came back with it quickly enough. I saw him patting the pockets before he handed it over. They were empty. I kept my secrets better hidden than that. I tested the lining of the coat at a certain spot then, *snip*, cut through a few threads, just enough to reach for the flat bundle within – papers and pictures.

I spread everything across the table for Francine. There was a birth certificate and a letter of commendation from a milliner in Vienna. An identity card bearing the name Brigitta Sara Igeul, stamped with a blood-red *J*. Jew. Two undated letters from an older brother, full of ink-blotched love, hope and rage. I had kept company with the photographs for so long they were part of my memory, as if I had known Brigitta and her family. They showed a Hanukkah meal with potato *latkes* and lit candles. A wedding portrait, dated 1925 – her parents,

211

before Brigitta was born. A studio shot of Brigitta herself, dated 1942 – a girl roughly my age, with fine dark hair, shadowed eyes and a shy smile.

Francine stared longest at this photograph. She nodded several times, but could not speak at first. Then she tapped the picture.

'When I knew her, in Auschwitz concentration camp, she only ever smiled with her hand over her face. Some beast had punched half her teeth out. I saw her last in January 1945, in the snow. Colder than it is now. All of us driven on by whips and gunshots, staggering from one hell to another. I lost her somewhere among the frozen corpses. You can't know what it was like. Nobody can. Are you even Jewish?'

I nodded.

'Were you in the camps?'

I shook my head.

She hissed and pulled away. 'So you are a liar.'

'Yes.' The word was rough on my throat.

'You stole her identity. Is this her coat? You stole that too?' She was breathing hard now.

'I don't know. I think it was hers. I mean, I was given it, towards the end. I had nothing. The Nazi Women's League, they were handing out charity clothes for bomb victims in Berlin. I took this. I had something precious, which I wanted to hide, so I thought I could put it in the shoulder pads. When I unstitched the coat lining I found all these things in the pads, among the horsehair. Brigitta must have hidden them there.'

'Huh. Possibly true.' Francine took her time mulling this over, then nodded. 'We all hid our valuables when we knew we were being deported. Wore our smartest clothes too, for the train

212

journey. Got to that stinkhole anus of a place – Auschwitz – and everything was stripped from us. I knew girls who worked in the warehouses at Auschwitz, sorting through all the stolen goods. Who'd've thought they were shipping the loot back to Germany?' She shook her head.

'I swear I didn't know where the coat came from, or the other things they gave me. A skirt. A blouse. A cardigan. Shoes.'

'Dead women's things. May the murderers rot for ever after. Amen.'

'I'm sorry about your friend. I took her name so that the Red Cross would look after me. I had no one. They set up refuges for Jews after Berlin was liberated. Going there for help meant coming out of hiding. I needed an identity. Taking on Brigitta's meant I had to declare myself as Jewish again, when this had long been . . . you know. A death sentence.'

Francine nodded, beginning to understand. 'You were one of the Jews who hid or passed as non-Jews to avoid the round-ups? Most of the people I knew who tried that got denounced by their neighbours and shot on the spot or packed off to be gassed anyway. You were one of the lucky ones.'

'Lucky? Living under floorboards or in a wardrobe?' Anger boiled for a moment. Then I remembered. I had been lucky. I'd had my mama. Music in my head.

Francine slumped. 'I'm sorry you've had it rough, kid, but I've been across Europe looking for Brigitta and she's not even here. I saw her name on the Red Cross lists in Berlin and tracked her – you – to England.'

'But how did you know I was at Summerland? I ran away from the Red Cross in London.'

'Someone reported a Brigitta Igeul to the police. Looks like they contacted the Red Cross, so Brigitta's name got put on a contact list for anyone searching.'

If Francine could find me, others could too. I looked up at Constable Ribble, who was squinting hard at us, as if that would somehow translate our words into a language he could understand.

'*You* told them I was here,' I said in English. 'You knew I'd run away.'

'That I did,' he answered, unflustered. 'Not much gets past me, flower. I saw a photo of you on the front page of the London paper. I like to keep abreast of what's happening in the city, seeing as I've got family down south. I just thought I'd let the Red Cross know you were here, safe and sound. They said you'd no business to be at Summerland, but if you'd found work, then that was all well and good.'

That wretched photograph! If they hadn't taken it, or no one had seen it, I could have been safe here at Summerland for as long as I wanted, and no one would have been any the wiser.

Except maybe that wasn't true. I couldn't hide forever, could I? Not the way things were going, the way I was changing. It was better to be myself, whatever danger that brought, than to live a lie for the rest of my life.

Ribble said, 'I put off saying anything for a while. Thought I'd watch and see what you were up to. Things at Summerland seemed to be working out all right. Next thing I know, half the village are out in the woods on New Year's Eve looking for you.'

'They found me.' I rubbed my sore neck.

'I don't mind telling you, this has put me in a bit of a spot.

It would help get to the bottom of all the fuss and bother if you'd just tell me your real name.'

I said nothing. Only Joe knew how completely I'd been hidden.

'Constable Ribble – Her Ladyship's asking for you . . .' Mrs Rover called from the kitchen.

Ribble left. Francine reached into her basket and pulled out a warm pot and two spoons. She set them on the table, having gently moved the documents aside.

'I might've known it was too good to be true, having Brigitta alive and well and living the high life in some fancy English house. Still, I did hope, and you've got to hope, right? I was all ready for me and her to go to America, to work in one of the New York factories where they need immigrants who can sew. I got tickets and sponsors and everything. Stupid.'

'You might still find her.'

'The boat sails in a week, and I'll be on it. Nothing to keep me here. My family were all murdered in the camps. The only people I care about now are the friends I made in the sewing workshop at Auschwitz. Brigitta in particular. So far I haven't tracked down a single one of them. Dead or scattered to the winds, I suppose. There's no place for Jews in Europe. Every lungful of Old World air makes me choke. Tastes of smoke and ash. So – to take the taste away, let's feast! Hungarian goulash like my mama never made it – she was a terrible cook! – and bread from your friend Madame Sophie.'

We ate goulash. We ate memories.

Finally, when we were both full, she belched comfortably

and asked for my real name. Surprising even myself, I told her: first name and family name.

'*Mon dieu!*' she said, drawing away from me a little. 'That complicates things horribly, doesn't it?'

Rabbit Pie

Angela and Andrew had danced about to a song once. They said it had been popular during the war – something about a farmer with a gun and a rabbit that had to run and run and run.

I wanted to run. Running, hiding, that was what I knew. Now I was facing something more frightening than a gun. The truth.

'What do you want me to tell those people, the English?' Francine asked me as she prepared to leave. 'I can say it's a mistake, that you're Brigitta, all is well.'

'*Alles ist kaput,*' I said, shaking my head. It's all ruined.

When she'd gone, I sat for a long time watching the shadows draw closer. Ursula came to sit with me. I'd miss her when I left, and I did have to leave. Summerland wouldn't welcome me now.

I called out for Constable Ribble. He'd obviously been keeping toasty in front of the kitchen range while helping polish off party-food leftovers.

'I want to see Lady Summer.'

As Ribble looked down to brush crumbs off his uniform, I sprang for a knife – one of Sophie Rover's big slicers. It wasn't planned. I didn't know what would happen. I was a rabbit – terrified. I ran past the ballroom and the beautiful grand piano, making Mrs Rover shout as she swept up party garlands. I ran up the grand staircase, making Vera Baggs squawk as she came to see what the noise was. I ran along the corridor to the Blue Room. To the wardrobe.

Part of me imagined I could step inside, curl up like a child and be safe like before. Most of me knew the time for hiding was over.

'Stop there,' I told Ribble, who had followed me and was huffing in the doorway. I didn't take my eyes off the mirror. 'Stop,' I told Joe, who ducked past Ribble into the room.

'Stop!' ordered Lady Summer once she'd swept the policeman out of her way. 'Whoever you are, put the knife down.'

'Look, it's all going to be fine,' said Joe. 'I told them you could explain.'

'Yes,' agreed Lady Summer. 'It is time you explained.'

'Yes,' I said to the mirror. It was time everyone explained.

I told them about the bomb, about the coat, about the real Brigitta. About the Red Cross helping me; about coming to England.

Lady Summer grew impatient. 'And Summerland? Why did you run away from the Red Cross and come here of all places?'

'Don't you know?'

She was so pale. So thin. I saw how her rings slipped on her fingers. 'No,' she said. She sounded genuinely baffled.

'You had a friend – Hélène Jacobs. She came here before the war.'

218

She smiled faintly. 'Yes, that's true. Many years ago, when I was new to Summerland before Joseph was born. What a golden summer that was.'

'Croquet and boating on the lake and strawberries with cream –'

'Yes, but –'

'Hélène wrote to you.'

'Yes, many times, and I do not see what –'

I interrupted, impatient with her ignorance. 'Just before the war. She wrote to you asking for help.'

'Money, yes. And I sent some.' Lady Summer looked more confused than guilty.

'No! Not money. Something called sponsorship, so she could get a visa. With a visa she could come to England and escape the . . .' What was the word? I needed my dictionary, and my grey glove. At least I had a knife.

'Escape the Nazis?' prompted Joe.

I nodded. '*Die Verfolgung* in German. Hunting. Attacks.'

'Persecution,' said Lady Summer in a hoarse voice.

'When she didn't hear from you, Hélène was desperate. They came for her.'

'Oh God, you *knew* her? What happened? Her little boy . . . ?' Lady Summer was pale as death now.

'They hid. For years. Every day hungry, every day afraid. Everyone else taken. At last in Berlin she was dead by a bomb, I mean, killed.' I couldn't stop myself looking at Joe. He wasn't her killer but he might have been. But if he hadn't bombed Germany how many more bombs would have fallen on England, making more Nellie Varleys motherless?

God it was a mess, the whole stupid war and everything in it. And if I hadn't been a Jew, would I have been fighting and bombing too, in the Hitler Youth, or as a partisan in the forest?

Lady Summer persisted. 'And the child?'

I smiled. I let dim light play on the knife blade for a second then stabbed and sliced, sawing to and fro, and *I didn't care*. When one hair braid was chopped off I did the second. I dropped them to the floor. God it felt good to ruffle my hair up and feel the back of my neck again. It had been years. First it had been short with a bow at the front. Then it was braided. Now it was gone. I looked in the mirror and saw myself.

'My name is David Jacobs Golanski. I am a Jew. That is who I am. My mother was Hélène Jacobs. That is the truth.'

I said the words and waited. The world did not end. Summerland did not crack down the middle and collapse all around me. Police did not come hammering at the door. I was not shot on the spot. Did I feel different? Yes. I felt like me. Me in a dress. I found I was smiling.

Joe was too.

Lady Summer wasn't.

'You . . . You're . . . I don't believe it! You're the boy? You're *David*?' Her hands trembled. She leaned against the door frame and hid her face. Then, 'Why? How?'

'Why do you think, Mother?' Joe's tone was harsh. 'The Nazis went for the males first. Being a girl was safer, right?'

'Yes.' I nodded. 'The police stopped to check the Jewish boys and men, their . . .' I waved my hand in the general area.

'Todgers,' said Joe helpfully.

'Joseph!' exclaimed his mother. 'You mean, circumcision, Brig— David?'

'Yes, the circumshich . . . what you said. To see if they were Jewish. We called it the *bris*.' My cheeks went pink. 'This is why I had to be disguised as a girl.'

Mama passed on lessons from her expensive school in Switzerland. How to stand as a girl, how to walk and sit and curtsy. *You can never whistle, or pee standing up, or swear, do you understand? You must learn all the female ways of speaking each language. You have to remember your new name, a new birthday, my new name. Forget everything else.*

'I had a new girl's name each time we moved. It was safer. I had to learn new languages. Mama taught me everything. She had a good education – you know that is true.'

Lady Summer was staring at me as if I'd performed a magic trick, when really I hadn't changed at all.

'Where were you?' she asked. 'In Germany or Austria?'

'We went everywhere looking for a safe place.' I'd forgotten our exact route across Europe, or it had all been flooded out by the fear.

The fear.

The fear.

You never lose it.

'Did you know?' Lady Summer turned on her son. He had come to stand near me. Not too near. I was too skittish to touch and I had that knife ready.

'No, not a bit. Not till last night.'

221

'You didn't know she was a . . . boy?'

He went red. 'No. I didn't think about it. I just saw her – him – dancing on the terrace the night I came back to Summerland. That was all it took. She – he – looked so free. We talked. We argued. We . . . The rest doesn't matter. The point is, I took girls on dates before and it was just nothing. Fun. They never got to me like he did. I didn't love them. I love him. I don't care about the rest, do you understand? *I don't care.*'

It was so dark my reflection almost disappeared. Eventually Lady Summer let out a long breath and stepped into the room. 'This is all very strange. Incredible! I . . . I am sorry to hear of your experiences, David. You must believe me. I had no idea –'

'I *don't* believe you! Get away from me!' I wrapped my arms around my chest, as if this would somehow contain all the anger I felt. 'Don't you understand? You could have saved us! We could have come here to be safe. Instead my mama is dead! I came here to find memories of her . . . To tell you. I hated you. To kill you. *I don't know!* To find my papa.'

'Yann Golanski is alive?'

Yann. Oh yes, that was his name. I'd forgotten. It was so long ago, buried under all the lies that had to follow. His face, his voice, were lost. I saw him as a big shadow against the sun, one day in the park when we'd taken my toy boat. I saw him as a giant who sang when we played piano. I last saw him when he was dragged away from us, shouting, *I will find you.*

My voice cracked. 'You knew my papa?'

'I knew *of* him. Hélène wrote about nothing else in her letters. How wonderful he was, how happy they were. It was wrong. He was poor. She was forgetting her music.'

'No! She never forgot her music. That is what she taught me. She kept me alive in every way. She was with me until the end. Even after the end. She pulled me from *Die Trümmer*, from the rubble. She was there. I heard her . . .'

Hold my hand, she'd whispered. *Don't let go*. I took her hand. She pulled me out. I was left holding her glove. Just one grey glove, stained with dust and blood. She was dead. I knew that, I saw the wreckage of her body, but she wasn't dead to me.

Softly I put words to what had happened in the end. 'I had to bury my own mother,' I whispered. 'I came to Summerland because I had nowhere else to go. I thought perhaps Papa would find me . . .'

Lady Summer drew herself tall. 'There's something I don't understand about all this. I received no communication about sponsorship from Hélène, or from your father.'

'Liar! They wrote, I know they wrote! They told me we would come and be safe!'

'David, drop the knife – please.' Joe inched closer.

I held the blade out. It flashed in the mirror. 'She's lying! She didn't want us in her big house. She didn't care!'

He edged closer. 'You can put the knife down. You're safe now. I promise.'

The knife fell as he reached me, the point stuck through a swirl of carpet, into Summerland floorboards. He held me. Tears flowed out. 'Boys don't cry,' I sobbed.

'Idiot. Boys cry their hearts out in private, muffled under a pillow usually, when punching someone isn't an option.' He pulled me closer so my face nestled in his shoulder. I

223

think he was crying too, because my dress was wet under his cheek. He kissed my hair. I lifted my face and he kissed that too. Finally he passed me a handkerchief and swallowed his own emotions down, saying, 'I am British, you know! Public displays of affection are a big no-no for the upper classes. Especially with an audience.' He waved vaguely at his mother, whose disapproval was matched only by her upper-class self-control. 'Can we go somewhere warmer to figure the rest of this out?'

Constable Ribble left by the front door, along a narrow alley through the snow: Mr Varley had been busy shovelling. The angel shapes and ambush mounds along the alley showed that little Varleys had been out to play too.

Lady Summer ushered us into the drawing room, where a small fire was lit. Vera Baggs was persuaded to unlock her bedroom door to join us. She bustled in, and stopped dead.

'Hasn't she been arrested yet? Constable Ribble is most remiss in his duties! Leaving innocent women and cripples defenceless against knife-wielding foreigners. Er, foreigners with short hair and trousers . . . Brigitta, what new disgrace is this?'

Lady Summer had insisted on Joe fetching me trousers, shirt and pullover to wear. 'No boy is to be dressed as a girl in my house!' she sniffed. I thought it was funny how a simple bit of cloth and stitching could take on so much meaning, as if putting on trousers made me male or wearing a dress made me female. It wasn't so funny trying to figure out menswear. The trousers chafed and the tie was fiddly. Had it all been normal when I dressed like this before? I couldn't remember. Standing in Summerland as a boy was strange and wonderful.

Miss Baggs simply would not believe I could be David Golanski. 'There's no likeness,' she gabbled when she'd heard the basic facts. 'Poor dear Hélène, a tragedy. Of course we can't know it's true. So many lies. He could be any boy off the street, looking to trick us. Looking for gullible rich people . . .' Her eyes slid to Joe.

He snorted. 'Rich? That's a joke. This place is worth more as firewood these days than as a family home.'

Lady Summer was browsing photographs. 'Here is one from our school days – the three of us.'

My mama, as a girl. No early grey hairs, no calluses, no frown lines. She smiled up at me from the picture. I smiled back.

'Ridiculous!' sniffed Miss Baggs. 'She's an imposter. She can't prove a thing.'

'I can prove I'm a boy,' I said dangerously.

She recoiled. 'I am not accustomed to being spoken to in such a way! My lady, you refused to meet the Golanski fellow when Hélène first took up with him. He wasn't *our sort* – you said so yourself. He was no *gentleman*. You should be glad I took it on myself to turn down their importunate requests.'

My brain scrambled to translate her words. I was getting flashes of memory. Vera Baggs sorting through the post . . . Vera Baggs jealously wanting Barbara Summer all to herself. 'Did you . . . Did you have letters from my mama?'

She twitched. 'There's no crime in reading a friend's

correspondence, and I often help my lady with her mail.' She turned to Lady Summer. 'Yes, Hélène dramatised her *situation*. They were in no real danger; they wouldn't really murder Jews – I wrote and told her so. How was I to know Herr Hitler was so nasty? What does it matter? They were only Jews after all, and this one survived, this *David*, as she calls herself now.'

She waited for approval.

Lady Summer had hold of Joe's arm to steady herself.

He was the first to speak. 'Good God,' he said. 'So it was *you* who turned them down when they asked for sponsorship, Baggs. I *knew* my mother would never do such a thing.'

'Don't you dare judge me! I was right. Give foreigners an inch and they'll take the whole country. Slippery, every last one of them. I was quite right to send that man packing when he called, with some flim-flam story about looking for his family. You'd have done the same, my lady. You can thank me that I dealt with it so discreetly.'

Lady Summer finally found her voice. 'Yann Golanski came here?'

'Can you believe the presumption? Earlier this year, in some trumped-up army captain's uniform.'

'This . . . This is monstrous!'

'Agreed, my lady, and I told him as much. It was lucky you were out. *No, we haven't had news about Hélène or any son*, I said. *And don't you come bothering us again.* Shall I telephone for the constable to return? He can escort this imposter from the premises.'

'Telephone for a taxi cab by all means Vera, if one can make

226

it here through the snow. You should be packed by the time it arrives. Do not expect a reference for your next position. Go. Now.' Lady Summer's tone was sharper than any knife.

I let the poison flow away. The thing I held onto was as joyous as a perfect chord on the piano. My papa had looked for me . . . he looked for me! The realisation played as a melody in my heart.

Lady Summer turned to me now, saying she wished I had explained who I was when I first arrived. As if I could have trusted that it would be safe to do so after so many traumatic years of hiding. She asked why I hadn't looked for Papa myself. I told her about the letters I had sent. The calls to Directory Enquiries. The hope that he'd find me first.

'You silly fool! All this could have been solved with a simple telephone call. I have contacts at the ministries, and not just with the imbecile tasked with removing those toilets.'

Within seconds her cut-glass voice was on the line to London. Joe and I listened in. He brushed the back of my hand with his. Every cell in my body hummed. Minutes passed. Lady Summer tapped a red fingernail against the telephone. Finally – 'Captain Yann Golanski? Yes, that's the man. You have his office and number? . . . Excellent.' She snapped her fingers for a pencil and paper, which Joe quickly passed her. She redialled the operator and asked to be connected.

I thought I might be sick. It was like in a wardrobe, hearing footsteps coming closer, not knowing when the door opened if it would be a friend or an enemy who found me.

Lady Summer set the telephone receiver back in its cradle.

'Captain Yann Golanski isn't in his office today, because it's New Year. We'll try again tomorrow.'

Tomorrow was too late. I knew it – just knew it.

We ate tea together in the dining room. It didn't seem right, being promoted from staff to family friend. We were all uncomfortable at first. Lady Summer's eyes scoured me, looking for her friend Hélène in my every move, my every molecule. At times Joe couldn't even look at me, and when he did his gaze was intense.

Mrs Rover broke the tension when she set down a magnificent dish, steam rising from a hole in the pastry. 'Rabbit pie! Heaven knows how Rom Varley flushed rabbits out in this snow. Come on, it's good to eat after a shock.'

Mrs Rover and I had a talk in the kitchen afterwards – just the basics. She took it all in her stride. 'When you've been in the army, nothing surprises you. I knew Bossy Baggs was a proper piece of work. Not helping your mum and dad come over here was downright wicked. The way I see it, there's room for everyone in this country if we all budge up a bit. You made a very convincing girl, I'll give you that.'

I jumped at the word *girl*, remembering things were different now. I still had the urge to straighten my braids and pull an invisible skirt over my knees. Had I been a girl, just by living as one? Was I an official boy now, just because I had trousers? My body had never changed, except to fill out and get older. That line of thinking took me to memories of my body next to Joe's, and that was too electric to dwell on for long, not while Mrs Rover was staring at me.

'Being male will take a bit of practice,' she said. 'Spread your legs out when you sit and slouch more, that's it. Obviously you've to respect women as the wiser sex now you're just a boy. Now, go practise walking with your hands in your pockets and whistling. I want to sit alone and savour the thought of Baggs being booted out on her bum – no more than she deserves.'

I sat at the piano and I couldn't rouse a single note. My fingers wouldn't move.

Without speaking, Joe came to sit on the piano stool behind me, his legs around me, his chest to my spine and his face turned, nestling into the back of my neck. His arm came around my body until his hand rested on top of mine.

'Play for me,' he whispered. When I didn't move his lips pressed softly against my skin. 'Play for me, please.'

I picked something I'd heard Connie sing, and my mama before her. It was low and melancholy. A bluesy number that told of aching loneliness.

Sometimes . . . I feel . . . like a motherless child . . . a long, long way from home.

Joe was kissing my neck, my throat, the line of my chin . . . I twisted to let his mouth find mine and dared to thread my arm under his to pull him closer. We couldn't get close enough. I had to unbutton my collar, it was choking me. He kissed where the collar had rubbed. His lips took away the pain of the noose. I heard my name reverberate along a pulse line.

I must have been crying again. 'It's OK, I'm right here,' Joe whispered. 'I won't leave you.'

'It's *not* OK.' My words were muffled. My face was buried

against his sweater. Just for a moment. Just for a minute while I got calm again. Finally I could speak without my voice shaking or breaking.

'I have to go. I have to go now.'

The rabbit had to run again.

Sloe Gin

'Absolutely not!' Joe said. 'Not without me.'

'I'm going to London.'

'I know. I'm going with you.'

I tried to talk him out of it. He was stubborn, and a bit irresistible.

It was only as we crept out of the house with a small bag each that it hit me – what it meant to leave Summerland. My refuge for a while. My taste of England. Kindness. Music. Love. I looked back at the house as we trudged up the snowy avenue. It was still, white and beautiful. Only one window was lit; the rest were dark and crowded with ghostly faces watching me go.

It was hard for Joe too. He was weary after only a few minutes' walking. 'I've been stuck inside too long, hiding. Feeling sorry for myself and wishing things could all go back to how they used to be.'

'Your mother called you king of the world.'

'Well, captain of the school cricket team, yes, which pretty much felt like the same thing at the time. I wonder if . . . Shh. What's that? Who's there?'

Two bundled-up figures were crossing the bridge from the village. I pulled my scarf up and my cap low.

One of them waved. 'Joseph, is that you? It's me, Colin, and Angela Goose. We're heading up to Summerland.'

Angela interrupted. 'Is Brigitta back? Is she all right? We heard she was all right. Tell us she's all right. I have to talk to her –'

'You can't,' said Joe harshly.

'But I feel so bad. There were things we did . . . things we said . . .'

'You tried to hang her!'

'It was all . . . I don't know . . .'

'We thought she was a Nazi spy!' said Colin. 'How do you even know she's not?'

I said, 'We haven't got time for this,' and punched Colin hard in the face. I lost the moral high ground, he lost his footing and went over in the snow. This time it was all blood and no blackberries staining him.

Angela stared. 'Brigitta? Why are you dressed like that? I didn't recognise you. Listen, I'm sorry about what happened in the Bomb House. I'm probably going to give up earthly pleasures and become a nun in a hair-shirt or something in penance, but I really, *really* am so sorry.'

'Good. Come on, Joe – the train!'

The London train called at Summer station at ten past the hour. It would be tight.

As we went through the village I said goodbye to the pond and telephone box and the shop and the pub. Smothered in snow, it all looked so safe and cosy. We didn't dare run in case anyone spotted us. Joe kept checking his watch.

I'd told him what little I knew from seeing the film clip at the cinema – that my father was a lawyer at the Nuremberg trials in Germany. That if he'd been in England – and how my heart sang to know he had – then it wouldn't be for long. There were new trials due to start in Hamburg . . . I had to get to him before he left.

Catch the train, get to London, trace the address Lady Summer had gleaned, find my father. That was our plan.

'Trains to London? You'll be lucky!' said the stationmaster when we rapped on the door of his office. He was huddled over a tiny pile of coal in a grate. 'Signals are down up the line, if you get what I mean. Ice – snow – I don't know.'

We stood on the station platform watching snow settle on the tracks heading south. I was thinking of the trains that had crossed Europe, taking people to be murdered. We'd seen a line of cattle trucks once, making slow and stately progress along the rails. There were no windows, just a slit, crossed with barbed wire, and dirty fingers pushed out to touch the air.

I took out the grey glove that Joe had retrieved before we left. My only memento of Mama. When they arrested Papa he had been holding my mama's hand. She was wearing her favourite gloves, from Gant's in England. As Papa was pulled away, he tore one glove from her fingers. Mama kept the other one tucked in her blouse, next to her heart. She said we'd all be together after the war; that the two gloves would make a pair again.

We left the station. A cold wind blew across from nearby

233

East Summer airbase. Joe looked haunted by memories.

'Old Rory grazes his cattle on the airfield over summer,' he said. 'And you go dancing in the aircraft hangars. It's all changed, as if it was for nothing. The war's gone, people move on.' He clutched his empty sleeve. 'Let's go back home and try again tomorrow.'

I saw my papa getting swallowed up in the ghosts and ruins of Europe before I even got to meet him. 'It will be too late tomorrow.'

Something growled down the lane. A silver ghost came out of the darkness and caught us in blinding twin beams of light. I turned to run, as I had three months before when I walked out of Summer station and into a policeman.

'Get in, you fools,' shouted the driver.

'Ma? Is that you?' Joe crunched a few steps forward in the snow.

'Do you think I'd let anyone else drive this beauty?' answered Lady Summer. 'Get in before the engine decides to stall – it's been sitting in the garage far too many years.'

'We are going to London!' I yelled.

'There are no trains . . .'

'Then we will walk!'

'Suit yourself. I'm driving. Let's see who gets there first.'

Joe laughed. 'You'll drive us to London?'

Lady Summer leaned from the open car window, spilling white fur out. 'Listen, darling, I drove an ambulance during the Blitz. I hardly think a bit of snow is going to stop me in a Rolls-Royce Phantom III!'

* * *

Mama once told me she'd been driven across London in a silver ghost. I didn't think she'd meant it literally. Now I found out Joseph's papa – Lord Summer then – had really owned a car called a Silver Ghost. He'd collected Mama from the boat train when she visited England that golden summer of her memory, before I was born. Off she went north on luxurious leather seats. Now I went south in just as much comfort. It seemed Mr Varley had been tinkering in the garage as well as helping transform the Summerland estate.

We saw a wintry England by night. Stars, headlamps, street lights and lit windows. No blackout now.

No bombers flying across the moon or rockets whistling to their targets. I had my name back. I had my body back. I had Joe. I fell asleep on his stumpy shoulder, there in the back of the Rolls. He slept on me. Perhaps Lady Summer looked back on us in her rear-view mirror as she drove. Perhaps she kept her eyes on the dark roads. She had a lot to think about. Me? I was tired of thinking.

The Phantom gave up the ghost in a little market town some miles out of London, just as the sun rose to shine through the morning mist.

Lady Summer popped the bonnet to glare at a steaming engine.

'We are definitely too late now,' I said, fatalistic.

Lady Summer began to roll up her sleeves. 'Joseph, fetch the toolbox from the boot. I will not be beaten by a mere machine . . .'

She was deep in the car innards when a jeep drove by with a sleepy-looking American lieutenant at the wheel. I remembered the Yanks from Berlin, before the city got divided among the Allies and I hid in the British sector. The Americans were good for gum and chocolate . . . or the butt of a rifle if you tried to pickpocket them.

This guy pulled up and asked if we needed help. Before Lady Summer could freeze him with a glance, he'd ducked under the car bonnet with her. They soon agreed the Rolls was going nowhere until the local garage opened for a spare part. Lady Summer explained it was imperative that we get to London without delay.

'Happy to oblige, ma'am,' said the lieutenant. 'At least as far as the next train station. Jump in.'

She looked at him with scorn. '*I* shall wait with my car. Joseph – do you need funds?'

'All good, Ma. We packed essentials. Rendezvous at the RAF Club on Piccadilly?'

'Very well. David, please give my best wishes and my apologies to your father. I hope to meet with him soon, as I should have done when Hélène first spoke of him. Forgive my arrogance all those years ago, and you should know that you are always welcome back at Summerland.'

Perhaps she said all that through gritted teeth, but she said it all the same. I could even believe she meant it.

In the jeep I asked the driver, 'Can you go any faster?'

'Sure, pal. If I want to skid on ice and kill us all.'

'Where are you from?'

'Madison, Wisconsin.'

'Is that near New York?' I was thinking of Brigitta's friend

Francine and her plans to start a new life in the New World.

'Only a thousand miles down the road.'

Francine – who had two tickets from the docks at Liverpool, and guaranteed work for two immigrant seamstresses. I knew the name of her ship and the date of sailing. We could get a message to Connie somehow ... through Lady Summer, since she owned Gant's factory where Connie worked. I saw a story unfolding. I told the American, 'Well, if you're ever in Harlem, New York, look up Connie Snow – she is going to be a big star.'

He scratched his head. 'Sure thing ...' He nodded at Joe. 'What's your story, chum?'

'Halifax bomb aimer. The rest of the crew bought it when we got pranged over Jerryland and had to ditch the crate.'

'Huh. War, eh? *Stinks*.'

Looking around London I was struck at how messy it all was. Traffic snarls, dirt, noise, bomb ruins. How could we find one man in all the mayhem?

'Wait,' said Joe, pulling me back from the kerb as a bus roared past, spraying us with slush.

'We have to be faster.'

'Let's get there alive at least.'

The address we had brought us to a tall building guarded with stone lions, not far from King's Cross station. I felt a rush of recognition. I'd seen this place before! The evening I crossed London I'd rested opposite those lions.

The doors were open. I ran up the steps and crossed the lobby to a secretary busy at a reception desk. His fingers typed while his eyes were on a page of notes.

'I would like to see Captain Golanski.'

Ta-ca-ta-ca-ta-ca, went the typewriter. 'Captain Golanski isn't here.'

'Are you absolutely sure of that?' asked Joe, suddenly sounding like a proper lord. 'Can you at least check?'

Ta-ca-ta-ca-ta-ca ching!

'He came in, made some phone calls, then left about fifteen minutes ago, to catch the boat train to the Continent. Is it important?'

Fifteen minutes. We'd missed him by only fifteen minutes.

'Do you have a forwarding address?'

The secretary sighed. 'No, I don't have an address. Or a telephone number, or a unicorn I could ride over to Germany on. Try again tomorrow. Someone may know more.'

Tomorrow.

We were too late. By tomorrow he could be anywhere in Europe.

Joe took one look at my face and said, 'What would Sophie Rover do?'

'What?'

'Let's eat – or drink at least.'

He took me across the street to a pub, somewhere I would never have dared enter when I was a girl. It smelled of beer and sweat and tobacco. He found us a ring-marked wooden table in one corner and sat me down. I was too shocked to move, in a sort of emotional wardrobe where I genuinely didn't know what to do next. He fetched two shandies over, one at a time. No one commented on his burn scars or his missing arm, probably because there were a fair number of ex-army types drinking at the bar.

Pretty soon I had to go to the bathroom. *Gents' not ladies', gents' not ladies'*, I told myself over and over. There wasn't a ladies' anyway. Standing at the urinal for the first time ever was just too nerve-wracking. I locked myself in a cubicle. Being a boy was strange. What did it even mean anyway? Was it what you felt inside, or what other people saw, or what you had in your pants?

I was in a daze when I got back to Joe.

'Play something,' he said, nodding towards the piano.

I looked at the crowds of work-worn men through their clouds of cigarette smoke. Not classical fans, I thought. Probably not big on jazz either. A man reeled over and breathed beer fumes on me. 'D'you know "Roll Out the Barrel", son?'

'How about "Nobby 'All"?' sniggered another drinker.

Joe casually came to shield me from any other requests.

The piano was clunky and barely in tune. Even so, the assembled drinkers were raucous with appreciation by the time I made it to the second chorus. Soon the whole pub was singing along to Vera Lynn's 'It's a Lovely Day Tomorrow'. By the end of it I was almost sick with loss. I had to get away from the crowds and the smoke.

Joe followed me out onto the street. 'Piccadilly isn't far. I'll get on the phone at the RAF Club and see what else we can find out . . .'

I felt a tap on my shoulder. Nothing momentous, just a man in khaki who'd come up behind us.

'Excuse me, did you drop this . . . ?'

He handed me something. A grey glove. But not mine. Mine was frayed and dirty and missing a button, and safely tucked in my waistcoat pocket. This glove was crisp and clean.

'No, it's not –'

My heart stopped.

It was almost identical. The left-hand glove to my right-hand glove. A pair.

I couldn't breathe. Didn't dare look up. I felt Joe at my side, suddenly tense.

I lifted my eyes.

A man in a British uniform, buttons a little dull, tie a little loose, hair a little ruffled.

A stranger. Real and not real.

'Papa?'

He gestured across the road to the lion building. 'I forgot my briefcase . . . went back . . . heard that song in the pub. It always makes me think of my wife . . . then I saw you. It is you, yes? You are David?'

The question nearly broke me. He didn't know if it was me or not.

Then I was crushed, my face pressed into those buttons, smelling the wool of his tie and the years-ago-familiar scent of him. I realised he was crying. His tears were wet on my hair. London ceased to exist. I was back in old Europe, in one-room apartments filled with cheap furniture and music and love.

'I lost you . . . I lost you . . .' came his voice in Polish. The voice of my childhood. My papa of tousled dark hair, firm warm hands and soft eyes behind round glasses. My papa who sang duets at the piano with . . .

'Your mother?' He held me by the arms and scanned my face. 'Where is your mama?'

Now it was my turn to hold out a grey glove. The right hand. The lost hand. *Hold my hand.*

'Dead,' I said woodenly. 'Bombed in Berlin.' Why soften the hard truth? There was no pretty way of putting it.

My papa crumpled, as worn as the glove, which he took and pressed to his lips over and over. Then he held me in his arms again. That was when I knew he loved her, had always loved her, and me; he had loved me too. Not enough. I pulled away.

'You left us,' I said in English.

'I had to! They arrested me. Don't you remember? I had your mother's hand and she said, "Don't let go!" and I pulled her glove off when they took me. I said I would find you.'

'You didn't. You survived and you didn't come.' My voice was flat. Where were my emotions? Why couldn't I feel anything more than a cold ancient horror? It was killing him to be punished like this. I knew it and didn't care.

We were buffeted by people on the pavement who didn't care either.

His voice became a whisper. 'David, I was in prison, do you understand? They were taking us east. To the gas chambers . . .'

While we had waited and hoped and waited and despaired, he had been as trapped as we were.

'How . . . how did you get away?'

He laughed. 'You can thank the RAF for that.'

I flicked a glance at Joe. 'What do you mean?'

241

'We were being transported by truck from a prison to a concentration camp – I don't know which one. There was a night raid. Heavy bombers. Pounded the hell out of the railway. Flattened me in a crater. I got away, got help . . . Eventually joined the Free Polish Army and got my captaincy with the British. None of this is important. I have been searching and searching for you ever since. I had almost given up hope. It's *you*, my dear, dear David-of-my-heart. My little boy grown big.'

He'd been looking. He hadn't forgotten me. *I'll find you*, he'd said. Now we'd found each other. Anger trickled away like a fading piano motif, replaced by heart's music of relief.

'Aw, save it, guv'!' came a rough voice from the pub. 'We ain't bleedin' wimmin to be blubbering in the street.'

I rubbed my eyes and thought of a saying I'd learned. 'Stiff upper lip and all that.' We both straightened, suddenly English-like. 'Papa . . .' How magical the word was! 'Papa, this is my friend Joe.'

Joe held out his left hand. Without the slightest awkwardness or hesitation, my father shook it, using his left hand too. 'Pleased to meet you.'

'And you, sir.'

I took a deep breath. Thought, *I might as well do this now, while it is still semi-bearable that my papa walks away again.*

'Papa, Joe is my friend.'

I took Joe's hand in mine. *Don't let go.*

Papa looked at our entwined fingers, then at both our faces. I was resolute. I would be me or no one. When he understood,

242

he did not recoil or turn on his heel. His eyebrows went up a notch – no hiding that. He nodded.

'Very well,' he said. 'Take love where you can find it.'

But not in the street. Never in public. Back we went into the lion building, businesslike now.

Ta-ca-ta . . . The secretary jolted alert as we came inside. 'Oh, Captain Golanski, I thought you'd gone.'

'I had. I forgot some files and found my visitors.'

'But, sir, the boat train, it leaves in an hour. You won't make it.'

'Call and cancel, will you?'

'Cancel? But the Paris meeting, the Hamburg trial preliminaries . . .'

'Can I introduce you to Lord Joseph Summer of Bomber Command?'

'Er, Your Lordship.'

'And this is David Golanski. *My son*. I haven't seen him for seven years, so perhaps the Paris meeting can wait?'

'Yes, sir, understood, sir. I'll sort that right away, sir.'

Papa took us up to a third-floor office overlooking the street. Seeing the windows and the view, I was reminded again of my first evening in London, when I sat in a doorway staring at this very building, and a silhouetted man looked out. The room was filled with towers of brown legal files.

Papa said, 'Sit down, if you can find a free chair. Are you hungry? Did you have a good journey? I'm sorry, I'm babbling.' He fell into Polish phrases. 'Seven years. Seven lost years! David – your mother – tell me. How . . . ? When?'

243

I heard an odd clink as Joe set his bag down. There was a pause as he looked inside. He laughed. 'You won't believe it, but Mrs Rover has sneaked a bottle of her notorious homemade sloe gin into my bag. Do not ask me how she managed that.'

'Gin?' exclaimed Papa. 'I suggest we celebrate.'

'Brace yourself, sir. It's heady stuff. Mrs Rover was an army cook.'

Papa's eyes twinkled. 'And I am Polish, Lord Summer. I thrive on distilled liquids.'

Soft-remembered moments of childhood came back to me, hearing Papa's voice now. After cautious sips of the sweet, sticky gin I told him what I could about Mama. Eventually the room went dark, save for the orange glow of the street lamps outside. When I could talk no more my father held me again and we both wept. Then he held his hand out to Joe.

'Thank you,' he said in English. 'Thank you for taking care of my son.'

'He took care of himself, sir. Rather well, given the circumstances.'

Papa smiled bitterly. 'If you knew what would have happened to him, had he been found. The places that were waiting for him – the concentration camps. These files, my work . . . Countless testimonies of ordinary people doing brave or bestial things. Risking their lives to save strangers, or murdering innocents to gain a bottle of vodka or a fur coat. Auschwitz, Belsen – they are just two camps out of thousands. They didn't spring out of nowhere either. They didn't run themselves. Here, this file . . .' He opened his briefcase and pulled out a folder. 'One of the SS guards I'm going to prosecute in Hamburg. A farm girl called Carla, only just turned twenty, says she did nothing wrong, yet we have proof she carried out multiple murders and horrible torture of Jews in at least three concentration camps. Her father wrote to me from the family farm in Germany, saying she was a *good daughter* and too young to know what she was doing.'

'Will she hang?' I asked.

'Probably not. She'll fake repentance and after a few years in prison be let out to run the farm, or marry and have children, or goodness knows what.'

Joe and I looked at each other. It could have been England, if Hitler's Third Reich had spread that far. It could have been Summer village put to the test, everyone having to decide would they embrace the violence or resist; would they denounce their neighbours or shelter them. I felt the sore welt round my throat and remembered how it felt to dangle by the neck. It didn't just take evil people to do evil things. Anybody could let themselves get swept along with the violence if they weren't careful.

'I have made you late. You have to go and continue your work. It's important,' I told Papa.

'*You're* important! I found you!' He shed his bitterness in an instant and, hugging me, almost swung me round, as he had when I was little. I remembered that – being spun round the room so fast my shoe fell off and hit the piano, and we were all laughing for some reason, or no reason, and now I could laugh again. I had my Papa back.

He stopped, suddenly stricken.

'I'm sorry, David, I have looked so hard, and there are no family left alive for you meet. They were killed – all killed.'

'Sir, David is welcome back at my home, at Summerland.'
Joe fixed his eyes on me, willing me to say I would stay. I took
his hand but I looked at my papa.

'If you are going to Europe, I will come too. There is someone
else I have to find, and you have to help me.'

'Of course. I have resources, a network. Tell me – who are
you searching for?'

French Fancies

I will find you.

I'd made the promise after talking with Francine at Summerland, after showing her the pictures and letters hidden in my Berlin coat.

I'll find you, Brigitta Igeul.

Papa got busy making calls. Men and women flowed in and out of the office in various levels of harassed preoccupation.

Over mugs of tea and plain biscuits Papa told me, 'I'm good at finding people, believe it or not. I've got a first-rate team of investigators.'

From the letters, I knew where Brigitta was from. Thanks to Francine, I knew where she'd been sent to – Auschwitz. After that, who knew? Papa said I wasn't to get my hopes up. He said there were few survivors from that place. He spoke with the Red Cross, with Jewish relief agencies, and with a sunken-eyed Slovakian woman who'd only just arrived in London as a refugee. She looked a hundred and was probably only twenty. I made her a cup of tea too. Papa interviewed her in private. He seemed both sad and excited afterwards.

'The things human beings can endure,' he said. 'But that lady knows someone who knows someone who's heard of someone else, and that's how it goes.'

There was talk of tickets for the boat train and a trip to France.

'I don't have a passport, or identity papers,' I warned Papa, when he told me I was coming too.

'Leave that to my mother,' said Joe. 'She's in London now and she means business. Give her five minutes with the man in charge at the Passport Office and you'll have your papers – all we need is a photograph.'

Cue: a studio trip. *Flash* – there I was, in black and white. Me, myself, David.

A day later a large package arrived at the RAF Club where Joe and I were staying. We each had a single room, up in the rafters. I loved looking out over the city, with its smoking chimneys and twinkling windows. We met up at midnight in honour of the Summerland tradition. Sometimes we talked, sometimes we didn't, and what happened then didn't need words.

I pulled the string off the parcel and unfolded the brown paper to find spare clothes, books – for Joe – and his awful, adorable purple pyjamas. There was also a strange drawing. I think it was a car in front of a house. The accompanying letter was written in military capital letters.

DEAR DAVID AND LORD J,
YOU'LL NEED CLEAN UNDERWEAR IN LONDON IF NOTHING
ELSE IN CASE YOU GET KNOCKED DOWN BY A BUS SO HERE

YOU ARE AND OTHER CLOTHES BESIDES. DAVID, I'M GLAD
YOU FOUND YOUR DAD, LOOKS LIKE YOU'RE AN ARMY KID
NOW. I'LL MISS YOU. I GOT A CAT, A REAL UGLY BRUISER.
I'M CALLING HER BAGGSY, SHE HISSES AT NOTHING, MAYBE
SHE SEES GHOSTS.
LOVE SOPHIE ROVER
PS THE GOOD LUCK CARD IS FROM NELLIE VARLEY. SHE
COLOURED IT IN, AND COLOURED IN MY KITCHEN TABLE
WHILE SHE WAS AT IT, CHEEKY MONKEY.
PPS A LITTLE BIRD TOLD ME YOU MIGHT BE GOING ABROAD
SO HERE ARE SOME FRENCH FANCIES. DON'T EAT THEM ALL
AT ONCE.
PPPS IF YOU MEET ANY NAZIS KICK THEM FROM ME

French fancies were little square sponge cakes covered in pink
and yellow icing. We ate them all at once. Joe tasted of sugar
when we kissed goodbye. That had to be in private, not on the
platform at Waterloo. He had offered to come to Europe, but
we both knew he should get back to Summerland, if only to
stop Mrs Rover overfeeding the builders.

'I'm going back to help, not to hide,' he assured me.

When the time came to leave, I felt as if I'd been torn in two.

'Keep dancing,' he whispered. 'Come back to me . . .'

How different my voyage back across the Channel was from
my journey to England. Papa booked a cabin so we could get
some sleep. We didn't. There was too much to talk over, too
many years to share. I told him about the Trautweins, the
Varleys and sherry trifle. About Mrs Rover's endless meals.

About Connie, fish 'n' chips, Land Girls and Gant's. About swing, jive, jazz and all the piano music I'd ever loved.

I said nothing about what had happened in the Bomb House.

He spoke of Mama's smile, and how she'd sung to me when I was a baby, and the time she took me onstage with her for a prestigious piano recital, bundled in a basket at her side, and I never made a single sound until the applause began, when I cried until she picked me up and let me play with the piano keys.

I wished I'd known that he hadn't forgotten us, that he'd been looking for us all along. I wish Mama had known I wouldn't always be alone.

Our search took us to the French capital. Mama called Paris the City of Lights. We arrived on a freezing winter afternoon. Parisians clattered out of the Metro on wooden-soled shoes. Young people wore their ski clothes in the streets it was so cold.

Papa commandeered a car and a driver. We drove round the main sights – the Eiffel Tower looked smaller than I expected and very grey in the rain – then headed out of the centre to a quieter neighbourhood with no bullet marks on the masonry. We got lost, found ourselves, stopped for a coffee and set off again, eventually slowing to a halt outside a dress shop of all places. The sign above the door read: *Le Ruban Rouge* – The Red Ribbon.

'Ready?' asked Papa.

'Ready.'

A bell chimed beautifully as I pushed the door open. Inside, the walls were painted white, softened with green plants and

250

displays of cheerful fabric flowers. There were neat wooden chairs with embroidered cushions and a table showing fashion magazines. Two Frenchwomen were admiring a dress on a mannequin. It had a narrow waist and a long, flared skirt. In a back room I heard sewing machines whirring and the chatter of happy young voices.

A girl about my age came to greet us. She was small with bright eyes and rosy lips that curved as if a smile was about to appear.

'*Bonjour et bienvenue, messieurs,*' she said with a smile.

It would take a while before I got used to being called a *monsieur* instead of a *mademoiselle*.

She looked us both up and down. 'I see from your clothes you are English, perhaps? And yet . . . not so English in manner. I sense a story?'

'Who is it?' called a voice from the back.

'Two intriguing strangers,' the girl called back. Then to us: 'Can I help you?'

I spoke French also, wincing a bit at my German accent. 'We are looking for someone – Brigitta Igeul. We had news that perhaps she worked here, or that you know of her?'

The girl tipped her head on one side, like a squirrel.

'Very well,' she said, after a moment. She whisked away to the back room and returned with another girl. This one I recognised at once. She was older and warier than her photograph. I'd been her, before I became me.

'Brigitta . . .'

The real Brigitta Igeul put her hand up to her mouth.

'You don't know me,' I went on hurriedly. 'My name is

251

David Golanski. This is my father, Captain Golanski. We're not here to make trouble. We come from a friend. You know a woman called Francine?'

Another girl came from the back room, wearing a pink dress with embroidered buttons. She was tall and strong, and looked ready to protect the others. All three of them now talked rapidly in a mixture of languages. They knew Francine all right. Just from listening in I could tell they had all worked together in the sewing room in Auschwitz. They hadn't known anyone else from the workshop had survived.

Brigitta turned to me. 'Tell me about Francine. Where is she? Is she alive? Is she well?'

'She is very alive and very well. I will tell you everything. First, allow me to give you these . . .' From my jacket pocket I took a bundle of papers and photographs. They'd had a long journey from Brigitta's Austrian home to the warehouses at Auschwitz, to bombed-out Berlin, to England and now delivered into the hands of their rightful owner. Brigitta had her memories back.

All three girls wept to see Brigitta's precious pictures and letters, then clapped with delight to hear of Francine and her voyage to New York. They invited us to stay in the shop to celebrate. We said we were sorry, we had another journey to make. We left, after exchanging addresses and kisses. I liked their lovely shop, even if I was glad I didn't have to wear dresses any more.

Papa bought pastries from the bakery next door. There were not a lot of cakes to choose from. Paris in 1947 was still hungry.

He got little squares of sponge covered in pink icing. Nowhere near as nice as Mrs Rover's French fancies.

We walked through the park opposite the shop and sat on a bench under an apple tree. Its branches were bare, waiting for spring and blossom time.

Papa asked, 'We have one night in Paris – what would you like to do?'

My answer came without hesitation. 'Go to a jazz club.'

'*Jazz*? Your mother went to see Josephine Baker at the Folies Bergère once, did you know that? She sneaked out there with a couple of schoolfriends; I remember her telling me. She loved every minute. I think the thrill of breaking rules was part of it. Very well. I'll treat you. I've got a lot of birthdays to make up for, after all. What's the matter? What did I say?'

It was silly really. I'd lived as Brigitta for so long, I couldn't remember when my own birthday was.

Jazz piano was on my fingertips as we left Paris and travelled by train across France and into Germany. Before we arrived in Berlin the music tempo slowed and I was back to playing Germaine Tailleferre, then Beethoven – the beautiful *Moonlight Sonata* once again. By the time we reached the suburbs of the city I had no music left. At the station Papa arranged an army jeep and a driver. The military were everywhere, just as I remembered. People still looked so thin. I felt guilty for my feasts in Mrs Rover's kitchen. It was desperately cold. My bones were chilled like ice even though the air was still.

Our first stop was along a street of ghosts. Bricks from bombed-out houses were now neatly piled on either side of

253

the road. The few intact windows had desperately respectable net curtains.

There, in that patch of wasteland, that was where the Trautwein apartment had been before the bombs dropped and I crawled from the rubble. Hitler's portrait frame, the piano and the wardrobe had long since been burned as firewood. That gap in the street was where I had spent cramped years hiding. They were not lost years. I had had my mama almost every single day.

There, on that corner, I had limped barefoot and bleeding to the help centre opened by the Nazi Women's League, to get clothes and a coat . . . and an accidental new identity. There, where flowers would bloom in spring, that was where I'd scraped a grave for my mother. The stony soil was flattened down now. The grave marker was gone, probably for firewood too.

'Shall we bury her gloves here?' Papa asked.

'No. Give them to someone whose hands are cold.'

Papa took my hand.

'I miss her,' I said.

'Me too.'

We stood there side by side as Papa recited a prayer, then we each picked up a small stone and placed it at the grave site. *Goodbye, Mutti, my amazing mama.* There was no ghost now.

It was a long journey north-west to Hamburg, where the next round of war-criminal trials would take place. Hamburg's ghosts clustered thick as weeds as we made our way to the law court. From Papa's office I dialled the operator for an international telephone call. Lady Summer answered after several rings. She made a few polite enquiries, hissed, *Get down, you wretched cat – that is not a scratching post, it's a Chippendale*, then called for her son.

When I finally heard Joe's voice across the crackling line I almost couldn't speak for happiness.

'You did it,' he said. 'You're out in the world.'

'The trials will be long, but then we are coming home.'

'To Poland, or Berlin?'

'To England, you idiot. To you. After that . . .'

He laughed. 'After that, it's wherever we want to go, whatever we want to do! I absolutely can't wait.'

People often talk about the war. How exciting it was, or how awful. Me, I'm done with all that. Done hiding from it, done talking about it, done looking back.

I am going to seize life hard, and I won't let go. I look forward to seeing Summerland in summer.

Author's Note

When I first visualised a refugee with a suitcase walking up the
drive to a Yorkshire country house, I imagined it was one of the
characters from *The Red Ribbon*, my previous novel. (Readers
had been asking me, 'What happens next?!') However, some
way into the story I was startled to discover all was not as it
seemed . . . Yes, even an author can be surprised by their own
plot twists. Suddenly everything fell into place.

I had set out to write a love story based on the experiences
of young people in the post-war period. I ended up exploring
many themes around secrecy and identity, as well as the lasting
trauma of Jewish children persecuted during the Holocaust.

Summerland is fiction – a work of imagination – but the
strands are drawn from many real wartime sources. David's
predicament was partly inspired by the true story of a hidden
child named Richard Rozen, as well as other memoirs that
mention Jewish children disguised for their own protection.
It was startling to learn how deeply children internalised
their new identities in order to survive in a world where
they could be denounced, deported and murdered simply
for being Jewish.

I had the good fortune to meet a gracious Holocaust survivor called Hanni Begg. When Hanni began to speak of her childhood, it was eerily similar to aspects of *Summerland*. Hanni had been a hidden child in Berlin during the war – a terrifying experience for any Jew. Then came the Allied bombing raids. Her father was killed. 'I had to bury my own father,' she quietly told me. Hanni made her home in England after the war and was happy here. Like many survivors, she seized life, worked hard and celebrated her new freedoms.

Sophie Rover – perhaps the real star of *Summerland* – is drawn from memories of being wonderfully overfed by my grandmother Ella, who made the best steamed-puddings-with-custard in the whole world.

* * *

I loved listening to the relevant music while I wrote this story, both classical and modern tunes. I even took a lesson on a grand piano, so I would know how it felt to sit and play the opening notes of Beethoven's *Moonlight Sonata*. By staggering coincidence, my piano teacher had, in turn, been taught by Nelly Ben-Or, a hidden Jewish child whose love of music helped her endure years of fear in World War Two.

Here are some of the music and songs that make up a soundtrack to *Summerland*:

Ella Fitzgerald sings *T'aint What You Do (It's the Way That You Do It)*
Adelaide Hall sings *I Can't Give You Anything But Love, Baby*
Elisabeth Welch sings *Stormy Weather*
Fats Waller plays *Ain't Misbehavin'*
Dinah Shore sings *The Nearness of You*
Flanagan and Allen sing *Run Rabbit Run*
Glenn Miller plays *In the Mood*
Vera Lynn sings *It's a Lovely Day Tomorrow*
Rebecca Clarke – *Rhapsody for cello and piano*
Wolfgang Amadeus Mozart – *Don Giovanni*
Claude Debussy – *The Snow Is Dancing*, from the 'Children's Corner' suite
Germaine Tailleferre – *Romance for piano*; *Fleurs de France for piano*
Ludwig van Beethoven – *Piano Sonata No. 14 in C# minor*, known as the *Moonlight Sonata*

Lucy Adlington

Lucy Adlington is a writer and clothes historian. Her novels for teenagers, including *The Diary of Pelly D*, *Burning Mountain* and *The Red Ribbon* have been nominated and shortlisted for the CILIP Carnegie Medal, the Manchester Book Prize, the Leeds Book Prize and the Rotherham Book Award. She tours the UK with dress history presentations and writes history books for adults, including *Women's Lives and Clothes in WW2: Ready for Action* and *Stitches in Time: the Story of the Clothes We Wear*.

Find out more at www.historywardrobe.com
or on Twitter: @historywardrobe

Want to read
NEW BOOKS
before anyone else?

Like getting
FREE BOOKS?

Enjoy sharing your
OPINIONS?

Discover

READERS FIRST

Read. Love. Share.

Get your first free book just by signing up at
readersfirst.co.uk

HOT
KEY
BOOKS

Thank you for choosing a Hot Key book.

If you want to know more about our authors
and what we publish, you can find us online.

You can start at our website

www.hotkeybooks.com

And you can also find us on:

We hope to see you soon!